YARD DOG

A.G. PASQUELLA

THE JACK PALACE SERIES

YARD DOG

DUNDURN
TORONTO

Cover design: Laura Boyle
Cover image: shutterstock.com/Dundanim
Printer: Webcom

Library and Archives Canada Cataloguing in Publication

Pasquella, A. G., 1973-, author
    Yard dog / A.G. Pasquella.

(The Jack Palace series)
Issued in print and electronic formats.
ISBN 978-1-4597-4228-4 (softcover).--ISBN 978-1-4597-4229-1 (PDF).--
ISBN 978-1-4597-4230-7 (EPUB)

    I. Title.

PS8631.A8255Y37 2018   C813'.6   C2018-901429-6
                                                C2018-901430-X

1 2 3 4 5   22 21 20 19 18

 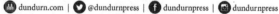

We acknowledge the support of the Canada Council for the Arts, which last year invested $153 million to bring the arts to Canadians throughout the country, and the Ontario Arts Council for our publishing program. We also acknowledge the financial support of the Government of Ontario, through the Ontario Book Publishing Tax Credit and the Ontario Media Development Corporation, and the Government of Canada.

Nous remercions le Conseil des arts du Canada de son soutien. L'an dernier, le Conseil a investi 153 millions de dollars pour mettre de l'art dans la vie des Canadiennes et des Canadiens de tout le pays.

Care has been taken to trace the ownership of copyright material used in this book. The author and the publisher welcome any information enabling them to rectify any references or credits in subsequent editions.

— J. Kirk Howard, President

The publisher is not responsible for websites or their content unless they are owned by the publisher.

Printed and bound in Canada.

VISIT US AT

 dundurn.com | @dundurnpress | dundurnpress | dundurnpress

Dundurn
3 Church Street, Suite 500
Toronto, Ontario, Canada
M5E 1M2

For Emma

CHAPTER 1

What does a man do when he gets out of jail? Gets drunk and gets laid, not necessarily in that order. Tommy picked me up in one of his dad's limos, screeching up to the front of the Don Jail with the sound system blasting, guards on the steps looking like they've been sucking lemons. The limo door swung open and there was Tommy in a ridiculous Hawaiian shirt covered in orange flowers, grinning at me over the top of his sunglasses.

"Come on in. The water's fine."

Did this guy have a Jacuzzi back there? I slid into the limo, feeling the guards' eyes boring a smouldering hole into the back of my neck. I knew what they were thinking. Who says crime doesn't pay?

Tommy, grinning like a sultan, leaned back into the limo's plush seats. "Tiffany, Amber ... I want you to meet a friend of mine. Amber, go over there and introduce yourself."

Now, I like to think I'm a pretty stoic bastard, but going from a tiny jail cell to the back seat of a limousine with two beautiful bikini-clad women in the space of five minutes is a bit of a mindfuck. Still, when Amber brushed her breasts against my arm I wasn't about to push her away.

"Jack, you want a martini? Tiffany, get my friend a martini."

"You got any beer?"

"Sure, we got beer! Tiffany, get me a martini and get my friend a beer."

How many nights had I laid awake in the clatter and gloom of jail dreaming of The Perfect Beer? The kind you see in the commercials, bits of ice and moisture rolling down the sides, ice-cold and delicious.

I savoured the first sip, letting it roll gently across my tongue. The taste of freedom.

I drank the rest of the beer in about three seconds. Amber laughed. "You were thirsty!"

"Take off your top," Tommy told her, and she did.

At the club, the music was so loud it shook my molars. A dark-haired waitress with impossibly long tanned legs swept away the third round of empty bottles. Fresh bottles appeared like magic. Tommy was swigging Grey Goose straight from the bottle because he was classy like that. Amber and Tiffany, now in party dresses, banged their heads together and laughed, white powder dusting their nostrils. Tommy did a line off the top of Tiffany's left breast and the ladies laughed louder. I glanced around uneasily. Then it hit me: there were no guards, cops, snitches, stoolies, or parole officers here. This was Tommy's place, and if he wanted to do a line off a stripper's fake tits, it was his fucking business.

"You sure you don't want some, Jack? This is good fucking shit!"

"You know why Mormons don't drink or do drugs? It's because they believe God gave them Free Will." I held up a bottle of beer, green glass glinting in the disco light. "Me, I like beer."

I downed the bottle as Tommy and the ladies laughed. "Doesn't he talk funny? I love this guy! Jack, you're a funny fucking guy!"

I grinned as Amber nestled closer. She smelled like vanilla. Goddamn, it was good to be free.

Tiffany and Amber were naked now, gyrating together in Tommy's V.I.P. lounge. Amber wriggled out of her little black party dress so sexily I almost asked her to put it back on and do it again. Tiffany ran her wet pink tongue along Amber's neck, both girls swaying to the soul music pouring from the speakers like molasses. Next to me in the darkness Tommy twitched and groaned. Tiffany's manicured hand rubbed Amber's tits and dropped lower, her finger dipping into Amber's folds before pulling away, teasing. Amber moaned and fell to her knees. Tiffany grabbed the back of Amber's head and pushed her face between her legs. They moaned together, swaying. They seemed to be genuinely enjoying themselves and that turned me on. Amber lay back on the stage with her legs spread, giving us an eyeful. I had just enough time to savour the view before Tiffany crawled over on her hands and knees and dove between Amber's thighs.

After five minutes Tommy couldn't stand it. He leapt up, charged toward the girls, and seized Tiffany's hand. "There's bedrooms on the third floor," he shouted back at me as he pulled Tiffany from the room. "See you in the morning. We'll talk business!"

I knocked back the last of my beer. The room wobbled. I must have been drunk because the idea of doing business with Tommy didn't bother me a bit.

Let's get one thing straight right now. I'm not a criminal. I believe in truth and justice and all that good shit. It's just that sometimes truth and justice and the law don't match up. Sometimes the path of the righteous man leads directly to jail. Do not pass go, do not collect two hundred dollars.

Amber stood over me, naked. "Are we going upstairs?"

I grinned. "Just try and stop me."

At some point in the night I woke up to Amber shaking me. She looked freaked the fuck out.

"Jack! Jack!"

My heart galloped as I fumbled for my knife. It took me a few seconds to realize the knife was long gone, sitting tagged and bagged in some police evidence locker. "What? What is it?"

"You were screaming in your sleep. Are you okay?"

My grey undershirt was soaked with cold sweat. "Yeah," I lied, "I'm fine."

CHAPTER 2

"You like eggs? They do the best eggs in the city."
Tommy squinted at the menu. "Chorizo? What the fuck is chorizo?"

A well-groomed couple with matching sweaters and silver hair edged their chairs away from us. We were sitting in a restaurant in Yorkville: waiters with ties and ladies with big purses. Yorkville used to be a hippie enclave before the hippies grew up and became investment bankers. Now it was fancy boutiques and million-dollar condos and nostalgia shops selling five-hundred-dollar lunchboxes.

"It's spicy sausage," I told him.

"Hell yeah," he said, slamming the menu closed. The waiter took our order and glided away.

Tommy rubbed his temples. "My fucking brain. You have a good time last night, Jack?"

I closed my eyes and listened to the rush and hum of my own blood. The whiff of vanilla. Amber, so warm and soft and good. "Yeah."

"Good." Tommy sighed. "It feels good to cut loose like that every once in a while. I tell ya, Jack, ever since my dad's been in the hospital, things haven't exactly been peaches and cream."

"Sorry to hear that."

Tommy shrugged. "That's life, right? First you're riding on top of the world and the next minute you're lying in the hospital with a tube up your ass."

Across from us the silver-haired couple in the matching sweaters got up and changed tables.

"He's been in there, what, a month?"

Tommy nodded. "One month and already the vultures are circling. You know Little Vito?"

I nodded. "I've heard of him."

"He had the gall to come by my club, offer his condolences. That fat prick. He was looking over my shoulder the whole time. I could practically hear him remodelling. Well, fuck him. He's got a club. He can't have mine."

"It's a nice club, Tommy."

"Damn right it's a nice club. I run things, kick a share up to my dad. That's how it works. That's how we all work." Tommy clenched his fist. "That fat prick."

I drained my water glass and gestured for more. "Let me guess. Vito's not paying."

"Oh, he'll pay. We've got a system here. An operation. My father spent years putting this together. It's a well-oiled machine. Guys like Little Vito, they gum up the works. Him and the rest of the pricks, they think that just because my dad's in the hospital, they can backslide. 'Oh, it's been slow this week, Tommy. We'll have it for you next Tuesday, Tommy.' Fuck that. It's a system.

They gotta understand that. A guy like Vito ... he's gotta learn the hard way."

I shook my head. "I don't do that kind of work anymore."

Tommy scowled. "Did I ask you to do anything? Did I?"

"No ..."

"No. That's right. We're just talking here." Tommy's face brightened. "Jack, I like you. We're buddies, right? I'm not going to ask you to do anything you don't want to do. Understand? I'm not going to put you into any awkward situations. Guys like Vito, we've got guys for guys like that. It's just that it's been pretty rough, you know, with my dad in the hospital and everything. I could really use a friend like you, Jack."

Something inside me screamed, *Get up! Get up and walk away now and don't look back. Go on, you stupid bastard — run!*

"What can I do to help?" I heard myself say.

Tommy grinned. "I just need an extra guy on a couple of runs. You don't have to do anything. You don't even handle the money. My guys will do that. You just stand there, all right? You're my eyes and ears. Who's paying? Who's not paying? Who could use some extra encouragement? Is there anybody in my crew with sticky fingers?" Tommy burped, coughed, and thumped his chest. "You're like an outside accountant. I know I can count on you."

"You want me to audit your routes."

"Yeah, audit! You're a smart guy, Jack." Tommy smiled. "So whaddaya say? Go on a few runs, keep your eyes open, and report back to me. Easy."

My hungover brain was screaming louder now. *RUN! RUN, YOU FUCKER!*

Tommy must have seen the look on my face. He laughed. "Don't you worry. I've got your back. I'll watch out for you, just like I did on The Inside. You made it out in one piece, didn't you?"

More or less.

"I go on your routes, I report back to you, and that's it."

"That's it."

"I'll do it."

"You're a good man, Jack."

The waiter materialized with artistic plates. Everything arranged just so.

Tommy tucked into his food. "What did I tell you? Good fucking eggs!"

CHAPTER 3

All right ... time to set my life in order. Tommy's driver dropped me off at Dundas and Spadina, deep in the heart of Chinatown. Throngs of people everywhere, carefully stacked mountains of garbage in front of all the grocery stores. Dirty sidewalks and the smell of rotting fruit. Hacked-open young coconuts with straws sticking out the top resting on every garbage can.

My apartment was long gone, of course. What was I going to do, pay two years worth of rent while I cooled my heels in jail? Fuck that. My stuff — a few books, some clothes — was boxed up and stored in a friend's basement. I'd get it later. It didn't matter. It wasn't my life; it was just stuff.

I pushed through the crowds and almost collided with a blind man playing the flute. His milky-white orbs stared right through me and I got the chills. *Stop freezing my soul, blind man. I've got work to do.*

Eddie Yao was right where I left him, right where he always was: smoking a cigarette in a haze-filled illegal basement casino fronted by a Chinese restaurant. Eddie was spread out on his stool like a frog on a lily pad. He had gotten bigger since I last saw him, his bulk almost hidden beneath a shiny black suit. Hair perfectly slicked back in an effort to distract from his pockmarked face.

Eddie saw me cutting through the blue cigarette haze and his eyes lit up. He stood and gave me an enthusiastic handshake. "Two years already? Man oh man, time flies."

"You look good, Eddie," I lied.

Eddie laughed. "You're full of crap. You look like crap, too. You look like you've been in jail for two years."

"It was a bullshit charge."

"Oh, I know, I know. Here in Chinatown we never get the police involved." Eddie smiled, his teeth glinting gold. "We handle things our way."

I nodded. "I've seen some Chinatown Justice. A few years ago I was walking down Spadina in the middle of the afternoon and I saw a guy come tearing out of a store like he was on fire. Six guys took off after him and boxed him in on the other side of the street. Then they picked this guy up and started carting him back across the streetcar tracks. You know how in the middle of the street there's a concrete strip with trees growing? This poor sucker latched onto one of the trees and was screaming as the other guys yanked on his legs. They finally pried the guy loose and disappeared him into a nearby store."

Eddie shrugged. "Probably a shoplifter. He would be, ah … *discouraged* from shoplifting again."

"He looked plenty discouraged, all right. What got me was that no one lifted a finger. The streets were packed — as I said, this happened in broad daylight — and everyone just watched calmly and then went back to buying Buddhas and cheap T-shirts."

Eddie grinned. "Forget it, Jack. It's Chinatown."

We headed upstairs, the dusty wooden steps groaning beneath Eddie's weight. The fluorescent hallway light flickered as Eddie fumbled with a giant dungeon-master-style ring of keys. Finally he got the right key in the lock and the door swung open.

"Here you go, Jack. Just as you left it."

If that was true, then I was one hell of a housekeeper. My office was covered in a thick layer of dead flies and dust. The brown and yellow plaid couch (straight from the 1970s to the Salvation Army to me) was piled high with cardboard boxes sealed up with tape. Otherwise there wasn't much to write home about — one wooden desk, one wooden chair, a battered set of iron-grey filing cabinets, a tiny bathroom with a toilet, a sink, and a shower almost big enough to stand up in.

"Whose boxes are those?"

"Hmm? Oh yeah, right. I'll take care of it." Eddie leaned toward the stairs and barked off some rapid-fire Cantonese. Then he leaned back toward me. "You want me to send someone up to take care of the dust?"

"Nah. I like it. It adds to the ambiance."

Eddie chuckled. "You haven't changed a bit. Come on downstairs ... let's have a bite to eat."

"Eddie."

"Yeah, man?"

"Aren't you forgetting something?"

Eddie snapped his thick fingers. He reached into his pocket and pulled out a wad of cash thick enough to choke a horse. "What was it? Ten thousand?"

"Twenty."

"Right, right." Eddie peeled off bills. "Now let's eat. I'm starving."

One platter of egg rolls later I was back in the office, scrubbing away on my hands and knees, getting rid of all the dirt and dust and grime, all the dead flies and mouse droppings and cockroach casings.

I stood up and surveyed my handiwork. *Not bad, Jack, not bad at all.*

Something was missing.

I went downstairs, crossed the street, and bought a plant. Back upstairs, I put the plant on my desk and rotated the pot until the leaves lined up with the sun. *There. Open for business.*

I creaked back in the wooden chair and stared at the water stains on the ceiling. Good times. No one called because I didn't have a phone. If someone wanted to call me, they'd have to go through Eddie.

The couch across the room was taunting me. *Hey, Jack,* the couch whispered. *Remember that first night with Cassandra? The way her eyes crinkled when she laughed, the way her straight black hair smelled just like green apples. The way she moved as she got undressed, so fluid, her clothes just sliding down her long dancer's limbs. The way you grabbed her and threw her onto the couch as she laughed, the two of you tumbling together, bourbon and aftershave and green apples.*

The walls were closing in. If I stayed inside I was going to chew off my own leg like a bear caught in a trap.

On my way out the door, Eddie stopped me and held up his cellphone. I looked at him questioningly as I took it, but he just shrugged.

"Hello?"

"Jack!" Nasal, keyed up, frantic and lazy at the same time. It was Tommy. "How the hell are ya? Settling in okay?"

"So far, so good."

"Listen, you got a place to stay tonight? I can put you up in one of our condos. You'll love it. Big-screen TV, surround sound, right on the lake."

"I appreciate it, Tommy, but I've got a place." *Did my office have surround sound? It did if you counted the Cantonese conversations that came floating through the walls like ghosts.*

"Oh yeah?" Tommy sounded disappointed. "I was thinking we could grab a bite to eat, see what's shaking at the club."

"I've got some things to take care of before tomorrow. Next time, okay?"

"Yeah, but —"

"I've got to go. I'll talk to you tomorrow."

On the other end I heard Tommy sigh. "Yeah, all right. Tomorrow."

Kee-rist. I handed the phone back to Eddie and rubbed my temples.

"Serious business, Jack?"

I managed a grin. "It's always serious."

Outside I cut through the alleys, back among the garbage and the loops and swirls of gang graffiti. Overhead, the gulls were circling in the bright blue sky, diving down into the alley ahead of me. When I got closer I saw what all the screeching and strutting was about: a fast food restaurant had thrown out a giant bag of half-eaten fried chicken and the birds were scavenging. The bag was ripped open and chicken bones were strewn across the alley. Two gulls went for the same drumstick at the same time and the feathers flew. I turned away, nauseated. Gulls eating fried chicken. It didn't seem right. Almost like cannibalism.

Maybe it was a mistake blowing Tommy off like that. Tommy was the type of guy who didn't forget a slight. I could've been nicer, maybe invented some kind of song and dance. "Love to hang out, Tommy, but see, my dog's real sick, and ..." And deep inside me there was a little voice saying, *Come on, Jack. We could've been sleeping on a king-size mattress with fine Egyptian sheets tonight instead of curled up on that busted-ass second-hand yellow plaid couch of ours.* But right there was the operative word. That couch was mine, not Tommy's or his father's. You gotta set limits. Let Tommy know you're not forever at his beck and call. Sure, I was grateful, and yes, I owed him. But I was no one's lapdog. Soon as I helped Tommy clear his books, I'd be free. In the meantime, I could use a drink.

I walked down the street to what used to be my neighbourhood bar in what used to be my neighbourhood. In a few hours, hipsters with goatees and orange-tinted glasses would take over the space, but for now the bar belonged to the junkies and the bums and the rest of the down-and-outers, dressed in fashions from twenty years ago, preserved in alcohol like insects in amber. Florid faces mapped with busted veins. My kind of people.

Behind the bar was a woman so beautiful I pulled a double-take and then looked for hidden cameras. What's the gag? A woman like that in a place like this … it didn't add up.

She came closer, smiling, dark hair and a low-cut top, skin white as milk, small emeralds in her earlobes, and silver sparkles on her eyelids.

"What'll it be?"

"Beer. No, wait — double vodka, rocks."

She laughed. "That kind of day, huh?"

"That kind of decade."

She poured expertly and slid me my drink.

"You're new."

She smiled. "New? I've been working here for at least a year."

"I used to come in here all the time."

"I've never seen you before."

"I've been away."

"Travelling the world?"

"Something like that. My name's Jack."

The bartender smiled. "Suzanne."

I settled into a chair with my double vodka and a crumpled-up newspaper. The ambiance had changed, but not much. Before I went away, this place was wall-to-wall smoke; now smoking inside bars was illegal.

Hours drifted by. I drank my drink, read the paper, had another drink. Time hung suspended, the outside world pushed away, the past and the future stopping their incessant drumbeats until there was only this, this moment, calm and perfect.

Of course it couldn't last.

A drunk with long, straight dark hair and a face cratered like the surface of the moon reeled up to the bar, closed one eye, and brought Suzanne into focus. He must have liked what he saw. His pink swollen tongue licked his nightcrawler-thick lips. He leered and muttered some incoherent pickup line and Suzanne instinctively took two steps back.

"I have a boyfriend."

The drunk leered and slurred and drooled. His hands, covered in the faded green-black ink of jailhouse tattoos, reached for her breasts.

Suzanne slapped his hands away. "You need to back off."

The drunk's face contorted into a horror show. Some people just can't handle rejection.

The drunk tried to climb over the bar.

Time to stand up. "She said BACK OFF!"

The drunk growled from somewhere way back in his throat. Alcohol overriding rational thought — primitive lizard brain kicking in. I knew what would come next and I wasn't surprised. The drunk smashed his beer bottle against the bar rail and lunged at me with a fistful of broken glass.

Remember that scene in the first Indiana Jones movie with the bad guy getting all fancy with a scimitar? The way the scene is set up you think Indy is going to out-fancy the dude with his whip, but he doesn't. Instead, Indy just pulls out his gun and drops the guy with one shot. Apparently the script did call for some fancy whip work, but Harrison Ford, the actor who played Indiana Jones, was feeling sick that day. It's a great scene. And it's true: when it comes to fighting, you can either get fancy or you can just drop the guy.

Suzanne pulled a baseball bat from beneath the bar and dropped the guy.

She looked down at the drunk crumpled on the floor. Then she glared over at me. "I don't need a white knight."

"Is that who you think I am?"

Suzanne ran a bar rag along the baseball bat, wiping off blood. "I can take care of myself."

I nodded. "I can see that." I pointed with my chin to the guy on the ground. "He still breathing?"

Suzanne shrugged. "What am I, a doctor?"

I tossed two twenties onto the bar. "Keep the change."

She watched me, considering. Then she pushed the twenties back. "It's on me." She grinned. "Your heart was in the right place."

I stepped toward the door. "I better go. I start a new job tomorrow."

"You sure you don't want a refill? You can be a little late."

I smiled. "I don't think so."

Back in my office I sat in my wooden chair, put my feet up on my desk, and waited for daybreak. It didn't take long … three, four hours tops. As soon as the sunlight started to slide through the blinds I walked over to the brown and yellow plaid sofa, lay down, closed my eyes, and fell asleep.

CHAPTER 4

A pounding on the door woke me with a start and once again I fumbled for my non-existent knife. Cautiously, I slid from the couch like an alligator into the swamp and drifted silently toward the door. My heart was pounding. *I hate this shit,* I thought. *One of these days I'm going to answer the door and BOOM, that'll be it for me.*

I undid four of the locks but I left the chain on.

Eddie shoved his cellphone through the crack. "You need to get your own goddamn phone."

"Morning to you, too, Sunshine."

I unlatched the door. Eddie rolled into the office and sat on the sofa, 1970s springs groaning beneath his weight.

The phone was cold against my ear. "Jack! I got a hangover like you wouldn't believe. You should've been there last night. There was this broad, she had these ping-pong balls ... hold on a minute." Tommy put his hand over the phone and I heard muffled thumps and either a sick cat or someone screaming his guts out.

Tommy came back on the line. "Jack, I gotta let you go."

"Everything okay over there?"

"Oh sure, sure. No problem. We're just working something out with one of the fellas. Look, be at the corner of Queen and Spadina at two thirty, all right? I'll send a car. Remember, keep your eyes open."

"I always do."

I hung up and checked my watch. Two thirty was half an hour away. That's one good thing about working for gangsters. Gangsters like to sleep in.

Eddie stood up and snatched his phone away.

"Eddie."

"Yeah?"

"Can you get me a knife?"

Eddie smiled. "Check your desk drawer."

Inside the top drawer, laid out on a black velvet cloth, was a glittering galaxy of knives. Long ones. Short ones. Skinny ones. Even a fat jewelled dagger that looked like Eddie might have swiped it from the British Museum. I pulled out a knife with a twelve-inch serrated blade and wrapped my hand around the handle. Perfectly weighted.

"Eddie, what would I do without you?"

Eddie snorted.

One brisk walk through Chinatown later and I was standing on the southwest corner of Queen and Spadina, right across from the McDonald's, watching the squeegee kids ply their trade. Soon as the lights turned red they'd be out there loping across the intersection, tossing water from plastic bottles onto windshields and then scraping it off, leaving dirty streaks. Hustling a buck here, a buck there.

An unmarked white van screeched up, and from the passenger side a weightlifter with sunglasses and slicked-back hair gave me the once-over.

"You Jack?"

What would happen if I said no? If I just shook my head and walked away?

I've never walked away from anything in my life.

"Yeah. You want me to do your windows?"

"What?"

"Forget it. Let's go."

The inside of the van smelled like spearmint gum and stale cigarettes. I sat in the back seat next to a tool-box and a rolled-up tarp.

The driver was another weightlifter, a massive man with no neck, just a solid trunk of muscle. The man in the passenger seat opened up the glove compartment, pulled out a photo, and held it up to my face.

"Yep. You're you, all right."

"Good to know. Here, let me hang onto that."

The passenger passed me the photo. "I'm Sully and that's Vince. You're a friend of Tommy's?"

"That's right."

"What kind of piece you got?"

"I don't carry a piece."

"What?" Sully was totally incredulous. "You gotta carry a piece. This is dangerous work, man — serious business."

"I can handle it." I grinned as Sully furrowed his brow. "My secret is, I love people. I'm a people person."

The white van cut straight along Queen Street, heading east.

Sully turned back toward me and peered over the top of his sunglasses. "Tommy tell you the ground rules?"

"Sure. But why don't you refresh my memory."

"Vince and me, this is our show. You're just here to watch. No heavy lifting. You just hang back and let us do our thing."

I didn't say yes and I didn't say no. I turned and stared out the window. The van slowed down and I realized where we were headed. There's a whole cluster of pawn shops running along the east side of Church and the north side of Queen. I thought the Russians owned most of them, but it figured that Tommy's dad had a piece of the action.

Vince bumped the van into the curb and cut the engine. Sully turned back to me. "Wait here."

"That wasn't part of the deal."

"Look, man, Vince and I, we're professionals. Understand? If things go south, we won't be there to hold your hand."

"I'll manage."

Grumbling, Sully walked to the rear of the van, opened it up, and pulled out a baseball bat.

Suzanne, I thought. *I wonder if she's working tonight.*

I walked toward Sully, keeping my eye on the bat. "Hey, is that really necessary?"

"Relax. It's an intimidation thing."

"You don't think you and Schwarzenegger over there are intimidating enough?"

Vince laughed at that, short angry barks like a pissed-off terrier. We headed toward a pawn shop, the baseball bat resting lazily on Sully's shoulder. Warning bells, flashing lights, and sirens were going off in my head. These guys didn't have the people skills necessary for a job like this. An operation like this called for some finesse.

Vince opened the door and Sully ran inside, swinging the baseball bat and smashing the owner's glass countertop. "WHERE'S THE FUCKING MONEY? GIVE ME THE FUCKING MONEY!"

Oh Jesus.

The owner, who looked like an older, balder version of Rasputin, dove behind his shattered countertop and came up snarling with a shotgun. In the narrow confines of the pawnshop the sound was deafening. Sully grunted as he got hit and went flying back, but I didn't see it — all I saw was the gun as I yanked it from the owner's hands.

Rasputin fell to his knees, blubbering and crying in a language I didn't understand. Turned out I was pointing the shotgun right in his bearded face. I lowered the gun. The poor old guy had pissed himself.

Behind me Vince stood up, his hands red with Sully's blood. "You killed him. You fucking killed him. I'LL KILL YOU!"

Vince charged toward Rasputin, bellowing like a wounded bull. I cracked him in the face with the butt of the shotgun and he went down. I hit him again just to be sure: the butt of the shotgun got sticky with Vince's matted hair and blood.

The old man was praying, praying and blubbering, down on his knees in the broken glass.

"Shh. Shh. I'm not going to hurt you. Where's the security tape?"

The old man's mouth opened and closed. His eyes flickered to the left.

I popped out the tape and stuck it down my pants. "You got a back way out of here?"

Soundlessly the old man jerked his head toward a beaded curtain. I ran through a maze of dusty shelves and boxes before exploding out into the sunshine. I quickly scrubbed my prints off the shotgun with my shirt, chucked the gun into a Dumpster, and emerged onto Church Street in a casual saunter, willing myself to breathe slow. In the distance I heard the sirens. I walked for two blocks, then I whistled for a cab and got the fuck out of there.

In the cab I looked down and saw blood on my shirt. *Fuck.* It was just a little bit. The cabbie didn't seem to notice. I got him to turn right and head east. He dropped me off at Gerrard and Parliament and I walked a few blocks to a thrift store, where I bought a plain black T-shirt. I wrapped the bloody shirt in the plastic thrift store bag. I hoped Eddie still had the fireplace up on the roof. Toss in the bag, the shirt, and the pawnshop security tape, break out the beer and marshmallows and the ol' acoustic guitar.

Fuck.

On the streetcar back west I kept my breathing under control and my anger in check. Did I forget anything? Security tape, check. Prints off gun, check. Photo of me from the van, check. Prints off the van? Shit.

Fuck. Fuck. Fuck.

Then there was Rasputin. He wouldn't talk. Or would he? One thing I've learned over the years: the Human Factor is the random X Factor that cannot be planned for. He could make up some song and dance, put the shotgun in my hands, not his. Robbery gone wrong. In Rasputin's scenario, it'd go like this: Vince and Sully and I come in to rip him off. I pull a double-cross, shoot Sully and bash Vince. Then I take the security tape, the money, and whatever valuables the old man's claimed on his insurance, and split out the back. Old man gets off scot-free with a pocketful of insurance money. Not a bad scam, but damned if I was going back to jail so an old man could buy himself another fistful of Viagra and some discount hookers.

I got off the streetcar at College and Spadina and walked south. Payphones were an endangered species in the Age of Cellphones, but I spotted one and dialed Tommy's number.

"Don't say my name. We need to meet."

"So soon? Sure, come on down to the club."

In the background I could hear house music throbbing. I had a headache already. "The club's no good. They could be watching the club."

Tommy laughed. "You're crazy, you know that? No one's watching the club."

"I'm serious."

"All right, all right. Meet me in the kitchen. Half an hour."

The kitchen was an actual kitchen in the back of one of Tommy's dad's restaurants. The maître d' arched his eyebrows when he saw me coming. I didn't look like one of the impeccably dressed suckers slurping down over-priced pasta in the main dining room.

"Table for one?"

"I'm meeting Tommy."

The maître d's eyes flickered. "Yes, sir. Right this way."

We walked through the crowded kitchen, past steaming vats of pasta and pans of frying veal. The maître d' led me to a private room tucked away just behind the dessert station. Inside the room was a long mahogany table with six chairs. I grabbed a seat and wondered how long I'd have to wait.

The answer: not long. Four minutes after I sat down, Tommy came storming into the kitchen, and he didn't look happy. He looked like I felt: tired and hot and pissed off. "My phone's been ringing off the hook all afternoon. What the fuck happened?"

I wanted to reach across the table and wring Tommy's fat, sweaty neck. Instead I calmly sipped my water. "There was a problem."

"Yeah, I'll say there was a fucking problem! I got one guy with his guts blown out all over the floor, I got another guy in the hospital with his head smashed in, and I got you sittin' there drinking fucking ice water. Where's my fucking money?"

Breathe in, breathe out. Maintain.

"We didn't get your money. Your boy Sully was too busy going apeshit with a baseball bat."

I filled Tommy in. My voice was calm. Just the facts, ma'am.

At the end of it Tommy didn't look happy, but he did look a little sheepish. "Really? He just started swinging?"

"That's right. Look, my fingerprints are in that van."

"Relax. My guys at the wrecking yard towed it. It's been crushed into a cube."

"And the old man?"

"He won't say shit."

I leaned back and let myself breathe.

Tommy shook his head. "Jack, you worry too much."

"That's why you hired me."

Deep down, though, I knew Tommy was right. I never used to worry about shit like that. I'd go in like a ton of bricks, do the job and split. Let someone else worry about mopping up.

I leaned toward Tommy. "You've got a problem. You've got weightlifters, and what you need are diplomats. I can't work with these guys. They're half gorilla, half steroids. I know, I know, they're perfectly nice guys and you've known them since grade school and they bring the best potato salad to the company picnic, but I'm telling you, they're not the right guys for the job."

An aging waiter brought over trays of meat. Tommy slowly cut a piece of veal. He brought a forkful to his mouth and chewed it slowly, contemplatively. "See, Jack? This is why I like you. You're not afraid to tell it like it is. Some of these guys, I tell 'em up is down and they all wag their tails like puppies. 'Sure thing, boss! Up is down, boss!' That kind of thinking, it's not good. That kind of thinking can doom an entire organization. But you … you've got a clean mind. You're a breath of fresh air." Tommy's knife and fork clattered to his plate. "Tell me what you need and I'll make it happen."

"I'll do your routes for you. Let me bring in a couple of my own guys."

"Nuh-uh. No way. Why don't I just hand over the combination to my safe? The keys to my safe deposit box?" Tommy leaned closer. "You gotta understand, Jack, in a business like mine there's certain, whatchacall, proprietary information that shouldn't fall into the wrong hands."

"I understand. Here's something else I understand: you need your money. You don't trust your own people to get it for you. So where does that leave us?"

Tommy hemmed and hawed over his last scraps of veal. He turned and beckoned the waiter closer. "What does this look like, Mothers Against Drunk Driving? Get us some more fucking wine."

I saw my face reflected in Tommy's eyes as he stared across the table. I looked like shit.

"You sure you can keep your guys in line?"

"Don't worry about that." I grinned and cracked my knuckles. "Management is my forte."

CHAPTER 5

I was nine years old when I first started taking karate. I hated it. All that bowing and scraping. For my mom it was an excuse to get me out of the house and be around a "positive male role model." Our sensei was a fucking tyrant. I swear he enjoyed hurting little kids. Grinning as he stood over me writhing on the mat, my arm broken.

When I was ten I won my first tournament. My mother wasn't there. I found her later passed out on our apartment couch, an empty tequila bottle keeping the empty beers company. I took no pleasure in the roar of the crowd, all those smiling faces, all those happy moms and dads. I hated the smug look on the sensei's face as he bowed to me, as if to say, "See, you little shit? I'm the best fucking karate teacher there is and you had better fucking believe it." I hated the stiff fabric of my karate gi, the strange plastic smell of the gym mats, the stinging chemical fizz of an orange soda someone's dad bought me afterward.

I remember a lot about that day. What I remember most is the look on the other kid's face as I swept his legs out from under him. Surprise at first, wide-eyed surprise, and then, as I moved in to finish him, a flicker of recognition. He knew he was beaten before he even hit the mat. He knew I had beaten him.

The look in that kid's eyes — that, I liked.

CHAPTER 6

It's just like riding a bike. Once you learn how to cut someone's throat with a set of keys, it's not something you're going to forget. I learned this trick from my good pal Grover. Remember those old Charles Atlas ads in the comic books? Ninety-eight-pound weakling on the beach gets sand kicked in his face by a big beach bully. Weakling gets pissed off, sends away for Charles Atlas's bodybuilding device (The Secrets of DYNAMIC-TENSION: Atlas's device was basically nothing but a giant spring) and bulks up and then kicks some serious ass. My buddy Grover was the before picture. Guy weighed about ninety-five pounds and he wore a bow tie. But he was one of the deadliest humans I knew, and no one ever took him seriously until it was too late.

Grover took the tiny paper umbrella out of his third margarita and took a sip. Salt crystals clung to his sandy-brown moustache. We had been sitting on the patio of this

Tex-Mex place on Baldwin Street for about three hours, shooting the shit and watching the world go by.

"You ever think about retiring, Jack?"

"Shit. Do I look that bad?"

We both laughed, but it wasn't funny.

"Look at me." Grover spread his skinny arms wide, causing his white linen suit jacket to fall open. "I've never felt better. I've got some money, my health, and a sweet gal. We sit in my boat, drink beer, and go fishing. When it starts getting cold, we pull up the anchor and haul ass toward warmer weather."

I shook my head. "I don't like fish."

Grover sucked salt from his moustache and leaned closer. "You've changed, Jack. I don't know what it is exactly, but you've changed. I can see it in your eyes."

"Contacts," I said.

This time nobody laughed.

"I sent you letters, you know. When you were Inside. Did you get them?"

"Yeah, I got them."

"You didn't write back."

"I know. I should've sent a postcard. 'Wish you were here.'"

"You know, Jack, some people use humour as a shield."

"Is that right? That's really fucking interesting."

"Why'd you call me down here?"

Enough bullshit. "I need to see The Chief."

Grover shook his head, finished his margarita, stood up, and threw fifty bucks on the table. "I'll see what I can do. Hey, Jack."

"Yeah?"

"You don't really wear contacts, do you?"

"Nope."

Grover squinted in the sunlight, staring out into some middle distance. "I got this old camping cooler that I keep on the deck of my boat, right by my fishing chair. I keep it stocked with ice and grape soda and at least twelve beers at all times. I'm saving those beers for you, Jack. Come get them sometime."

Then he was gone, just a little man in a white suit, fading into the crowd.

CHAPTER 7

I met The Chief on one of my last legit security jobs. He and I were added at the last minute to the security detail surrounding a multinational entertainment company's latest product to roll off the teen idol assembly line: three fresh-faced, non-threatening boys who could sing like angels.

You couldn't hear anything over the screams and shrieks of the basically all-female crowd. An ocean of arms, all with outstretched hands and cameras and posters, all desperately reaching out toward the boys as they walked the red carpet in front of MuchMusic. It was fucking crazy.

The Chief was out front — "on point," as they say in the military — then came the fresh-faced boys and their regular security goons. I tagged along, bringing up the rear. Suddenly, this freak with a knife tried to jump the fence. Back then I thought I was fast, but The Chief was there before me, hands moving in a hummingbird blur, breaking the guy's arm in three different places. The Chief caught the knife before it hit the red carpet and handed it to me: "Here." Then he hauled the guy to the ground, snapped the cuffs on him, and hustled him away before the cameras and the news crews even realized what was happening.

After the concert, with the boys tucked safely away while the roadies dismantled the gear and tried to score with the groupies, The Chief cocked his head toward me and said "Let's grab a beer."

We didn't go far. The Chief had parked his car in the MuchMusic parking lot. He plopped down in the driver's seat, grabbed two beers from the cooler in the back, and grinned. "That was something, wasn't it? An ocean of girls."

"I've got a girlfriend."

The Chief snorted. "The boys don't. Not if you believe the press releases. They say they're saving themselves for marriage." The Chief guffawed. "Freakin' altar boys move more product — keychains and teddy bears and shit. The corporation's got an image to uphold."

The Chief killed his bottle and then unscrewed his silver flask. "Whisky?"

"No thanks."

"You smoke crack?"

"Hell no."

"Reefer? Uppers? Downers? Leapers? Screamers?"

I held out my bottle. "I like beer."

The Chief laughed. "Me too, kid. You ever break any legs?"

"I broke my arm once."

"No, not *your* legs. Other people's."

Finally I caught his drift. "Like for money?"

"That's right."

I shook my head. "Nope."

The Chief grinned. "Would you like to?"

It didn't go quite like that, of course. There's the obligatory song-and-dance. You've got to get to know a person a little bit before you ask them to break someone's bones.

"Do you agree there are people in this world whose legs need breaking? Speaking hypothetically, of course."

"Of course, I mean, yes. I agree."

"Then it stands to reason that there are people who must break those legs. Right?"

"Well … I guess. But those people don't have to be me."

"You're right about that, kid. But think about this. You're performing a valuable service. We're not talking about civilians here. You aren't walking into the family butcher shop and taking out Grampa. These are degenerates we're talking about. Thieves. Drug addicts. Compulsive gamblers."

"Those people need help."

"That's right. That's exactly right. And that's what we do. We help them realize they've got to straighten up and fly right. Nothing like lying in an alleyway screaming in agony with your legs broken to help you see the error of your ways."

"But you're working for gangsters."

The Chief leaned back, his face half-hidden in shadow. "I had an epiphany a few years back, kid. I was sitting in my trailer drinking a G&T and watching a show about monkeys. Apes, really. Chimpanzees. The British voice-over was droning on about how these apes get organized. Basically they form a gang with the alpha chimp on top. Chimps are our closest animal relatives, did you know that? So it makes sense that we're no different. That's how all of society works. It's all gangs. You got your corporations fighting each other. Each one is a gang. You got gangs of cops fighting gangs of crooks. Think about a university. Each department is a gang fighting for funding. It's all gangs, each one with an alpha chimp on top."

The Chief's silver flask gleamed in the moonlight as he tilted it back. "And if it's all gangs, then we're all gangsters."

CHAPTER 8

I was on the roof with Eddie Yao, perched on a rusted and busted lawn chair, the kind with the green and white plastic latticework, both of us kicking back and sipping a few beers in the splendour of the asphalt beach while down in the alley below two dogs were yowling and snarling and trying to tear each other a new asshole.

Eddie finished his beer, set the bottle down, and looked over at me. The sun was setting, disappearing pale pink and purple behind the rooftops. Eddie was still wearing his sunglasses. "You like dogs?"

I leaned back and grinned. "You know me, Eddie. I love all of God's creatures."

"You're a lover, not a fighter."

We both burst out laughing.

Eddie snapped his fingers. "That guy called for you. Tommy."

"Oh yeah?" I reached out my hand and Eddie slapped

his phone into my palm. In the darkness the phone looked different. No, wait … it was different.

"You get a new phone?"

Eddie snorted. "Because of you I have to keep chucking them in the lake."

The wind whipped through my hair as I walked out toward the edge of the roof. From there I could see the blinking lights on the CN Tower, warning airplanes to back the fuck off.

As I punched in Tommy's number I wondered if he threw his phones into the lake, too. He wasn't exactly a cautious guy. In fact, you could sum up his credo with a T-shirt slogan I saw once writ large across the belly of a slouchy teen: I Don't Give a Fuck.

Tommy picked up and just started talking. "So I'm on my fifth Scotch and soda when suddenly it hits me. I haven't heard from my pal recently. My good pal Jack."

Tommy was slurring his words but I caught the menace in his voice. He was at the club. Eddie's phone throbbed with bass.

"So where the fuck are you, Jack? Didn't we have a meeting scheduled?"

"Um … no, I don't think so."

Tommy was talking but he wasn't talking to me. "Leave that. Leave the whole fucking bottle. What's that, Jack?"

"I said I'm on my way."

The cab cut through Clubland, past lineups of beefy guys with gold chains and gel in their hair and skinny gals with sparkly silver tops and micro-miniskirts, rubbing their bare arms against the evening chill.

The cabbie, big guy in a newsie cap, shook his head and let loose a grunt. "Damn shame. All these young girls done lost their pants."

The cabbie grinned at me in the rear-view mirror and I knew he was waiting for me to laugh. *Sorry, my man — not tonight.* Tonight Tommy was both pissed and pissed off, which meant anything could happen.

I got off about two blocks from the club, stepping onto the sidewalk just as a police horse took a huge steaming crap at the intersection. The light turned green and the mounted cop trotted off, past the lineups thrumming with anticipation. Everyone was happy, but I knew how this game ended: Last Call and then 2:00 a.m. and the clubs vomit out the stragglers, all those guys with gold chains who came in from the suburbs to get laid and instead got shot down again and again and now they're boozed up and angry, beer and testosterone coursing through their veins, surging onto the streets with their fists clenched because, hey, if you can't fuck, you might as well fight.

At Tommy's club a fat man with a shaved head stopped me at the door. He must be a real cool guy because he was wearing black pants, black shirt, black tie, and a headset. Two huge guys stood behind him with their giant arms crossed, flanking the doorway like Greek pillars.

Headset turned up his nose at my sweatshirt and rumpled pants.

"This is the Red Carpet Entrance."

I grinned and pointed to the ground. "That explains the red carpet."

The fat man cocked his head. "There's another door over there."

Time was I would've taken this guy's headset and made him eat it. Then I would've gone loco on the two guys behind him. But I've matured. That kind of shit, as good as it may feel, doesn't get you where you want to go. That's the kind of shit that lands you in jail.

Instead I got right up into Headset's face and I smiled. "I'm a friend of Tommy's."

"Name?"

I kept smiling. In a quiet, even voice I said, "My name is 'Tommy is going to cut your balls off with razor wire if you don't get the fuck out of my way.' Go on, check your list. Should be on there."

Headset's eyes narrowed into slits. "Name?"

"Jack. Jack Palace."

A quick scan of the list and Headset stepped aside. "Go right in, sir."

I stepped through the door and the metal detector started to kick up a ruckus. Headset waved me back. *Shit*, I thought. *The fucking knives.*

Headset's huge buddy shook his head. "Forget it. Let him through."

"But —"

"Listen to your boy, Headset."

Headset glowered as I breezed through the door.

———

Tommy was flying high when I saw him, a wild shock of receding hair bolting straight up from his head, his pupils like pinpricks, sweat running down his face. His Hawaiian shirt hung open, buttons either undone or missing. Four deeply tanned party girls clustered around him, two servers bringing champagne by the bottleful.

"Jack! About fucking time. Come on." Without waiting for a response, Tommy turned around, his arms and legs jerking like a Claymation cartoon. He moved off toward a circular staircase leading up to another level of the club. The party girls obediently trailed behind.

Outside the door to his private office, Tommy lurched around and growled at the girls. "Beat it." He reached out and caught one of them by the wrist. "Not you. Get in here. You, too, Jack."

Inside, Tommy's office was long and lush. Black leather couches and black tables and white shag carpeting, like a bachelor apartment from the 1980s. A black and chrome bar stretched across the entire length of one wall. The other wall was one-way glass looking out over the sweaty madness of the club. Tommy could see out, but nobody could see in.

Tommy staggered over to the bar and poured himself five fingers of Scotch. Then he grabbed a bottle of soda and splashed it all over the counter. Maybe a drop or two hit his glass.

"Jack, you want a drink?"

I knew better than to say no. "Sure. Scotch." The woman beside me was standing statue-still. I could hear a faint tremble with every breath she took. She wasn't just scared, she was terrified. Something told me she had been in this room before.

Tommy almost tripped on the white shag as he jerked and lurched toward us, thrusting a highball glass full of Scotch into my hand.

"*Salud.*" Tommy tilted his glass to his lips and drained it in two gulps. The black leather couch hissed softly as he plopped himself down.

"Darla ... Starla ..."

"My name is Janet."

Tommy smashed his highball glass against the table-top. "Your name is Shut the Fuck Up!" Arm twitching, Tommy jerked down his zipper. "Get over here and suck my cock. Jack, you want to get your cock wet?"

"Tommy, man. Come on. Let's talk business."

I focused on Tommy's eyes, those tiny black pin-pricks burning with rage and hate. *Leave her alone*, I thought.

"You want to talk business? Let's talk some mother-fucking business. Where's my money, Jack?"

"You'll get your money. I'm putting my team together."

"Your team? Your team? The Brooklyn Dodgers, now that was a fucking team."

This was a waste of time. I might as well be wearing a leprechaun hat and dancing a jig. Tommy wouldn't remember any of this in the morning. Hell, Tommy probably wouldn't remember any of this fifteen minutes from now.

A knock on the door and one of Tommy's guys stuck his head in. I recognized him. An older man with a long face and sad, droopy eyes.

"Boss —"

"What the fuck? Can't you see I'm busy?"

"Yeah, but … we got The Leopard outside."

Tommy blinked and twitched his nose and wiped sweat from his brow. "The Leopard, huh? The Leopard. That prick. Where is he? He's here? Fuck him. Fuck him right up the ass with a telephone pole." Tommy noticed Janet cowering in the corner. "You still here?" Tommy lurched to his feet and almost tumbled face-first into the table. I caught him before he fell, but one look at Janet weeping silently in the corner made me wish I'd dropped him.

"Get your hands off me. Come on, we got work to do. Carlo! Send that prick in."

Carlo pushed the door open wide. Two huge guys stuffed into charcoal-grey suits lumbered into the room. There was a tall, nervous man in a white suit and an open-collar blue shirt wedged between them. The Leopard.

The nervous man's hands twitched. "Tommy, I —"

Tommy screamed, "Shut the fuck up!" In the corner, Janet jumped and hid her face behind her hands.

Tommy closed one eye, bringing The Leopard into focus. "You fucking guys. You don't talk first — I talk first. I ask the questions, you answer. You got that?"

The Leopard nodded mutely.

Tommy fumbled a cigarette into his mouth and then turned to me. "Jack. You got a light?"

I knew what it was all about. Power. A display of dominance. The alpha chimp. I stepped forward and lit Tommy's cigarette.

Tommy blew smoke right into The Leopard's face. The tall man coughed.

"So where's my fucking money?"

"Tommy, you know me. You know I'm good for it. I've had a real bad run recently. Sometimes you just don't get the cards, you know?"

"No, I don't know, because I'm not a degenerate fuckin' gambler like you, you prick." Tommy leaned closer. For one crazy minute I thought he was going to bite off The Leopard's nose and spit it out onto the carpet. "I gave you one last chance to get my money. What did you do? You fucking blew it."

Tommy slammed his fist right into The Leopard's stomach. The tall man doubled over, his arms caught by the two goons in the charcoal suits.

Tommy jerked his head toward the exit door on the far side of his office. "Let's take a walk. You, too, Jack. Let's all go get some fresh fucking air."

Janet stayed weeping in the corner. I left the door open and gestured with my head. *Go*, I thought. *Go far, far away and never come back.*

Deep down I knew she would stay in that room, waiting for Tommy.

Outside the club a cool breeze was blowing off the lake, ruffling The Leopard's hair. We marched into an alley and the whole scene was strangely familiar: garbage, rats, graffiti. Back-alley business.

The Leopard was whimpering now. I stepped forward. "Tommy, I got to get going."

"You're not going anywhere. I want you to see this. Understand? You fucking stand there with your eyes wide open."

One of the bouncers wrapped his giant hands around The Leopard's arms and held him tight. The other bouncer stepped forward and slammed his fist into The Leopard's sternum. The Leopard let out a sound that was half a whimper, half a groan. Silently, almost bored, the bouncer started to really work the guy over. Just another day at the office.

I wanted to look away but I didn't. I wanted to step between the bouncer and The Leopard and say, "That's enough," but I didn't. I just stood there next to Tommy, listening to him breathe, smelling the Scotch fumes rolling off him in waves.

The bouncers stepped back and The Leopard crumpled to the ground, startling the rats pawing through the trash. I breathed a sigh of relief as the bouncers turned to leave. At last, it was over.

Then Tommy started to kick the guy, really stomping him with this savage look in his face. And he wouldn't stop.

CHAPTER 9

The plant needed water. I needed something stronger.

I shuffled slowly across my office, the yellow light so dim it was almost brown, and poured myself and the plant some drinks. "What do you think, plant? Do I need this shit? I don't need this shit. I could be sitting on the beach in sunny Acapulco drinking a margarita. I could be touring the grand canals of Venice."

"You could be dead."

I dodged and whirled, stiletto leaping into my palm.

The Chief held up his hands. "Relax, relax."

"Jesus. I almost slit your throat."

The Chief grinned. I didn't ask how he got in. It didn't matter. He wouldn't tell me.

"Grover said you wanted to see me."

"Yeah. Drink?"

"No thanks. I gave it up."

"Oh yeah?" Back in the day The Chief could booze with the best of them.

"That's right."

"You go to AA?"

"Yeah, right. And put my life in the hands of a Higher Power?" Lightning-quick, The Chief unholstered his Glock 9mm. The gun gleamed evilly in the feeble yellow light. "Here's my Higher Power."

I set my vodka down on the desk. "It's good to see you, Chief."

It had been about seven years, but the man looked exactly the same. Squat, compact frame wrapped up in jeans and a white T-shirt and a black leather jacket. Short black hair starting to turn silver at the temples. Maybe a new scar twisting across his face, leathery as a catcher's mitt.

The Chief shuffled over to the window and peered down onto the neon streets below. "So what's the hustle?"

"Collections."

The Chief turned and grinned. "Since when are you an errand boy?"

"I met this guy in prison. I owe him a favour."

"And I owe you a favour."

"Run these routes with me and we're square. But I've got to warn you, this guy I'm working for, he's a real vicious prick."

The Chief shrugged. "They all are."

CHAPTER 10

Mostly it was smooth like butter. Walk in, get the envelope, walk out. There were a few holdouts but they didn't hold out for long. The Chief could be very persuasive.

We hit bars, restaurants, night clubs. We went out to Chinatown B on the East Side and stopped off at the off-track betting parlour. The air was dense with cigarette smoke. Outside on the sidewalk faded old men were smoking and coughing and spitting on the sidewalk. Tuberculosis City.

I frowned. "Tommy's dad doesn't have any pull in Chinatown. The Chinese run their own show."

The Chief grinned. "I know. I just had to put some money down. Got a real hot tip."

Back in the car The Chief stretched and yawned. "What's next?"

I brought up my mental list. "Joey Economy. Numbers

runner. He's got a place out in the Beaches."

"Beaches, huh? I should've brought my swimsuit."

You know you're getting close to the Beaches when the stores get cutesy. Rustic furniture, scented candles, and spas for dogs. Yuppie shit. The Chief cocked his head. "You want an ice cream? Let's get an ice cream."

The Chief licked his ice cream as we strolled along the boardwalk. Dogs barked. Joggers pushed two-thousand-dollar baby buggies. Girls in sunglasses and bikinis played volleyball on the beach. We stopped to watch, blue skies above, white sailboats cutting across the lake.

The Chief wiped his mouth and dropped his crumpled-up napkins into the trash. "All right, let's go get that money."

A receptionist with wild red curls piled atop her head looked up as we came piling into the front room.

"You're here to see Mr. Mezell?"

For the millionth time I was glad The Chief was standing next to me instead of one of Tommy's goons. One of the weightlifters would've blurted out something stupid like, "Nah, bitch, we're here to see Joey Economy." Steroid-laden brain too dense to separate the street name from Joey's civilian life. Which was ... what? Some kind of dentist?

The receptionist muttered into her phone. Then she looked up. "Go on in."

Joey Economy was old, older than I expected. He

must have been at least in his midseventies. He was skeleton-thin but still dapper, wrapped up tight in a light linen suit.

"Gentlemen, come in, come in. Sylvia said you wanted to see me?"

The Chief's eyes were fixed on Joey, so I took a few seconds to scan the office. Something didn't feel right.

"Tommy sent us."

"Oh?" Mr. Economy turned to his desk and picked up a big black ledger. His skeletal fingers expertly flipped the pages. "Tommy, Tommy …" Joey gave his skull a shake. "Sorry, I'm afraid I don't know any Tommy. Perhaps you have the wrong address?"

"You're Joey Economy?"

The skeleton smiled. "Now I know you have the wrong place. My name is Mezell. And now, if you'll excuse me, gentlemen, I have another appointment."

Outside in the sunshine, The Chief scratched his head. "What the hell just happened?"

I blinked as a babe on Rollerblades went gliding by. "The old man's some kind of hypnotist. Must've been a stage magician in a previous lifetime."

"Yeah, right." The Chief darted his hand beneath his coat and settled on his Glock. "Let's go back in there and get that fucking money."

I shook my head. "Something's wrong. I don't like it."

"We going back in?"

"No, not yet." Over the years I've learned to listen to my gut. Right then my gut was standing up and rattling my ribcage trying to get my attention. "We're done for the day. We need more information. Let's see what Eddie can put together."

CHAPTER 11

I did a favour for Eddie once. Some guys had caught on to Eddie's extracurricular activities and they wanted in. Eddie figured his casino was running just fine without them, so he turned them down. These guys weren't too happy with that. Turns out these guys were members of a Jamaican crew run by a killer named King Diamond. King Diamond mostly ran drugs, but he was trying to branch out. He had big plans, this King Diamond. He was going to take over everything: all the drug-running, all the gambling, all the girls ... everything. Sure, he was crazy. No one man can control all the rackets. It's an ebb and flow, a give and take. Plenty of vice for everyone. That's not how The King saw it, though. King Diamond wanted to be on top, sitting on his throne in his penthouse overlooking the city, cackling as his subjects bowed and scraped their way forward, arms laden with bags of tribute. The King let his nickname go to his head. He was capable of anything, and that's what made him dangerous.

When King Diamond's crew told him that Eddie turned him down, he was none too happy. If Eddie wasn't going to let him have a piece, then he was going to take the whole pie. He was going to put the squeeze on Eddie, force him out of business, drive him from the city. To make it happen, The King kidnapped Eddie's daughter.

Big mistake.

Eddie frowned. "You were right, Jack. Something's screwy. Joey Economy isn't a numbers runner. He's a hit man."

The Chief and I went silent. I knew we were both thinking the same thing. An old hit man equalled a dangerous hit man. Sure, he was a bag of bones now, but he was in a dangerous game and he had stayed alive a long, long time. That meant he knew his shit.

"And Joe Mezell is Joey Economy?"

"That's right. Mezell is one of his aliases. Joseph McIntire, Joey Machine —"

The Chief: "Wait a sec. Joey Machine?"

"Yep."

The Chief's chair scraped back. "I'm out."

That's not good. "Wait a second, Chief —"

"Nope. Sorry, Jack. I signed on to help you with collections. I didn't sign on to go against Joey Machine. This guy … he's a legend, Jack. The baddest of the bad. Shit, I didn't even think he was real."

"But —"

"I ran the routes with you. But now I'm out. If you're smart, you'll get out, too."

Across the table Eddie nodded. "Chief's right, Jack. Joey Machine is bad news. My guys were asking around and they didn't like the looks they were getting. You know Tony Talks-A-Lot? Soon as he heard 'Joey Machine,' he clammed right up."

I shook my head. "I can't get out. I owe Tommy."

The Chief stuffed himself into his leather jacket. Had to be 32 degrees Celsius outside, but The Chief never sweats. I'd never seen him back down from a fight yet, but there he was, leaving.

"You're an honourable guy, Jack. I respect that. We all do. But sometimes you got to do what's right for you. You got to look out for yourself, or you'll end up dead."

CHAPTER 12

The Chief, The Chief. I remember walking through the snow toward his trailer lit against the darkness, a string of red Christmas lights pinned to the roof. I had been coming out here for almost three months. There was an old abandoned barn nearby that still smelled like horses and hay. That's where The Chief brought me the first day, pushing open the barn doors to reveal his own private gym. Boxing ring, heavy bag, blue gym mats — standard stuff. Then there were the human-shaped targets pinned to the walls. Not so standard.

"Come on, kid," The Chief had said, grinning. "Show me what you got."

I got in the ring. "No gloves?"

"Very few people wear boxing gloves in the street, kid."

That first fight lasted all of two seconds. I thought I was fast but The Chief was faster. I swung with my right.

The Chief sidestepped easily and then slammed his foot into my groin.

"No rules in the street, either," The Chief said as he picked me up and dusted me off. "You'll learn."

The Chief was as good as his word. We were still working legit jobs back then — security for nightclubs, a bit of bodyguarding. After work and on my days off we'd go out to the barn. I only had to go to the hospital twice. I was getting better.

That Christmas, though …

The Chief and I had just finished babysitting a bagful of diamonds with a man attached. After we got the diamonds and the man safely from one side of the city to the other, we dropped into a dive bar to have a few pints. There were half-assed decorations pinned to the wall above the bottles: limp tinsel, a faded Santa, a sad-looking snowman.

"You got plans for Christmas, kid?"

I didn't say anything. I kept on drinking.

"Going back home? Gonna see the folks?"

"Nope."

The Chief slapped my shoulder. "Come by the homestead. We'll do it up right. Turkey, eggnog … the whole nine yards."

"I don't think so."

"What are you gonna do? Go back to your rooming house and sit alone in the dark? Fuck that. Come on over and have some cranberries."

"I'm not too big on holidays."

The Chief leaned closer. I could smell the beer on his breath. "You're not going to be alone for Christmas, Jack. You got that?"

So there I was, trudging through the snow toward The Chief's trailer, the Christmas lights kicking up an eerie red glow. I had a gift-wrapped box of chocolates under my arm. I felt fucking ridiculous. "Thanks for teaching me how to kill a man with a playing card, Chief. Here, have a nut cluster." In retrospect I should've brought a bottle of whisky, but what the hell did I know?

The Chief was already blitzed when he threw open the door. Puffs of steam and smoke and ragtime music poured out into the night. "Jack! Get your ass on in here."

Inside, the trailer was bright and warm and homey. Half-empty whisky bottles covered the table. The Chief's gun was on top of the television. A frozen TV dinner (turkey and gravy) was abandoned on the counter. The air was blue with cigarette smoke.

This was a mistake.

"Chief … I've got to go."

I stood outside the trailer blinking, trying to catch my breath. In the distance a lonely truck rumbled down the highway, its headlights lost in a mist of snow.

"Jack."

I almost leapt out of my skin. I never heard The Chief coming. "I'm okay."

"What's wrong, kid?"

"Nothing."

The Chief stood there waiting, the snow settling on his shoulders.

I let out a deep breath. "I remember good Christmases. I remember my mom laughing as we opened presents, stockings hung by the fire, cat sleeping on the carpet. Thing is, we didn't have a fireplace. Or presents. My mom was passed out drunk. It's like … I made it up, you know? My brain filled in the missing pieces."

The Chief was silent for a while. The snow fell.

"I know." The way he said it, I had no doubt that he did.

Embarrassed, I turned away. "I'm sorry."

"You've got nothing to be sorry for. Here." The Chief passed me a long box wrapped in green paper covered in cartoon snowmen. "Go on, open it."

I ripped through the wrapping paper and opened the box. Resting on blue velvet was a double-edged Bowie knife with a handle carved from a deer antler.

"I saw you looking at that in the barn the other day."

"Chief … I can't."

"Go on, take it. It's yours." The Chief grinned. "You know how to use it?"

"Yeah," I lied. "Sort of. Not really."

"I'll teach you."

I turned away. Something caught in my throat.

The Chief's eyes twinkled. He thumped my back. "Merry Christmas, Jack."

I still had that knife. It was in storage, gathering dust in its blue velvet box.

The Chief, though … The Chief had packed up and left, and I was alone.

CHAPTER 13

The ice rattled in my vodka as I paced across my office, back and forth, restless as a caged panther. In my head the wheels were turning, cogs and gears connecting, synapses shooting blue sparks. Something was screwy. Tommy sends me to collect from a hit man who's never heard of him — or at least claims he's never heard of him. Tommy says the hit man Joey Machine is actually Joey Economy, numbers runner. But Joey Machine is bad enough to scare The Chief, and The Chief doesn't scare easily.

So … possibilities: Tommy's wrong. Tommy got confused. It's possible. Maybe Tommy only knows Joey Economy, numbers runner. But then why would Joey deny knowing Tommy? To keep the money. No, that doesn't make sense. Think about the other stops on Tommy's route. Bars, nightclubs, pawnshops. A thousand here, a thousand there. Real nickel-and-dime shit, in the grand scheme of things. A few two-bit operations thrown

Tommy's way to keep him busy. Like Tommy's nightclub. Keep him busy and away from his dad's table, where the real deals go down.

Outside in Chinatown it was still dark. Hours before sunrise. I poured myself another vodka. The first sip cleared my head and the second sip kicked up mud. For a brief minute I thought I had it — Eureka! — but then as quick as it came, it disappeared in a cloud of mental smoke.

I turned to the plant sitting on my desk. "Tommy. This is all about Tommy, isn't it?" But if he was pulling some scam and I was just an unwitting cog in his vast machine, it's not like he was going to come clean and tell me. "Ah, you got me, Jack. I was totally setting you up! Ha ha ha. Come on in, have a beer."

The dusty floorboards creaked as I kept on pacing. Man, I hated this shit. My brain felt like a snake eating its own tail. Tommy, the hit man, me. The money. Somewhere down near the bottom where things got murky it had to be about the money. It always was.

CHAPTER 14

I tossed Tommy a backpack full of envelopes. "Here you go."

"Jack, hold on a second. Where ya going? Come on, sit down and have a beer."

"I ran your routes. You wanted to know who was holding out on you. Tex at the Starlight, Carl at the Cavern, and Bobby Rich at the Bullfighter. Okay?"

Tommy looked like a whipped dog. "So that's it?"

"That's it."

"You're just gonna walk away?"

I shrugged. "Don't see why not."

"Come on, sit down, have a beer. For old time's sake."

Ah, fuck it. I sat down. Tommy snapped his fingers — classy guy, that Tommy — and summoned our server. "Gimme another beer. Dos Equis. Same for my friend. And maybe some chips and salsa or some shit like that. You know, something to nibble on." Tommy shot our server a wink and I swear to God I could see her shudder. Tommy started pawing through the envelopes in the backpack. "I knew I could count on you, Jack. You say it's all here?"

"That's right. You think I'd hold out on you?"

Tommy barked out a laugh. "Not you. But some of these mutts … " Tommy looked up curiously. "So you got out to the Beaches okay?"

"Yeah, we got out there. Joey … what was his name again?"

"Joey Economy."

"Yeah, that's it. Joey Economy. You know, it was interesting. He said he never heard of you."

The server returned and set down our beers. Mine looked so cold and delicious I wanted to jump into the bottle and splash around awhile. Two gulps and the beer was gone. "You might want to check into that. Thanks for the beer, Tommy. I've got to split."

"Wait, wait!" Tommy's eyes went sideways. "That guy Joey … he's not really a numbers runner."

"You don't say."

"No. But I figured you and your guy might be able to talk to him, you know, shake some money loose."

"You sent me to rob a hit man?"

Tommy jumped as if stung. "No! Come on, Jack. Would I do that to you?"

"I sure hope not."

"No way, no how. It's legit. He owes my dad some dough."

"He said he never heard of you."

Tommy's face screwed up like he just sucked a lemon. "Yeah, well, my old man's not much for introductions. At least not where I'm concerned." Tommy tilted his head back toward his bodyguard sitting at the next table, eating scrambled eggs with a knife and fork. "Rocco ... go check on the car."

Rocco stared down at his plate. "My eggs'll get cold."

"I'll get you some new fucking eggs. Get the fuck up and go check on the car."

If I was Tommy I'd be a little more courteous toward the man who had my life in his hands. But I wasn't Tommy, and thank God for that.

Tommy watched Rocco as the big man trundled away. Then he turned back to me. "Jack. I'm gonna let you in on a little secret."

"Don't. I don't need to know, and I don't want to know."

"It's not really a secret. You're a smart guy, I'm sure you've already figured it out. This ..." Tommy hoisted the backpack stuffed with envelopes stuffed with money. "This is bullshit. Penny-ante bullshit. Pawn shops and night clubs. Fuck that. I'm thinking big, Jack. I've got my eyes on the prize."

"You want The Empire."

"Damn straight I want The Empire. My dad was going to give it to me, Jack. I swear to you, he was going to turn it all over to me, make a big announcement in front of the guys and everything. Then he got sick, went to the hospital, and fell into a coma. Now he ain't saying shit to anyone."

"And the guys ..."

Tommy nodded. "Yeah, you get it. The guys all want to be boss. They're going to rip The Empire to shreds.

They're going to get out their carving knives and kill the goose that laid the whaddaya call it, golden eggs."

"I can't help with that, Tommy."

"Hey, I'm not asking you to get caught in the middle of a civil fucking war. I'm just saying I need your help. Same shit you've been doing. Same song, different tune. And it's not like I'm asking you to do this out of the goodness of your heart. There's plenty in it for you, Jack. Plenty."

"I'm sorry, Tommy."

Tommy's eyes flashed black lightning. "Jack. You can't just fucking walk away. I saved your goddamn life!"

Caught like a fly in a motherfucking web.

I sat back down.

Tommy grinned. "That's more like it. We're old friends, you and I. This is a friendly chat, that's all. I'm not asking you to do anything new. I'm just saying the job you started isn't quite done."

"Collections."

"Yeah, that's it, collections. No more penny-ante bullshit. I need your help to collect on some big debts."

"Like from Joey Economy."

"Yeah, like that. I want to square the books, Jack. Collect my dad's debts while he's still alive." Suddenly Tommy choked up. "Let the old man know I'm not a complete screw-up, you know?" Tommy hung his head, embarrassed by the sudden display of emotion.

I knew how he felt. I've got a long white scar burrowing into the back of my head like a worm from where my mom's beer bottle found its target. "You're fucking useless! Useless!" Screaming, crying. Broken glass and blood.

Still, it wasn't all teardrops and violins. If Tommy collected his dad's debts, then Tommy would emerge with the keys to the kingdom. Little Vito and the others would have to doff their hats in respect. At least, that was the theory.

I stumbled out of the restaurant and headed for home. Another night with my feet propped up on my desk, waiting for daylight. At the last minute I turned and headed back to the neighbourhood bar so I could soak up some sanity.

Suzanne was working behind the bar. She grinned as I walked through the door. "Here to save me some more?"

"It's been a long day." I plopped down onto a bar-stool. "Why don't you save me?"

Suzanne frowned, gesturing toward the bottles. "Alcohol's a depressant. This shit won't save you."

She poured me a Scotch anyway. She looked so damn beautiful.

"What was your name again?"

"Jack."

"All right, Jack. What's your story? You go into bars and try to stop fights? You a good Samaritan?"

I sipped Scotch. "That story, The Good Samaritan. It's from the Bible. Luke 10:25–10:37. It's all about showing mercy to others." I shook my head. "Mercy isn't really my thing."

"You a priest?"

I laughed. "No."

"Married?"

"Nope."

"Girlfriend?"

I shook my head. "Not anymore."

"There's a story there. I can tell."

I shrugged. "She left me. I'm not going to sit around moaning with my thumb up my ass. Sometimes shit goes south and it's not your fault."

"Sorry."

"Don't be. Things happen."

"Yes." Suzanne smiled, her hand brushing mine. "They do."

We bumped through the doors of Suzanne's apartment still lip-locked, hands ripping at clothes, massive erection pushing against my pants.

"Wait." Suzanne broke away and sashayed toward the bathroom.

I took a deep breath and looked around. Postcards of 1950s books on the walls. Paintings of tough dames and gun molls, cold, flinty stares, sneering at the world with a gun in each hand. Fantasy Gangsters.

She came out of the bathroom draped in a light-green dressing gown. I could see the silhouette of her body through the flimsy fabric, backlit by the moon.

"Martini?"

"Sure."

The martini was cold and delicious. Her lips were soft, so soft. She stepped back and dropped her gown. Her alabaster skin glowed in the moonlight. I stood up and dropped my pants. No more waiting.

She moaned as I entered her. She pushed me back on the couch and climbed on top. Her hair flicked my chin, my chest. She bit my lip. I thrust inside, faster and harder.

At some point we moved to the bedroom, because that's where I woke up. My mouth tasted like blood and gin. I didn't remember getting here. From the bed I could see into the living room: the lamp beside the couch was in pieces on the carpet. One of us had kicked it over. I didn't remember that, either.

I rose silently to find my pants.

Suzanne snored softly. It was adorable.

I got back into bed and the next morning she made pancakes and we sat outside in the sunshine and laughed and drank coffee and read the newspaper and then the next day I built a patio and the week after that we had the neighbours over for a barbecue and we took our kids to the park and we walked our dog and everything everywhere was just hunky-dory, forever and ever, Amen.

I blinked. I found my pants and put them on.

Suzanne opened her eyes. "You going?"

"Yeah. I've got to go."

"Fine." She rolled away, turning to face the wall.

Good job, Jack. Together one night and you've already blown it. You swore you'd never hurt another woman and now look what you've done. Go on, look.

"Suzanne —"

"It's cool. Maybe I'll see you around sometime."

I walked over to her side of the bed and sat down. "I want to stay. Believe me. I really do."

Suzanne sat up and stretched. "I'm serious, Jack. Stay, go … whatever."

Fuck it. I'm not about to bury another relationship under a steaming shitpile of lies.

"Suzanne, I'm going to be honest with you. Okay? Let's cut through the crap and get down to the nitty-gritty." I took her hand in mine. Her skin was rough from years of work. My skin was rough, too. "I've been in some bad shit. I don't sleep very well. I get nightmares … really bad nightmares. I wake up screaming. I punch walls. Once I woke up and I had a knife in my hand. Bad shit. I don't want you to see that."

"Wow." Suzanne blinked. "You're really fucked up, huh?"

"Yeah. I guess."

She smiled, leaned toward me and pulled me close. "Me, too."

Back in my shack I cracked open another bottle of Scotch, put my feet up, and waited for sunrise.

CHAPTER 15

Sunlight sparkled on the water. A parade of geese honked by. Gulls circled and dove. Sails unfurled and boats floated lazily toward open water.

Grover grinned, shuffling across the deck of his boat in an all-white outfit complete with white canvas shoes. "You want a margarita, Jack?"

I shook my head. No, I didn't want a margarita. I wanted this. I wanted the boat and the money and the freedom. I wanted the wife sunning herself in a dark-blue bikini on the top deck. I wanted to be able to hoist the anchor and unfurl the sails and head out to see the world. This was what I wanted. A nice quiet life with a woman who loved me.

"How about a beer?"

"Yeah, sure."

Grover settled back in his chair, sipped his margarita, and wiped salt and foam from his upper lip. I sat down next to him, wind ruffling my hair. Grover inhaled deeply and grinned. "You smell that? Fresh water smells so different than salt water. Fresh water is …"

"Fresher?"

"Well, yeah. It's that kind of earthy, after-the-rain smell." Grover was still grinning. "It smells fucking fantastic."

No argument here. "You talk to The Chief?"

"I did. He says he helped you out."

"He went on a few runs with me. But then he left."

Grover frowned. Behind him a gull landed on the boat rail and fluffed its feathers. "Not like The Chief to abandon a job. You two have a falling out?"

"The job description changed."

Grover laughed, short sharp barks. He sounded like a sea lion. "Sounds like Tommy, all right. I ever tell you about the time I did some work for his dad? Tommy was just a punk kid back then, a real snot-nosed brat. All zits and hair. Anyway, his dad has called this conference, right? Real heavy-hitting guys. There's this problem in Montreal — bikers, guns, money, the usual. A week earlier Poppa sent Tommy to check it out and report back. So Tommy gets called into the conference. It's all these old guys in undertaker's suits sitting around a polished mahogany conference table, all eyes watching this punk kid as he struts toward his father. "So," Poppa says, "what's the situation?"

Grover's grin was wider now. "And Tommy says, 'What situation?' There's this rustling, guys crossing and uncrossing their legs, a bit of coughing, that sort of thing. Tommy's dad is scowling. 'The situation in Montreal,' he says. 'Oh yeah,' says Tommy. 'I didn't go.'" Turns out instead of doing his fucking job this kid made his body-guards take him to Niagara Falls. He's going on and on about how much money he made at the casino and these old guys at the table are rolling their eyes; they can tell it's bullshit, they can smell it from a mile away. I'm standing behind The Old Man trying not to bust out laughing. Finally The Old Man just cuts him off and points to the door and says, 'Out.' Well, surly Tommy packs up his attitude and slouches off through the door. Then The Old Man stands up and the room goes dark and silent. I swear to God, it's as if the light bulbs all went out at the same time. I had chills shooting up my spine and I'm sure I wasn't the only one. It's like suddenly the room was frozen. No one wanted to even breathe for fear of disturbing the air. And Tommy's dad says, 'Never send a boy to do a man's job.' And everyone kind of flinches. We know he's talking about Tommy, but it's a warning to all of us at the same time, you know?"

Grover took another gulp of margarita. Above us his wife rolled onto her stomach, reached up, and untied her bikini strap. I kept my eyes fixed on Grover's blindingly white shoes. "The next day I go out to the compound to pick up Poppa to take him to a dentist appointment. Can you imagine that, Jack? I'm going to be standing guard while this dentist is scraping the don's teeth. You never think about a crime boss getting his teeth cleaned, but it happens. The dentist probably has no idea. Shit, if I was a dentist, I wouldn't want to know."

"Tommy," I said.

"Oh right. So I show up at the compound and Tommy's slouching on the couch in the living room. I think he's watching TV — music videos, some shit like that — but nope, the TV is off. I say something like 'How are ya, kid,' and Tommy looks up with two black eyes and a busted lip. I don't have to tell you who busted him up."

"The Old Man."

"Of course The Old Man. Who else is going to beat up a gangster's son? Poppa was always wailing on Tommy — in private, you understand, never in front of me or his crew — trying to knock some sense into that shaggy head of his." Grover shook his head. "I don't think it worked."

I resisted the urge to grab Grover's scrawny body and throw his ass overboard. "That shit never works."

"It's in the Bible, Jack. Spare the rod and spoil the child."

"Since when did you find religion?"

"Oh, I've always believed in God, Jack. Look around." Grover threw his arms open wide, encompassing the lake and the boats and the birds. "You think all this happened by accident? All things move according to a divine plan."

The sun hit my face and I squinted. "Yeah, well, Tommy's divine plan is to seize The Empire. He wants me to collect on his dad's debts."

"His dad's debts? That's going to be tricky."

"I know."

"The Old Man's in the hospital. He's in a coma, Jack."

"I know."

Grover fished a long, thin joint from his front pocket and sparked it up. "So what's your end? Two percent? Five?"

"We haven't talked money."

Grover shook his head. "Jack, what I'm about to say I'm saying as a friend, okay? This guy Tommy, he's got his hooks in you. He's hooked you and you're dangling on his line. You know what comes next?"

"Why don't you tell me?"

Grover squinted. "You get gutted."

CHAPTER 16

The receptionist, Sylvia, peered at me over the top of her glasses. "You're hear to see Mr. Mezell?"

"That's right."

"Do you have an appointment?"

"Tell him it's regarding the two guys who came to see him the other day."

"You really should make an appointment. Mr. Mezell is a very busy man."

"Would you do me a favour? Could you see if he can squeeze me in?" I turned on what I thought was a charming smile. Sylvia reeled back like I just threw dung in her lap.

"Wait here."

One hushed conference behind closed doors later, Sylvia emerged from the inner office and held open the door. "Go on in."

Joey put his elbows on his desk and steepled his fingers. "So, you're back."

"I'm back."

"I must say, I'm surprised to see you here. Can I offer you a drink? Mineral water?"

"No thanks."

Joey leaned back and waited for me to explain myself. I didn't. I sat straight and stared right at him. Finally Joey Machine grinned. "That's a good trick. The ol' Silent Treatment. But I'm afraid I can't help you if you don't tell me what you want."

"I told you what I want. Tommy's money."

"You sure I can't offer you a drink? Espresso? Tea? I believe I'm going to have a little something." Joey Machine leaned into his intercom. "Sylvia, could you send in some tea, please?"

"Right away, Mr. Mezell." Only one wall separated us but Sylvia was in another dimension. A dimension of tax forms and appointment books, wall calendars and clocks. Joey Machine and I lived in a different dimension. A dimension of blood.

I waited until the hit man finished stirring his tea. Then I kept waiting.

"I'm afraid you're wasting your time …"

"Jack."

"I'm afraid you're wasting your time, Jack. Say I was this person you think I am. And say this person had debts to this young man's father. Tommy, was it? Tommy's father. If that was true, then any debts that may have accrued are to Tommy's father, not Tommy."

"Tommy doesn't see it that way."

"No." Joey Machine smiled sadly. "I suppose he wouldn't." Joey started to stand, so I stood, too. I kept glancing down at the hit man's hands. The Chief taught me that years ago. "Always watch the hands. They can't pull something on you if you're always watching the hands."

The old man laughed and held up his liver-spotted hands, palms facing me. "Nothing up my sleeves, either. Jack, you seem like a competent guy. Why are you really here?"

"Just trying to pay off a debt."

"Mine? Or yours?" Joey's eyes narrowed into slits. "They've got something on you ... I wonder what. Did they threaten your family? No, no, nothing like that. You're not a family man. In fact, you hate your family. Oh yes ... I'm right. You live alone in a small apartment. You own almost nothing. You move through this world like a ghost."

Joey stepped closer. I stepped back. I kept watching his hands.

"In some ways we're a lot alike. All this ..." Joey gestured to his office, "all this is nothing. A house made of smoke. One puff and it disappears, and so do I."

"And Sylvia?"

The hitman smiled. "A generous severance package. She'll never have to work again. She'll spend her time with her bridge club, talking about the nice old man she used to work for."

I nodded. "That's real sweet. And here I thought you would just kill her. Abandon her in a shallow ditch. Move on to the next person you can use."

Joey's face went hard. "You can think what you want."

I shrugged. "I've been wrong before. You're the hit man with a heart of gold — why not?"

Joey Machine stared at me with flat, cold eyes. Snake eyes. "Your information is wrong. I'm not who you think I am."

"You say you're a nice guy — I believe you. I believe you're nice enough to help me help a son make his old man proud. Let's clear the air. You give me the money, I give it to Tommy, he gives it to The Old Man, everybody's happy. The Old Man's happy because he got his money and his son did a good job for once. Tommy's happy because The Old Man is happy. I'm happy because Tommy is happy. And you … you're happy because you've done the right thing."

Joey suddenly smiled again, his Dapper Old Man mask once again clamped tight against his skull. "I would love to help you spread the joy, Jack. But as I've said, this is a case of mistaken identity. I'm not who you think I am."

So this was how he wanted to play it. All song and dancey. An elegant, elaborate routine, a magic show complete with smoke and mirrors and a glued-on goatee. "Well … as I've said, I've been wrong before. Sorry to have wasted your time."

"Not at all, not at all."

I walked sideways toward the door, keeping the hit man in my line of sight. At the door I turned. "Just one more thing."

Joey Machine looked annoyed. "Yes?"

"Say you are who I think you are. And let's say you do in fact owe Tommy's dad some money. If that's the case, then you owe that money to Tommy now. He and his business associates are not going to let that slide."

"I'm sure this man Tommy realizes there's certain costs to doing business. In any business there are write-offs. In my business we call it Goodwill. If Tommy is smart, he'll write this off."

"Let's say for the sake of argument that Tommy's not that smart. Then what happens?"

The hit man leaned back. "You know, Jack, when you get to be my age you've learned a few things. I like to think of myself as a student of history. Fascinating subject. The study of history is the study of epic conflict. The grand cavalcade of human experience rampaging across the earth. Armies clashing in the night. Empires rising from the dust. Amazing if you think about it. First a collection of tents by the river, or maybe some mud huts. Then someone steps forward and says, 'the people who live in those huts across the river … let's go get them. Kill the men, enslave the women, steal the horses, steal the grain.' Then you do that again, and then you do that again. That's how empires get built. It's been said that Peace brings Prosperity, but that's wrong. Peace brings Death. To achieve prosperity, you have to take it. You form an empire from blood and sweat and mud, one brick at a time. I've learned this in my studies. Do you know what else I've learned?"

"Tell me."

"No empire lasts forever."

CHAPTER 17

I wanted to get the fuck out of Dodge. Hail a cab, pass the driver a hundred, and tell him to floor it. Leave a trail of burnt rubber across the city, CN Tower looming on the horizon. Rush into the bar and grab Suzanne with one hand and an ice-cold bottle of vodka with the other. Call Tommy from a roadside stop and tell him to go fuck himself. Then Suzanne and I would nestle back in our hotel hideaway. We'd eat pancakes with sausages and syrup in the morning and make love all afternoon as the big rigs blared by, rattling the windows. It'd be a good couple of days, maybe weeks. Then there'd be the knock on the door. Would Tommy come himself? Yeah, probably. Him and a couple of guys. They'd shoot first, and if they were lucky they'd get me in the stomach or the knee. That would take me down but not out. I'd still get to hear Tommy's nasal voice drone on about Loyalty and Betrayal. If they missed, though … that would be it for them. No second chances. I'd paint the room with blood.

In the end, I'd still be dead. The knock on the door could come at any time. Why fear it? To be happy one must accept the inevitable. What do they say in AA? "The serenity to accept the things I cannot change."

The situation with Tommy, though. That I could change. There was a light at the end of the tunnel. This game would end with Tommy shaking my hand and wishing me well. Then I could walk off into the sunset with a briefcase full of cash and the woman of my dreams.

To get the dream payoff I would have to hustle. I would have to collect Tommy's dad's debts and I would have to do it fast. Joey Machine was going to pay up, he just didn't know it yet. I'd be back for him, but for now there were plenty of others on Tommy's list.

The racetrack was like a video game except no one was tossing barrels as you advanced up the levels. First floor you've got your hoi polloi, guys with five o'clock stubble and rumpled shirts. Air electric with anticipation, the crowd surging forward as the trumpet sounds. Next level up you've got a central bar and fat guys with florid faces drinking G&Ts from plastic cups. There's a few women here and there and shorter lineups at the betting booths. To access the next level you have to go through a turnstile and pass by a security guard. Still no barrels. This next level is pretty swanky: a nicer bar, women in dresses and sun hats, guys in suits drinking red wine. The crowds thin out up here. Then there's another set of stairs leading up to an even nicer bar, wood-panelled and totally enclosed, isolated from the rest of the racetrack.

A jockey about the size of a sack of potatoes was perched on a stool at the bar, drinking whisky and talking to a beautiful brunette in a low-cut black dress.

I tapped the jockey on the shoulder and he didn't even look up. "Sorry … no autographs."

"Tommy will be so disappointed."

The jockey jerked at the sound of Tommy's name. That's the reaction I was looking for. None of that *Who's Tommy* bullshit I got from Joey Machine.

The jockey put his tiny hand on the brunette's exposed knee. "Sorry, darling. I'll deal with this and then I'll be right back."

The brunette looked confused. "Who's Tommy?"

"A guy I know. Business associate. I'll tell you all about it later."

With a flick of her hair the brunette glided away. The jockey swivelled on his stool. I could tell he was nervous, but he was trying to play it cool. "Look, man —"

"Jack."

"What?"

"The name's Jack."

"Uh … look, Jack. I told Tommy he doesn't have to worry. He'll get his money."

"I've got some bad news for you. If I'm here, that means Tommy's worried."

"No, seriously. Trust me." The jockey's arm darted up and the little prick threw his glass of Scotch at my face. I deked to the left and the heavy glass tumbler sailed on by, splashing me with amber drops of booze. I reached out and tried to grab the jockey, but he was fast, faster than me. He vaulted from the bar stool and skittered off down the stairs.

I was off and running before I even realized what was happening, taking the stairs three at a time and then cutting through the crowds, eyes fixed like lasers on the jockey as he disappeared beneath a flock of sun hats.

I caught the back of the jockey's suit and shoved him into a bathroom. I pinned the little prick against the wall and held them there, wriggling.

"Tommy wants his money."

"Fuck Tommy!"

I shook my head. "There's two ways we could've done this. The hard way and the easy way. You picked the hard way."

"Fuck you!" The jockey's foot lashed out, but I caught it before it slammed into my groin. It was over in seconds. I flipped the jockey backward into the wall. He got acquainted with the concrete face-first, blood spraying against white paint. There was a sharp cracking like the splintering of wood as I broke both the jockey's arms. The heel of my shoe ground down on the little man's hands. Another kick to the chin and he went down for the count, lying against the wall at an awkward angle, blood bubbling from his mouth, a dark stain spreading on his fine white shirt.

"Hold it right there!"

I bolted, plowing through the security guards at the door. Outside a woman screamed. There was blood on my shirt. I bumped into a guy carrying a hot dog: yellow mustard smeared my shirt and mixed with the blood. Someone threw a random punch and I blocked it, running purely on instinct. I saw specks of bobbing blue in the crowd ahead: the cops closing in.

I dodged past the bar and ducked through a door marked EMPLOYEES ONLY. I jogged through concrete corridors, pipes twisting overhead, a faint tinny radio blaring from somewhere. Up ahead a door said EXIT and I was free.

I took two cabs, a streetcar, a subway, and another cab. I walked the remaining four blocks to Suzanne's bar. She grinned as I stumbled in.

"Back for more, eh? What is it about this place? The ambiance? Must be the ambiance."

"Ambiance is everything," I croaked as I eased myself down onto a bar stool. My hands throbbed. "Do you have any rubbing alcohol?"

Suzanne shot me a sly smile. "Sorry, Jack. We don't serve that stuff here. If you've hit rock bottom, you'll have to take your business elsewhere."

"Not to drink. I ran into some trouble down at the track."

I hauled my bruised and bloody mitts up from my sides and Suzanne winced.

"Jesus, Jack. What the hell happened?"

"I beat up a jockey."

"Did he come in last?"

"I'm serious."

Suddenly Suzanne looked sad, so sad. Eyes wet, she turned away. Her eyes said it all. For her I was just another violent man in a long line of violent men.

"Babe, look at me. That man I beat up … he attacked me. I didn't like hurting him, but he was a bad guy."

"And you're not."

"No. I'm just a guy trying to do what's right." I held up my bloody hands. "Some day all of this will be over. We're almost there. I just need a little more time."

"How much time?"

"A month, tops. A couple of weeks. Soon. Very soon."

"I don't believe you."

"It's true."

Suzanne watched me, weighing my words. "You promise?"

"I do." I reached out and took her hand in mine. My hand was warm from heat and blood. Hers was cool and pale. Blood slid from my hand to hers, raspberry on white linen. "I promise. Soon all this will be over, and you and I will have the lives we deserve."

She smiled, her eyes lighting up the bar's twilight murk.

We headed back to her place. On the couch I tried to kiss her but she turned away.

"What's wrong?"

Suzanne hid her eyes. "I've never talked about this with anyone before. I come from a violent family. My dad, my mom, my brother … screaming matches, hurled bottles, broken windows. My dad, red-faced drunk and sweating, my brother and me screaming and crying as he loomed over us with a belt in his hand. You see these scars? Cigarette butts. My mom was a smoker. I made the mistake of telling her once what my brother was doing to me late at night. She blamed me ..." Suzanne choked back a sob. "The first time I ran away from home I was twelve years old. I got as far as the truck stop about half a mile from my house. These two truckers ... I threw sand in their eyes and kicked one of them in the crotch and ran. Back at home I wanted to go to the doctor but Mom wouldn't let me. 'Just wait until your father finds out,' she kept saying. That night my dad beat me so hard I shat blood for a week. My brother thought it was funny. He kept sneaking into my room at night. One night I told him to stop but he wouldn't so I hit him with a water glass. Cut him pretty bad. He hurt me worse. I ran away again six months later, but this time I brought my dad's gun. It wasn't easy, but I've been on my own ever since." Suzanne fell silent. She glanced at me, her eyes shining with moonlight. "At the bar you talked about 'the lives we deserve.' I don't deserve to be happy."

"Bullshit. Of course you do."

Suzanne laughed a horrible hollow laugh. "You deserve happiness. You deserve someone ... better than me." She brushed away a tear.

I took her hand. "These things that happened to you ... they're terrible things. They don't make you a terrible person. Your parents, your brother ... they're terrible people, and they will burn in hell. You went through something that no one should ever have to go through, ever. You'll always bear the scars and the memories, but in time even the worst scars fade. You've been through some bad times, but you're not a bad person. You hear me? It's not your fault."

Suzanne laughed through her tears. A snuffly laugh but a real one. "The way you say that, it's almost like you believe it."

"I do."

That night we tossed and tumbled, once again moving from her living room to the bedroom, buttons flying from my shirt as she yanked it open, her own shirt long gone, black lacy bra barely containing her milky-white breasts. I spun her around and got my hands around the waistband of her jeans and panties and yanked them down, jeans and panties around her knees, my hands gripping her fabulous alabaster ass as I gently pushed her toward the bed.

She shoved me away and wriggled out of her jeans and panties and looked at me with a crooked smile. Then she reached around and popped off her bra. She fell to her knees in front of me, tugging at my pants, but I grabbed her wrists and hauled her up and threw her onto the bed. She moaned, writhing on the sheets, touching herself, her legs spread wide. It took me about two seconds to shed my clothes and then I dove between her legs.

She moaned louder and slammed herself against my face. Then she pushed me away, gently protesting. I lifted her legs over my shoulders and angled myself in. She gasped as I entered her with a sudden thrust and then I slowed down. She felt so good.

She grabbed my ass and said, "Faster ... faster." I obliged, pushing in and out, pounding her hard and then harder. She yelped and bit me like an animal, then pushed me away and climbed on top. I slipped back inside and she rode me fast, trying to jam every inch of me inside her wet slickness, her centre hot like lava, radiating heat and need and want. We went harder, faster, trying to fuck out all the hurt and pain, smash out the suffering and replace it with bliss.

I don't know if we succeeded, but we came damn close.

CHAPTER 18

Rise and shine, up with the roosters at the crack of dawn. I was nestled up snug beneath Suzanne's lilac-scented sheets, feeling like I had just slept for a thousand years. Best sleep I'd had in a long time. Possibly The Best Sleep Ever.

I looked over at the beautiful woman sleeping beside me, her dark hair spilling across the light-blue pillow, and my stomach did this strange thing where it seized up and then dropped. That's when I realized that if anyone ever tried to hurt this woman again, I would kill them. No questions asked.

I spilled out into Kensington Market, with its espresso bars and fruit stands, college kids, hobos, and punks. It was just a quick jaunt back to my office and that's where I was headed.

Eddie cocked his eyebrows quizzically as I barrelled

through the door. He wouldn't ask any questions and that was just fine by me. That was one of the reasons we were such good friends. We operated on a need-to-know basis.

"Any calls?"

"Tommy. Couldn't really make out what he was saying. Sounded really drunk."

"Sad, angry, or happy?"

"Sounded happy."

"Good." Tommy could wait. "You had breakfast?"

We went next door and chowed down on bacon and eggs and melon and fresh Chinese pastries. Eddie called the server over and got a refill of steaming hot coffee. I stuck with water.

"Eddie. Who does your suits?"

"My cousin Vin. Want me to set you up?"

"Yeah. Thing is, I need the suit today. Like in an hour."

Eddie nodded. "My cousin's got fast hands."

An hour later I stepped out into the Spadina sunlight all spiffed up in a black suit with a light-blue shirt and a maroon tie. Eddie kept pushing me toward the pinstripes. "C'mon, man, live a little. Get some flair, some pizazz." He missed the point. For this next stop I needed to be invisible, faceless. Just another drone trapped inside the corporate cogs.

I hailed a cab and two pulled over right away, almost running a bike messenger off the road. The cyclist yelled, "Watch where the fuck you're going!" but the cabbies didn't hear him because they had their own argument going, shouting back and forth in rapid-fire Hindi. Fighting over who had dibs on my wallet. I stepped into the first cab and the argument was over. The second cab roared away.

"Bay Street," I told the cabbie, and I saw dollar signs going off in his eyes. Must be fresh on the job. I drove a cab briefly, and let me tell you, Bay Streeters don't tip for shit. The rich don't get rich by handing out money. The good tips come from either happy drunks or working-class folks who know how hard it is to make a buck.

We drove east on College Street, past the University of Toronto, past Queen's Park, and then we turned right onto Bay, driving south toward the lake. Bay Street, the heart and soul of the city's financial district, Canada's Wall Street, the location of my next meeting. On Bay Street it was all about the right suit and the right pair of shoes and the right platinum watch. Image was everything. Back when I was a surly teen, I'd hated that shit. I still hated it, but I'd come to a grudging acceptance of the biological facts. We humans are visual animals. In my new suit I should blend in fine. I'd be invisible if it weren't for my taped-up knuckles. Hopefully I'd come across as just another coked-up asshole who liked to fight on Friday night.

"Stop here." I threw some money at the cabbie — tip not too big, not too small, nothing memorable — and then I was out on the street, breathing in smog, cutting through the crowds toward the revolving doors of an office building. The elevator took me up to the seventeenth floor. At the end of the hallway was a wooden door with a small sign on the wall next to it: APEX INVESTMENTS. I rang the buzzer, touched the knife beneath my shirt, and waited for the door to open.

A tall, reedy man stuck his bald head out. "Yes?"

I shot him a shit-eating smile. "Hi there! Is this Apex Investments?"

The tall man turned sour. "That's what the sign says."

"I've got an appointment with Hiram Greenstein."

The man peered at me suspiciously. "What's this regarding?"

"I represent a client who needs Mr. Greenstein's procurement services."

"You've been misinformed, son. We don't procure anything except investment advice."

"I understand. This is about investment advice. Namely, how to move one planeload of investments to the proper … ah … bankers."

"Wait here a minute."

The door shut and I let it click closed. Either they'd be back or they wouldn't.

I flexed my still-healing hands. I shouldn't have given the jockey the business. That was incredibly stupid. Woodbine was crawling with cops and security guards. Sheer dumb luck I was able to get away.

Inhale, exhale. Play it cool. Unfortunately, not all problems can be solved by grabbing a guy and throttling him senseless.

The door slid open. There was the tall man, and behind him was a shorter man with slicked-back hair. If my source — that would be Tommy — if Tommy was right, I was staring at two of the biggest arms dealers in the world, Hiram Greenstein and Mohammed Joe.

Hiram cocked his head back toward his office. "All right, come on in."

Once I was past the threshold, Hiram grinned. "We can talk freely here. We sweep for bugs daily."

"Attention to detail. That's good."

Mohammed nodded. "In our business, everything is detail. You want us to ship a planeload of goods?"

"That's right. You have contacts in the Middle East. My clients need to use those contacts to ensure the safe arrival of their cargo."

"And this cargo —"

"You don't need to know that."

Mohammed Joe broke out laughing. "Attention to detail, yes? The contents of the cargo is a pretty big detail."

Hiram's face hardened. He looked like a pissed-off snapping turtle. "We can assume it's guns. Otherwise why come to us?"

"Maybe he admires our work ethic. Our spirit of camaraderie."

"Look, you want guns moved anywhere in the Middle East, you come see us. And what do you see? The future. One Jew and one Palestinian, working together hand in hand. We're doing our part for world peace. Isn't that right, Jo-Jo?"

"You can shove world peace right up your ass. If there was world peace, you and I would be out of a job."

Hiram shrugged. "So we sell white doves instead of missiles."

I shook my head. "This isn't about guns."

Hiram stood up. "Then you've wasted our time."

"It's about money."

"Of course it is."

"The two of you happen to have some of my client's money. My client would like this money back."

"And your client's name? Before you tell us this isn't important, let me assure you that this information is very important indeed."

I told them the name of Tommy's father. The gun-runners shot each other looks. Mohammed Joe stood up and strolled from the office. Hiram sat down behind his desk. His right hand dipped out of sight.

"Jo-Jo is going to make some calls. If you check out, you're going to be walking out of here with a briefcase full of cash. If you don't —"

"Let me guess. You'll slit my throat with a letter opener."

Hiram Greenstein grinned. "If you're trying to run a scam, we'll just shoot you in the back of the head."

I stood up and began slowly manoeuvring myself into the best fighting position. Hiram watched me, then brought up his gun. "Why don't you sit back down."

I sat back down.

Mohammed Joe marched back into the office. "The Old Man's in the hospital. No one knows shit about this guy."

"Really." Hiram's voice was ice cold. "You thought you could waltz in with some little con and waltz back out with a briefcase full of cash. Well, you just fucked up our entire day. Jo-Jo?"

"WAIT! Wait. Call Tommy. The Old Man's son. That's who I'm working for."

"We don't owe Tommy anything."

The common refrain. More and more it was looking

like Tommy wouldn't be inheriting the keys to the kingdom. Tommy hadn't exactly made a lot of friends during his twenty-eight years of existence.

"Call him. He's the one who set up this appointment."

Tommy, you fucker. You better be home.

I sat in Hiram's office watching the light flicker off the man's gun.

Mohammed Joe's shadow stepped into the office followed by the man himself. "It checks out."

"Well." Suddenly ol' Hiram was all smiles. He kicked back, gun disappearing back into his desk. "Thank God for that. Did you know the last time we had a disgruntled client in here we had to replace all the carpeting? My suit was ruined, Jo-Jo's suit was ruined ... messy, messy work."

I had these guys pegged as soon as they opened the door. These guys ... they weren't hands-on guys. They might've been at one point. Hiram probably had some Israeli military training under his belt. Mohammed could've trained with any number of military or paramilitary groups. But now ... now they sat in their air-conditioned office and moved millions of dollars' worth of guns with phone calls and computer clicks. One click of the mouse and tens of thousands of guns poured into the streets. For those who got killed in the crossfire, that was the reality. Explosions and blood. Shattered bone and screams. For these guys, it was all abstract. Moving units. Shipping product. *If we don't do it, somebody else will. Sure, people die. People die every day. It has nothing to do with us. The war is Out There, not In Here.*

In Here was a world of soft offices and polished shoes. *Out There* was a four-year-old on fire with her face ripped off.

I pushed back and stood up. "Let's have the money, gentlemen."

Hiram shook his head. "As we've explained, we do business with the father, not the son."

"The father's business is now the son's business. Would you like to continue doing business? Then you deal with the son."

Hiram craned his neck and looked over at Mohammed Joe. "I don't think this guy likes us very much, Jo-Jo."

There was a pause. Three heartbeats. This situation could turn to shit so easily.

Hiram chuckled. "We value all our business relationships. Jo-Jo, get the man his money."

CHAPTER 19

Somewhere out there was a poor sucker who had left a briefcase just like this one in the back seat of a cab. Maybe the briefcase was full of money, maybe it was full of drugs. Maybe both. And you know that poor sucker was shitting bricks when he realized that briefcase was missing. Provided the poor sucker lived through the night, there was only one thing he could do: replace the drugs, replace the money.

My hands were locked iron-tight around the case. I could replace the money, but it would take a few days and all my bankroll, and then I'd be in debt to some seriously bad guys. Forget the rigmarole of changing cabs and streetcars. I was heading straight for Tommy with the cash.

At the club I breezed through the front door and got a nod from the bartender. *Shit, I'm a regular now. Might as well have a vodka soda.*

"Tommy around?" I asked the bartender.

"Upstairs," he replied with a jerk of his goateed chin.

"Thanks." I knocked back the vodka and headed for the stairs.

Outside Tommy's office there was a new guy guarding the door. Another weightlifter gorilla-type dude. Maybe Tommy grew them in tubes.

The gorilla shook his head as I approached. "Can't go in. Private office."

"I'm here to see Tommy."

"Tommy's busy."

"Tell him Jack's here."

"I said he's busy."

I stepped into Tommy's office and the door swung closed behind me, bumping up against the gorilla now stretched out dreaming in the hall. Tommy, looking tired and tousled, looked up from the middle of a huddle. Three guys with scars and dark suits narrowed their eyes. I smiled and jerked my thumb. "Your guy out there might need some medical attention."

Tommy snapped his fingers. Fluorescent light glinted off his rings. "Rocco! Take care of it."

One of the dark-suit guys, a little rat-faced man with slicked-back hair, twisted up his lip. "Who's this fucking guy?"

Tommy slapped rat-man's back. "Friend of mine. Don't worry about it." Tommy turned to me and shot me a nervous smile. "Howya doin', Jack?"

I hoisted the briefcase. "I've got something for you."

"Hey, yeah ... that's great. Hold on to it for a minute, will you?" Over by the bar Tommy's cellphone rang. He ignored it and lurched over to me. In a stage whisper he hissed, "Take the case downstairs and wait." Then he straightened up and smiled. "Go down to the bar, get yourself anything you want. On me!"

I nodded and smiled. *Yessuh, yessuh. Yo' the boss, suh.*

Three vodka sodas later Tommy came downstairs, sweeping the sweat off his brow with an embroidered linen handkerchief. He and the dark-suit dudes hugged and kissed each other's cheeks and then the suits were gone, heading out the back. Tommy stumped over to the bar. Without being told, the bartender had a double whisky ready and waiting. Tommy drained it in one pull.

"Everything all right?" I asked.

"What? Oh, yeah. Yeah, yeah. Everything's fine. A few problems to take care of, that's all. We —" Tommy cut himself off. "Ah, you don't want my worries." His cellphone rang again. He ignored it.

I patted the briefcase. "I got the money from the gunrunners."

Tommy didn't even look at the case. He sat on his bar stool, twisting and fidgeting. He grabbed a paper napkin and started ripping it to shreds. "The what?"

"The money."

"Yeah, yeah. Put it over there. No, wait. Give it here. I'll throw it in the safe."

Tommy's phone kept ringing.

"You going to answer that?"

"What? Fuck no. Let it ring."

I sipped my drink.

Tommy chugged another, then rubbed his eyes. "Thanks for bringing me that case, Jack. Jesus! I haven't slept in days. Do you know that? There's all kinds of shit going down. Little Vito, that prick … he's trying to muscle us. My dad's in the hospital hooked up to a fucking ventilator and this prick is trying to muscle us." Tommy bared his teeth. "But don't you worry about him, Jack. I'm going to cut the fucker's nuts off. Feed them to my dogs. You just keep doing what you're doing. Get the money from Joey fucking Economy. Fuck that guy. FUCK 'EM ALL!"

Tommy's face twisted with rage. Eyes flashing, he snatched his ringing cellphone and smashed it to shit against the bar.

CHAPTER 20

It didn't take a genius to see that Tommy was living right on the fucking edge. He was a primed powder keg burning an extremely short fuse. He was gonna go off, and when he did, I planned to be far, far away. Costa Rica, maybe. Monkeys and mosquito nets. But before I left, I had to finish the job.

Eddie knocked on my door as I was suiting up, strapping on knives. "Hey, you need another guy? I got a cousin who could use the experience."

"The tailor?"

"No. Another cousin."

I shook my head. "This isn't a job for rookies."

No cabs for this job, either. Eddie had found me a souped-up Honda Civic CRX with bogus plates. About the only thing this car didn't have was a Gatling gun.

But I was too late. Joey Economy was gone. His house near the beach was empty. There was a pile of newspapers on the porch and a FOR SALE sign stabbed into the lawn.

My stomach sank as I thought about Sylvia. Sylvia the receptionist with her piles of red curls and her bifocals on a chain. A little voice of hope bubbled up from within: Maybe Joey Economy had told the truth. Maybe she did get a big pension and now she was sitting somewhere on a beach getting fanned by burly cabana boys as she sipped a peach margarita. It's possible, right? Right?

Yeah, right. Godspeed, Sylvia. Rest In Peace.

I called Grover from a payphone. "I'm coming over. We need to talk."

"Tonight's not really a good time, Jack."

"This can't wait."

Muffled voices on the other end of the phone. Then Grover was back. I could hear him smiling. "All right, Jack. Meet me on the water."

I made one more call. "Eddie, I need a boat."

"How big?"

"Little."

"Done.

The water churned as I steered the little boat toward Grover's yacht. I could hear music and laughter drifting out across the lake. A party was in full swing.

I climbed aboard. A woman with long black hair jiggled by, wearing nothing but skimpy red bikini bottoms. Grover, in a straw Panama hat and an all-white linen suit, appeared at the top of the stairs.

"My invite must've gotten lost in the mail."

"This isn't a Tough Guy party, Jack. This is a different kind of party. Tough Guy parties are so boring. Bunch of men sitting around some smoky bar knocking back beer and whisky, watching a scabby woman strip for crack. Guys just waiting to be insulted so they can go out back and beat the shit out of each other. Those parties always end the same way: either out in the woods digging a shallow grave or down by the docks with a weighted gym bag. That atmosphere is too tense. Sometimes you just want to have a good time, you know?"

A naked man and a naked woman with all-over tans walked by hand in hand.

"So what's the deal, Grover? You've gone nudist?"

"You've got it all wrong, Jack. These are Margarite's friends. None of these people know who I am. I mean, who I *was*." Grover chuckled. "They think I'm CIA."

In the hot tub, naked women shrieked and splashed. A plump woman laughed and rose from the steam, water trickling down her slick pink curves.

I nodded at the hot tub women. "They seem nice."

"Margarite has friends all over the world. Swingers. You didn't know? I admit it was a bit of a shock for me at first, but the bottom line is I love her and want to make her happy. It's an interesting lifestyle, Jack. Have you ever thought about it?"

I shrugged. "Never really had the time."

"Well, if you're interested, tonight we're short-staffed. There's more ladies than men. I'm sure they wouldn't mind if you wanted to join in."

I sipped my G&T and glanced back toward the hot tub women. "I didn't come here to get laid."

"Right, right. Of course not. I know that look in your eye. You're on a mission."

"Joey Economy is in the wind. I need to track him down."

"How about The Chief?"

"The Chief would be perfect but he took a fucking powder. Soon as he heard Joey Economy was involved, The Chief turned tail and headed for the fucking hills."

Grover frowned. "That doesn't sound like The Chief."

I shrugged.

Grover leaned closer. "You didn't hear it from me, but The Chief needs money. He's been doing some heavy gambling. He's in the hole for two hundred large. Maybe for the right price, you could lure him back." He shook his head. "He should've given up the ponies when he gave up the booze. Ah, well … we all have our vices." Grover grinned and slapped the ass of a passing brunette. She squealed and giggled and plopped down in his lap. Grover's small hands ran up the length of her tanned and oiled legs.

The party rolled on. The gin scorched my throat. With unsteady legs I stood and made my way toward the bathroom in Grover's cabin. Inside the cabin, a nude blond woman was sitting on the bed. She smiled when she saw me and spread her long, tanned legs.

"You like what you see?"

"Yes."

"Why don't you come on over?"

I thought of Suzanne, and I turned away.

CHAPTER 21

Grover told me where to find The Chief. He was in a dingy motel room complete with buzzing neon sign out front and fly-swarmed Dumpster out back. Right next to a liquor store and not far from an underpass where fifteen dollars could buy you a blowjob and a rock of crack.

"Who the fuck is it?"

"Jack."

Click-clack of the chain coming off. The door swung open into hell. Cigarette smoke, overflowing ashtrays, broken beer bottles, a hole punched in the wall. Spilled beer, half-eaten food, dead cockroaches. Broken lamp shattered on the floor. Water from the busted toilet seeping into the mouldy orange carpet.

The Chief stood in the middle of the chaos wearing his leather jacket, with no shirt or pants. His boxer shorts were streaked with either blood or ketchup. "Jack! How the hell are ya?"

I nodded toward the woman wearing matching black bra and panties stretched out across one of the double beds. "Is she okay?"

"What?" The Chief whirled. "Is that bitch still here?" He marched over and gave the woman a shake. She mumbled something incoherent and swatted his hand away. The Chief turned. "She's fine. Drank too much. Speaking of —" The Chief yanked a tall boy from its plastic collar and tossed it to me.

My eyes narrowed. "I thought you quit."

"Yeah ... I did." The Chief grinned. He was missing one of his front teeth. "But I'm back, baby!" He popped the top of another beer. MuchMusic was blaring from the TV speakers. The Chief shuffled over and turned it up.

"THERE! NOW WE CAN TALK!"

"WHAT?"

"I SAID NOW WE CAN TALK!"

I cocked my head. "Shhh! You hear that?"

There it was again, unmistakable: a loud, angry knocking at the door.

"What the fuck?" The Chief pushed through the empty bottles on the carpet like he was an icebreaker moving through the Arctic. He reached inside a pizza box sitting on the cigarette-scarred table and came up with a Glock 9mm.

"Chief ... be cool, baby. Be cool."

I stepped in front of The Chief and cracked open the door. A balding man with glasses and a white undershirt stood shivering outside the motel room. "Excuse me ... could you turn your TV down, please?"

I turned on my shit-eating grin. "Absolutely. Sorry about that."

"I'm presenting at a conference tomorrow and I really need my sleep."

"Hey, I know how it is. No problem. Sorry to have disturbed you." *Sorry whatever cheap-ass company you work for stashed you here at the No-Tell Motel.*

Behind me I heard The Chief muttering curses under his breath. I quickly closed the door on Conference Man: he blinked rapidly as the door slammed closed.

The Chief waved his gun at the FIRE SAFETY sign stuck to the back of the motel room door. "Motherfucker ... tell ME to be quiet."

"Chief ... just let it go, man. Let it go."

The Chief turned and punched his fist right through the motel room wall. "HOW'S THAT? TOO FUCKING LOUD?"

If this were a game show a gigantic buzzer would have been going off right about now. The rhinestone-suited host would bounce up and clap me on the back and say, "All right, Jack, your time is up!" Time's up, all right. Time to get gone.

"Take care of yourself, Chief."

"What?" The man turned his scarred face toward me. His lips were wet with saliva and beer. "You goin' already? You just fucking got here. Come on, have a drink."

"Some other time." I kept my eye on The Chief's gun hand. Here's something I've learned over the years: friends are friends, but drunks do stupid shit. I didn't want the cleaning crew finding us in the morning, The

Chief weeping over my body, a 9mm bullet hole sitting right between my eyes.

"Fuck you, then." The Chief turned his back. Stomach hollow, I slipped out the door into the cool night air.

CHAPTER 22

The pigeons outside my office were having an orgy. The fuckers would not stop cooing and flapping and beating their wings. I kept my eyes closed, lying on the couch, trying to sleep. Fucking pigeons. I cracked open one eye and gazed over at my desk full of knives. *Filet of Sky Rat.*

A knock at the door. I shuffled over all bleary-eyed. "Yeah?"

"Eddie."

I peeked through the peephole and sure enough, there was Eddie, standing in the hallway all by his lonesome. I opened up and he passed me his phone. "It's Tommy."

I held the tiny phone up to my ear.

"Jack! You madman. You fucking genius. The jockey came through."

Thoughts and words pushed through my sleep-addled brain. *The jockey, the jockey ... oh right, the jockey.*

Tommy continued: "Yep. That little fucker showed up at the club last night all bandaged up like a fucking mummy. His little knees were knocking, he was shaking so bad. He apologized and paid me off."

"That's great, Tommy." I yawned, deep and long like a jungle cat.

"You make any progress with our other friend?"

"Joey?"

"No, the fucking Tooth Fairy. Yeah Joey."

"He's in the wind. I don't have the manpower to track him down."

"Don't you worry about that. That fucking guy has been running around too long. My father and him were buddies or something, but not me. There's gonna be a reckoning, Jack. We're gonna drag his headless fucking corpse through the streets."

I heard Tommy's teeth grinding. "That'll send a message to all the other stiffs and deadbeats. Fuck with me, you end up dead."

Jesus Christ, I thought. Didn't anyone ever tutor this guy? Phone calls and death threats don't mix. That's the kind of shit that makes the cops get up on their tippy-toes and cheer.

"You need me today, Tommy?"

"Is the job over? No? Then I fucking need you today, and tomorrow, and the day after that until it's done. You got that?"

"Got it."

"Good.

I hung up and tossed the phone to Eddie. He sighed. "Another one for the lake?"

"I'll pay you back. How much?"

Eddie shot me a lazy smile. "It'll all be in your item-ized bill at the end of the month."

I couldn't get back to sleep. *Fuck it, I'll go run some errands.* Pick up some toothpaste, new razors, soap. You never hear about tough guys buying groceries. Did Sam Spade send his secretary?

Outside on the streets Chinatown was as busy as ever. The summertime stench of rotting garbage hung over everything. In the middle of Spadina a streetcar angrily slammed on its breaks and rattled its bell as an old Chinese man hobbled and weaved across the tracks. I'd never seen anyone get hit on these tracks, but it happened. I saw the aftermath once: streetcar at a standstill, paramedics loading a black body bag into the back of an ambulance.

A long black car cut me off at the corner of Spadina and Sullivan. The passenger door swung open and a mean-faced man with lips thick as sausages beckoned me closer. "Get in."

"No thanks." I smiled sweetly. "It's such a beautiful day, I think I'll walk."

The big man let loose a grunt. "I heard you were a joker." The big man lifted his coat, letting me see the gun in his hand. "Get the fuck in or you die."

It took less than a second. In one fluid motion my hand darted into the car, snapped the gun out of the man's hand (I heard the green-wood *snap* of the man's wrist breaking), and hit him over the left eye. Head wounds bleed plenty; the man yowled, blinking back blood, holding on to his shattered wrist.

"I said I'll fucking walk."

Up front the driver was frantically fumbling, trying to get his own gun out of his side holster. I levelled Big Man's pistol at him. "You really want to do that?"

The driver panicked and gunned the motor. The car leapt ahead, passenger door slamming closed as the car screamed around the corner. I ran into an alley, wiped down the gun and ditched it.

I've made a few enemies over the years. I like to think I'm a pretty decent guy, but I guess I just rub some people the wrong way. There's plenty of folks cooling their heels in prison who wouldn't be there if it wasn't for me. I'm sure some of them stay up at night, sharpening their claws and dreaming of revenge. Those guys in the car were no friends of mine. Were they sent by Joey Machine? Probably not. Too roundabout. I had a feeling Mr. Machine preferred the personal touch.

Then it hit me with clarity and surety: those were Little Vito's men. Tommy's troubles had washed up on my doorstep.

There's a martial art called aikido. If you've ever seen a Steven Seagal movie, then you've seen it practised. Aikido is all about defence, using other people's actions against them. It's not about acting, it's about reacting. Just like Bugs Bunny. Bugs Bunny doesn't go out looking for people to fuck with. He just chills in his rabbit hole, snackin' on carrots until someone tries to fuck with him. Then what happens? Elmer Fudd gets shot with his own gun. This is how I live. Send hate my way and I will deflect it back to you. However — and I think Steven Seagal and Bugs Bunny would agree with me on this point — sometimes the best defence is a good offence.

I flipped open one of Eddie's phones and punched in a number.

Grover picked up. I could hear gulls in the background. I envisioned white fluffy towels, sunscreen, and bare breasts.

"It's Jack."

"The boating life's growing on you, eh, Jack? You just can't stay away."

"Forget the boat. Tell me something about Little Vito."

"I've heard a few things."

"I figured you had."

"Nothing I'd want to repeat over the phone, mind you."

"Dinner?"

"Dinner."

One more call. "Hello?" Suzanne's voice was warm and sweet like honey.

"It's me. Let's reschedule."

The silence of Suzanne's disappointment filled my ear.

"Something's come up. Business stuff. You know how it is."

"Yeah, sure." Her voice was flat and far away. "Don't get killed, okay?"

"Will do." *That's what I do every day. I wake up, do my job, and try not to get killed.*

I hung up and pushed my way through the crowds, heading for one of those stores that sold everything. Out on the sidewalk a group of old Chinese ladies were arguing about multicoloured cheap plastic bowls. The bowls were stacked next to a bin full of flip-flops, and next to the flip-flops was a bin full of feather dusters. Down the street there was a man with a shaved head and a rumpled all-black outfit hunched down by the curb. I gave him the once-over. Trained assassin? The man was intently scratching symbols on the curbside bricks with a rock, ignoring the crowds swirling all around him. A crazy man, or a killer in disguise? I watched him more closely but he just kept scratching, carving protective symbols onto the street. No disguise. He was an actual Crazy Man.

It was The Chief who taught me how to pull off "The Crazy Look." We had been hired to shake down a bank exec, some real smooth Johnny who had gotten in over his head. He started with drugs and then moved on to women, one woman in particular: his coke dealer's girlfriend. The coke dealer wasn't happy, so he called up The Chief.

We decided to stake out the bank from across the street. "Here," The Chief said, opening his giant black duffle bag and pulling out a moth-eaten coat. "Put this on."

"Are you kidding?" I responded. "It's hot as fuck out here."

The Chief grinned. "Exactly. If you look crazy and homeless, you might as well be invisible."

Sure enough, The Banker blew right past us. We trailed him for three blocks before we saw our opening. The Banker crossed the street and buzzed his way into an apartment building. The Chief caught the door before it closed.

The Banker was there to see the coke dealer's girl-friend. She was surprised to see us, but not as surprised as he was. "Keep an eye on her," The Chief said as he led The Banker into the bathroom. We didn't hear any screams, just muffled thumps. The girl started blabbing a blue streak: *my boyfriend* this and *my boyfriend* that.

"Your boyfriend," I told her, "isn't very happy with you."

With that her eyes widened and her mouth slammed shut.

The Chief came out of the bathroom with his hands wrapped in bloody towels. "Let's go."

"What about her?"

The Chief grinned. "Sister," he said, "your boyfriend just sent you a message. Do you understand? If I were you, I'd get the fuck out of Dodge."

Outside, The Chief lit a cigarette. "Sad, isn't it?"

I scanned the street for cops. "What do you mean?"

"She won't leave. I bet you a thousand bucks she's on the phone with him right now, crying her eyes out and begging for forgiveness."

"What'll happen to her?"

The Chief flicked away his cigarette. "Nothing good. But if she doesn't leave ... not much we can do." The Chief turned to me and grinned. "You did good in there, kid. Come on ... I'll buy you a beer."

The Scratcher kept scratching. I moved past the arguing Chinese ladies and into the store, stepping past piles of woks and giant jolly Buddhas. *Toothpaste, razors, soap. Might as well throw in some deodorant while I'm here.*

I kept one eye on the street, but nothing happened on the walk home. Back in the building Eddie was bustling around his restaurant, barking orders. A man in a long white butcher's jacket hustled past me carrying a whole dead pig on his back. Lunch.

"Eddie, you going to be around for a while?"

"All day, man. All goddamn day."

"All right. I'll be in the office. No visitors, okay?"

Eddie clapped my back. "You got it, Jack."

Inside the office I stashed my toiletries and poured the plant a water and myself a vodka. I raised my glass to the plant. "Here's looking at you, kid."

Down the hatch. I had a few more hours before my dinner with Grover. I kicked off my shoes, curled up on the couch, and in seconds I was waltzing through dreamland.

CHAPTER 23

Turned out Little Vito was one vicious fuck. I mean, I figured this guy wasn't Captain Kangaroo, but it's one thing to think something and something else entirely to hear it out loud.

Grover picked a restaurant on Queen East near Parliament, which surprised me. The neighbourhood was a little downscale for Grover's tastes. Not far from here was Queen and Sherbourne, which used to be basically an open-air crack market until a guy got shot and the cops finally stepped in.

Outside, a scabby woman with bird's-nest hair lurched through a parking lot. Inside, it was all elegant lighting and dark, polished wood. Men in suits with no ties held hands across the table with their dates, smiling women with perfect hair.

Grover was already seated. He saw me coming and stood up.

"What did I tell you? Pretty nice place, eh?"

I looked around and had to agree. "How'd you find out about this place?"

"My wife. She belongs to the club upstairs."

We sat down, encased in dark wood. "Tell me about Little Vito."

Grover swirled his wine. "You know, people get into our line of work for a variety of reasons. Some guys are just angry, with short fuses, hair-trigger tempers. Some guys see it as "just business," like in the army — soldier versus soldier. Some guys really enjoy the work. And some guys can't feel a thing." Grover held his wineglass up to his nose and breathed in deep. "Little Vito is the last kind of guy. He's a stone-cold sociopath, Jack. They say that's the reason Vito never rose as far as he wanted within The Family. Tommy's dad … sure, he's a vicious killer, but the man has a heart. Vito's the kind of guy who would step on a puppy if it got in his way."

"So he doesn't care about anything."

"Wrong. He cares about one person — himself. He thinks the world revolves around him and gets plenty pissed when he encounters evidence to the contrary. For this guy, too much flattery is never enough."

"Any other weaknesses?"

"There's another reason he never got to be the big boss: he can't relate. You, me, that empty chair over there — to him it's all the same."

"Have you ever seen him in action?"

Grover paused. "Once. It was a thing in Hamilton. Wintertime — you know, dirty snow piling up on the street corners, steam and smoke rising from the steel mills. The Chief and I were downtown, freezing our asses off in a borrowed Cadillac outside the bingo parlour. We were there to pick up an envelope. You know the drill. This guy Louie had an envelope, our guy needed the envelope … Louie hands it to us, we hand it to the boss, we get paid, everybody's happy. Only it didn't go down like that."

Grover sipped his wine. "I was about to lapse into hypothermia, I was so cold. Sitting there in the front passenger seat with crumpled-up McDonald's bags scattered all over everything. I was jiggling my feet, trying to get warm, when suddenly The Chief went tense. I did, too; I trust The Chief's instincts."

I nodded. The Chief had been right about Tommy. He knew I'd get pulled in too deep.

Grover continued. "The Chief didn't look over at me, but he said, really quietly, 'There's our guy.' I casually glanced out the driver's side window and saw a beat-up, mud-splattered white van pull into a parking spot right in front of the bingo parlour. I blew on my hands and reached for the door handle, but The Chief shook his head. *Wait*.

"So we waited. Across the street Louie got out of his van. The man looked like a circus bear, this big hairy beast that some poor sucker had to dress up in a vest and a little hat. Louie reached into his jacket pocket — he had one of those quilted jackets — and pulled out the envelope. 'There's the envelope,' I said. 'I'm going in.'

"The Chief said, 'Wait.'

"So we waited some more. At point I wanted to scream, I was so fucking tense. I turned to The Chief again and said, 'What the fuck is this, a Beckett play?

Let's go get the motherfucking envelope.' Yeah — I was more profane back in my younger days.

"It had only been only about four minutes since Louie pulled up in his mud-splattered van, but it seemed like it was twenty-to-life. Louie was rummaging around for something in the back of his van and suddenly the door to the bingo parlour swung open and these two guys in suits walked out. I don't know if you've ever been to the bingo parlour in downtown Hamilton, but there aren't a lot of suits in there. Track pants, rhinestones, sweatshirts with airbrushed wolves howling at the airbrushed moon — I don't mean to stereotype, but that's what you wear to bingo. The Chief slid down in the driver's seat, way down. Without being told, I did the same. I was still looking out the window, so I saw it all. I saw these two guys in nice suits and overcoats walk straight toward Louie, still rummaging in the back of his van. One of them said something and Louie looked up. He must have known the guys because he smiled. Just then a long black Caddy pulled up, and somehow this car was spotless. I mean, the roads were a mess, right? Mud and snow and road salt all over the place, but not on this car. Louie reached for the door, but one of the suits popped it for him. Laughs and smiles all around.

"I turned to The Chief. 'I don't want to follow that car around all the goddamn day. We've got to move now.'

"The Chief said, 'Wait.'

"Across the street Louie ducked his head to climb into the car. The guy in the suit — the doorman — he was still smiling. The other suit, he was smiling, too, but suddenly he had a gun in his fist. Four shots, five.

Louie spun around dead. The Caddy took off. The smiling guy chucked his gun into a snowbank and then he and the other suit casually sauntered across the street and climbed into a long black town car as if they were going for a Sunday drive. The town car zoomed away. Louie was lying dead in the snow. A woman screamed. The Chief turned to me and smiled. 'Aren't you glad we waited?'"

I sipped plain water that cost six bucks a bottle. "You think The Chief knew about the hit?"

Grover shrugged. "Hard to say. I think it was instinct. Like The Chief could feel the electricity in the air and it felt wrong. You ever get that?"

"All the time."

"So you know what I'm talking about. But wait, it gets better. The Chief leaned over to my side, popped open the glove box and pulled out a stethoscope. A stethoscope! 'Wait here,' he said. I'm about ready to vibrate through the fucking floorboards, I'm so keyed up. I've been waiting and waiting and waiting for fucking forever and now I've got to wait some more? The Chief threw this stethoscope around his neck, got out of the car, and ran across the road, shouting, 'I'm a doctor! I'm a doctor!' The Chief strode over to poor Louie's body, knelt down, opened Louie's jacket, and damned if he doesn't palm the envelope. The Chief played doctor with the stethoscope for a few minutes and then stood up. 'This man ... is dead.' Oh, shit, Jack, you should've seen it."

"And Little Vito?"

Grover frowned. "Didn't I tell you? Little Vito was the trigger man. *POW POW POW*, right in broad daylight.

You know what I remember most about that day? It was the look on Vito's face. Just smiling gently, like he was talking to his next door neighbour or his dentist's receptionist. Just a soft, gentle smile." Grover shuddered and shook his head. "Gave me the creeps."

Grover handed our server his menu. "I'll have the lamb. Jack, you should really try the lamb. It's excellent."

"Steak," I told the server. "Raw."

CHAPTER 24

Grover drove me home along King Street, tracers of headlights and sparks from the streetcar wires lighting up the night. Soft quiet jazz floated from the speakers. I sank back into the soft, buttery leather of the passenger seat.

"The Chief's in trouble."

Grover frowned. "What do you mean? Don't get me wrong, I'm not disagreeing with you, but let's make sure we're on the same page. He's drinking again, right?"

"Yes."

"But that's not all."

"No. He's ..." I trailed off. A clarinet blew hot and sweet. Outside the lights flashed past. How to put it into words? The trashed motel room, the woman in her undies, The Chief's death's head grin.

Grover glanced over at me. "Don't worry about The Chief. The Chief's a big boy, Jack."

"There's plenty of big boys in the boneyard. They get buried in special big boy coffins."

Grover floored it, staring straight ahead. The Lexus leapt forward, bumping over the streetcar tracks and cutting off a green van in the far righthand lane. The van's driver, a young East Asian kid, slammed on the brakes and leaned on the horn. Grover spun the wheel, sending the Lexus squealing into a gas station parking lot. Inside the brightly lit gas station convenience store a bored teen looked up briefly, then went back to his porno mag. Grover stared over at me and cut the engine. I kept one hand near the knife in my coat.

"All right. Cut the shit, Jack. Are you seriously worried about The Chief?"

The broken bottles, the dried blood, the ocean of booze.

"Yes, I am."

Grover sat quietly for a minute. "Do you remember the first time The Chief brought you to see me?"

"Of course."

"You were scared shitless. No, don't deny it. You were just a rookie back then. Greener than Kermit the Frog, and just as wet behind the ears."

"Frogs don't have ears."

"Forget about it. The Chief introduced us and I paid attention. You know why?"

"No, why?"

"Eleven years before we met I asked The Chief to find me someone just as vicious as himself. Someone young and rough but willing to learn. You were the first person he ever brought by."

Grover sat quietly. Cars passed by. A fat man walked out of the gas station convenience store, unwrapped his sandwich, and took a big bite. "You never disappointed me, Jack. Not once."

My hand inched closer to my knife. This would be a hell of a way to die. Killed in a gas station parking lot by the man who's been like a father to me. What did Grover say, so many years ago? "Never Trust Anyone." That's harder than it looks. Or maybe I'm just a trusting sort.

Grover stared straight ahead through the wind-shield. Two kids with baggy jeans and long white shirts rode up to the convenience store on tiny BMX bikes. The kids reached into their back pockets and pulled out nylon masks. One of the kids reached into the front of his pants and pulled out a handgun.

Grover groaned. "Oh for fuck's sake. Hold on a minute." He stepped out of the Lexus and sauntered over to the kids, who were working up their nerve to storm the store. Grover turned on his shit-eating grin. "Hiya, kids! You're up pretty late, don't you think?"

The kid's gun jerked up. "SHUT THE FUCK UP, MAN!"

Rapid-fire gunshots. The young would-be robber was blasted backward through the glass front of the con-venience store. Grover had a gun in each hand and was blazing away. The other kid was screaming and waving his hands in the air. Grover strode toward the scream-ing kid and shot a red hole smack in the middle of his forehead. Grover kept firing, blasting the kid's body, the bicycles, the store windows, the sidewalk.

The gunfire stopped. A car alarm was going off.

There was a screeching of tires: nearby cars hauling ass out of there. Grover screamed at the dead body sprawled out on the sidewalk. "I'M TRYING TO HAVE A CONVERSATION HERE! WHAT THE FUCK IS WRONG WITH YOU?" Grover's face twisted into a mask of hate as he unloaded the last of his bullets into the dead kid's body.

Grover ran back to the car and I realized I'd missed my chance to slip away. The door slammed shut and Grover floored it.

Quiet jazz, double bass, and vibraphone. Grover shook his head. "My wife's going to kill me."

"Not literally."

"No, not literally. This was a brand new car and now I've got to ditch it. Goddamn punks!"

"I'm sorry."

"Don't be." Grover grinned. "Maybe this time I'll get a Bimmer. What do you think? Get it painted British racing green." Grover shook his head. "Can you believe that shit? There we were, trying to have a nice quiet conversation and they came waltzing in and made me break my concentration. Where were we?"

Two kids, dead on the sidewalk.

"Um … we were talking about The Chief. You said I never disappointed you."

"That's right, Jack. You never have." Grover cocked an eye over at me. "But I've got to know. The Chief … should he be worried about you?"

"Who, me? I'm fine." That morning I'd woken up screaming with blood on my knuckles. I had been punching the wall in my sleep.

A.G. PASQUELLA

"No, I mean … say you see The Chief sitting by his lonesome in an out-of-the-way sidewalk café. Should he be worried?"

"What?" I reeled back, incredulous. "Hell no. The Chief is one of my best friends."

"So you haven't been given a contract?"

"You sure you're all right to drive? You know I don't do that kind of work. And besides, if anyone ever tried to give me a contract on The Chief, that would be the last thing they ever did."

Grover relaxed. He smiled. "That's good to hear. I believe you, Jack."

If Grover didn't believe me, I'd have been dead by now. They'd find my headless, handless body tucked away neatly in the Lexus's truck. That is, if they found my body at all.

"What's this all about?"

"You're right to be worried, Jack. Someone has taken out a contract on The Chief."

"Who?"

"I don't know yet. But I'm working on it. Any ideas?"

"He's got a lot of enemies. It wouldn't be Joey Machine …"

"No. He wouldn't take out a contract. He'd do the work himself. Don't worry, Jack. I'll find out who did it. In the meantime, you hear anything, you let me know."

"Always."

The jazz played. Grover gunned the engine and the car glided through Clubland. "I'll drop you off here. I'm going to go dump the car."

"Grover …"

"Yeah, Jack?"

"Has anyone taken a contract out on me?"

"You mean like Little Vito?"

"Whoever."

Grover smiled. "Not that I've heard, my boy. But you never know."

CHAPTER 25

From Clubland I walked toward Spadina, past the reeling drunks and cops on horseback. A party bus full of drunk girls shouting out the window roared past. A rolling bachelorette party. One of the girls spotted a crowd of hair-gelled guys and shrieked, "Who's got a big dick?" The guys laughed and the party bus rolled on.

On Spadina I looked down and noticed my hands were shaking. I closed my eyes and saw Grover's hate-filled face, his guns barking fire. Two teenagers dead on the sidewalk. I tightened my fists and kept walking, fingernails digging into my palms.

The stale beer smell of Suzanne's bar hit me instantly as I slouched through the door. Suzanne wasn't behind the bar. Instead there was some joker with bushy eyebrows and a ponytail. There was an old man with hair like a haystack camped out at the end of the bar, half of a half pint of beer forgotten in front of him. The old man stared straight ahead at nothing. The Rolling Stones'

"Sister Morphine" droned from the jukebox. A crowd of artsy hipsters was slumming it at the big table over by the window. A girl with 1950s-style thick, black-rimmed glasses and purple dreadlocks was laughing too loudly at everything this guy with a goatee and a porkpie hat said. One drink, I told myself.

Four drinks later my hands had stopped shaking and Bruce Springsteen was on the jukebox and I was so relaxed I wasn't even thinking about the two teenagers Grover had gunned down earlier. Not thinking about their bodies being laid out in cheap coffins and lowered slowly into the ground as their mothers wept and then were helped back to their sad apartments where they would sit at their kitchen tables and cry all night.

I signalled the bartender. "Another vodka."

Something fluttered behind me. A hand touched my shoulder and I ducked to the right and lashed out with my left leg. I spun around just in time to see Suzanne falling back, her eyes wide open, her mouth a surprised O.

"Oh shit!" I reached down and helped her up. "You okay?"

Suzanne brushed off her backside. "What the hell, Jack?"

"I don't like people sneaking up on me."

"Yeah, I got that. Now you get this: you do not get to hit me. Ever. Got it?"

"I got it. I'm so sorry. I thought ..." I shook my head. "It doesn't matter. It won't happen again."

"Damn right." Suzanne exhaled and pushed back her hair. "What are you doing here, anyway? I thought you had a business thing."

"Business thing's over, babe. I dropped in to see you."

"I don't work tonight. I'm just here to pick up my cheque."

"Well," I said, grinning, "can I buy the pretty lady a drink?"

Suzanne scowled. "I'm serious about the hitting, Jack."

"I get it. I really do."

"In that case, tequila."

Booze burned down my throat like amber fire. The jukebox shook, rattled, and rolled. The lights went dim, then dimmer. The hipsters moved off, laughing. The old man with the haystack hair limped toward the bathroom, and after what seemed like three days he limped back to the bar. The server ("That's Mark," Suzanne said. "He's a nice guy.") refused to serve the old man another beer. Without a word the old man turned and limped through the door, haunted eyes staring into another world.

Suddenly Suzanne and I were outside in the cool night air, laughing on the sidewalk, supporting each other's bodies. She smelled so good, like talcum powder and vanilla. Then we were in a cab that smelled like doublemint gum and the speakers were blasting salsa tunes and I blinked and I was sitting in Suzanne's apartment in Kensington Market, kicking back on her bright red couch as she passed me a martini and sashayed over to the record player. Soft jazz trickled from the speakers.

"Let's listen to something else," I said.

Suzanne frowned. "You don't like jazz?"

"I like it plenty. It's just ... let's listen to something else."

"Dub reggae okay?"

"Perfect."

Bass rattled the room. Echoey guitars leapt from speaker to speaker. Suzanne danced slowly toward me. I gulped my martini.

She stopped short and smiled, shaking her head at her living room window. "They're at it again."

"What?"

"The neighbours. Check it out."

I staggered to my feet and shuffled across the shag. Suzanne's living room window looked out into an alley and directly into the apartment next door. *Nice place*, I thought. Black-and-white tiled floor, ceiling fan, lots of bookshelves. On the couch a woman with pale skin and long black hair was straddling a brown man with muscles. Hot 'n' heavy makeout session in progress. I blinked as the muscle man peeled off the brunette's purple sweater. She wasn't wearing a bra: her massive breasts swung free.

"Sweet Jesus!"

Suzanne nodded ruefully. "I know. They're real, too."

The brown man yanked off his own shirt and then buried his face between those tremendous breasts. The brunette pushed him back against the couch and leapt on top of him, with his hand clutching her ass. Then she popped up and wriggled out of her jeans and her lacy pink thong. The brunette stood facing her lover, her perfect white ass exposed in the window. The muscle man reached for her and she twisted away playfully, giving Suzanne and myself an eyeful: breasts and legs and a clean-shaven pussy. I was rock-hard. The muscle man leapt up, yanked down his pants and pushed the brunette onto the couch face down. He was hard, too, his soldier standing at attention. He lifted up the brunette's hips and pushed in from behind. Suzanne and I watched the brunette gasp with pleasure. The muscle man started to rock, each thrust setting those massive breasts swaying like pendulums. I stepped closer to Suzanne and ground against her tight, denim-clad ass. The muscle man was moving faster now, really socking it to the brunette. She had her mouth open and her eyes closed, gasping and moaning, pleasure carrying her into a different dimension, his strong hands locked tight around her hips, pushing her this way and that, then grabbing tighter as his body stiffened and his face contorted ...

And then the muscle man collapsed on top of the brunette and they lay there breathing heavily, clutching each other on the couch.

I knocked back my martini and grabbed Suzanne's hand. "Bedroom. Now."

Suzanne grinned drunkenly. "I love that caveman talk."

CHAPTER 26

I didn't stay the night this time, either. It was damn hard to leave and Suzanne made it harder, stretched out nude on the silky white sheets, her black hair fanned out across her pillow as she smiled up at me with sleepy, half-lidded eyes.

"Why don't you stay? If you start to freak out in your sleep, I'll wake you up."

I grinned. "Damn decent of you, darlin'. Maybe another time, okay?"

Disappointment flickered in her eyes. She turned away. My stomach churned like I had been sucker-punched. I'd let her down again.

Useless … you're fucking useless. Memories of Mom, drunk and red-faced and screaming her guts out. Bottles smashing as I ducked and weaved through the house. Piles of crap everywhere. Dirty clothes. Newspapers. Dishes. Bottles, everywhere the fucking bottles. I had to get out of there but I wasn't leaving without my kitten.

"Inky?" Mom snorted the day I brought the little shivering stray in from the cold. "That's a dumb name for a cat." She didn't mean it; she was just drunk. That's what I kept telling myself. "Inky! INKY!" I called for the kitten as I ran past the ripped-up window screens curling and rusting in their frames, past the smells of rotting food and cockroaches coming from the kitchen, Mom raging like a typhoon behind me. "What do you care, you never do anything to help out around here. Look at this fucking place! That fucking cat shits all over the goddamn house!" She was really getting worked up and I knew what came next and that was why I was getting the fuck out of Dodge. Once when I was little she got into one of her rages and threw me through a plate-glass window. At the hospital she said I ran through it and they believed her. They always believed her.

Inky was cowering under my bed. I picked her up, this little soft bundle of fur, and I held her close, feeling her warmth on my chest, feeling her little heart beating fast, so fast. "Shh," I said, smoothing out her fur. "It'll be okay. It'll be okay."

Suzanne watched me get dressed. She blinked as I taped knives to my arms and legs. "You sure have a lot of knives."

"It's a crazy world out there."

Shadows fell across the wall of Suzanne's bedroom as she sat up, suddenly covering herself with the sheet. "Jack ... there's something I ... I want to ask you. I mean, I don't want to ask, not really. I don't really want to know, you know?"

"So don't ask."

A sweet, sad half smile appeared on Suzanne's lips. "I know I shouldn't. But I can't stop thinking about it."

"So go ahead. Ask."

"Jack … have you ever killed anyone?"

It was bound to happen. Curiosity is a powerful thing.

I sat down on the bed and looked into her eyes. "I used to lie a lot. Especially to women. It was easier on everyone if I kept my business separate from my personal life. But those lies caught up to me."

"Is that what happened with what's-her-name?"

"Cassandra? No. What happened with her is I told the truth."

The moonlight shone on Suzanne's face as she turned away. "Was it the same question?"

"Phrased a little differently, but yeah, more or less." I looked down at my hands, gnarled and red and raw, sitting on my lap like two hunks of diseased meat. "The truth was too much to take. Too much for both of us."

Suzanne shook her head firmly. "Forget it. I don't want to know."

I took her hand. "Yes, you do. Otherwise you'll always wonder. We'll be having dinner at a nice restaurant and you'll look over at me eating my steak and think, 'I wonder how many people he's killed.'"

"But if you tell me … then I might look over at you and think, this man killed … how many people? Forget it. Forget I said anything."

The bedroom lapsed into silence, broken only by the hum of a neighbour's air conditioner. I smiled at Suzanne. "I'm not a killer, babe. I've hurt people — a lot of people — but I've never willingly set out to kill anyone."

Suzanne smiled. "Good. I mean, don't get me wrong, there are people out there who could use a good killing."

"You got that right."

We hugged. She smelled good, like vanilla cookies.

"So … self-defence?"

"Here's the thing about that. I don't like to toot my own horn, but I'm a pretty good fighter. I can usually take someone out without putting them down permanently."

"You said *usually*. So …"

Shadows shifted on the wall. I stared straight ahead. "When I was a little kid I had this little kitten. An all-black stray named Inky. I loved that cat."

I took a deep breath and continued. "My mom drank. Sometimes I had to leave the house for a while. But every time I left I would bring Inky with me. She was —" My voice choked off. I stared at the wall. *Come on, get it together.* "She was the best thing in my life, you know? Little Inky. She never did get very big.

"In high school my mom got a new boyfriend. Karl, with a *K*. He drank, too. But even when he was sober he was a fucking asshole. He was like some throwback 1950s greaser — wore his hair all slicked back like that guy in *Laverne & Shirley*.

"One day I came home from school and a lamp came smashing through the living room window. I could hear my mom and Karl shouting. My stomach clenched up. I didn't want to go inside. I wanted to keep walking. Just turn my back and keep walking forever. But I couldn't leave Inky.

"So I went inside. The place was trashed — more trashed than usual. Mom and Karl could barely stand up.

They were lurching around the living room, screaming at each other, holding on to the furniture. I tried to sneak past them and go up to my room to get Inky — I figured she'd be hiding under the bed — but Karl saw me and started talking shit. 'Look at this lousy kid you raised, can't even look after your kid,' shit like that. Mom went ballistic and charged. Her nails really ripped his face up pretty good. Then he hit her, and I mean really hit her. Spun her around and knocked her to the ground. She was lying there writhing in pain, holding her face and screaming.

"I stepped forward to help my mom. Karl saw me coming and raised his fists. 'Don't get any bright ideas, kid,' he said. 'This bitch had it coming.' I took a swing. I was so angry the swing went wide. Karl jumped back. That's when …" I shook my head. "It was the worst sound I've ever heard. This yowling, this tortured, unearthly howl."

Suzanne's eyes went wide. "No."

"Yes. That 1950s-looking motherfucker stepped on my cat. Broke Inky's spine. He killed my cat."

My fists were clenched. "I lost it. Everything went red. I might have killed him." I looked up. Suzanne was staring at me. "I hope so. He needed killing."

Suzanne reached out and took my hand. "You don't know for sure?"

"Nope. I walked out of the house and I never went back. Never went back to school, either. Got a fake I.D. from a guy I knew and hopped a bus to Toronto. That was a long time ago."

Suzanne snuggled closer. "I'm glad you hopped that bus."

"Me, too," I told her. "Me, too."

CHAPTER 27

So it didn't go down exactly like I told Suzanne. But I wasn't lying. The basic truth was all there.

The plant needed more water. I walked back from my office bathroom, humming, with a pint glass with a chipped rim brimming with nice fresh water. Yeah, I was feeling pretty good. It was one of those mornings where you wake up well-rested and crisp, optimism brimming in the belly. Sure this world is fucked and we've all got our problems, but that morning it seemed like everything was possible. Sunlight was pouring through the windows and the plant was already perking up, roots drinking deep, sucking up that sweet ol' H_2O.

"Whaddaya say, plant? You and me, baby." When Suzanne and I made our Great Escape out to the country (why not?), I'd take this plant with us. Maybe replant it in our yard with a bunch of plant buddies. Yeah. A big ol' yard with plants and trees and rolling green grass, dogs rompin' around, little kids zipping all over the place fast as neutrinos. Suzanne in a billowing white dress, me in tan slacks and a yellow cardigan, standing on our porch holding hands, watching the kids and the dogs tumble in the yard.

A fresh start. We'd make a clean break — no loose ends. Our friends would gather at the depot to wish us well. Grover could wave his monogrammed handkerchief as our train tooted and pulled away.

There was a knock on the office door. Two short raps, then a third, then two more. Eddie's code: possible trouble. I pointed to the plant. "Stay cool. Just stay cool." I cracked open my desk drawer and pulled out the biggest motherfucking knife I had. Gargantua. The knife to end all knives. It was like a sword crossed with a freakin' butcher's cleaver.

The dusty floorboards creaked as I sidled up to the door. "Eddie? You okay?"

Eddie's voice was muffled through the thick wooden door. "Yeah, Jack. Maybe it's nothing. But you should come downstairs."

I followed Eddie down to the basement. I heard the whimpering even before Eddie threw open the storeroom door. In the middle of the room was a little weasel-faced guy with a moth-eaten goatee, sitting terrified on a wooden chair, surrounded by three of Eddie's guys. I jerked my chin toward the weasel. "Who's this guy?"

"Nobody, I'm nobody," the weasel whined. "I'm just a delivery man. I'm just doing my job."

I turned to Eddie. "What did he deliver?"

Eddie pointed to a cake-sized box wrapped in brown paper sitting on a rickety table. "That. It's got your name on it, Jack."

I stalked over to the terrified guy. His eyes were fixed on my meat cleaver. He started babbling. "I'm telling the truth! I'm a delivery guy, I get paid to deliver packages, that's what I do!"

"How did you know where I was?"

"This old dude gave me directions. 'Deliver this package to this address,' he said. He paid me two hundred bucks!"

"Old dude? What old dude?"

The weasel shifted, sniffed and coughed. "This skinny old dude came into the courier office. Real dapper, you know?"

"Did you get a name?"

"He … I …" Weasel couldn't stop goggling at the cleaver. I turned and handed it to one of Eddie's guys, who held it behind his back. "I don't know. He paid cash."

"Return address?"

Eddie shook his head. "Nope."

"Give me your wallet."

Weasel blinked. "What?"

"You heard me."

Weasel fumbled through his pockets and pulled out a fraying blue vinyl wallet like the kind you'd have if you were in the fifth grade. I flipped it open and pulled out his driver's licence.

"Herman Soto. Elizabeth Street. Herman, I want you to forget we ever had this little conversation. You stay forgetful, we don't come visiting. Understand?"

Herman was moaning. "Aw jeez, aw jeez —"

Eddie rolled up on Herman, all angry eyes and towering menace. "He said, 'Do you understand?'"

"Yes! Yes! I won't say shit! It never happened! Please don't hurt me!"

I tossed Herman's wallet into his lap. "Go on, get out of here."

Eddie's guy handed my knife back and escorted Herman upstairs. Eddie turned to me. His face looked jaundiced in the glare of the overhead bulb. "Skinny, dapper old guy. Joey Machine?"

I nodded. "Could be."

"How did he know you were here?"

"Someone told him, or he followed me. Either way, someone knows I'm here. Did your people —"

Eddie shook his head vehemently. "My guys don't say squat."

"Yeah. Anyway, it might not be Joey Machine. Could be another dapper old guy."

"What? Like Little Vito's father?"

"Shit, I don't know."

Silence descended. Eddie and I stood in the musty basement. At the same time the two of us took a step closer to the box sitting on the table.

"What do you think is inside?"

"Birthday cake. Anthrax. One way to find out."

I raised my cleaver. Eddie took a step back. "Anthrax? You don't really think it's anthrax, do you?"

"Beats me. I don't have x-ray vision."

"One of my cousins works security at the airport. She can run it through the machine, take a look inside."

I grinned. "Too late."

The cleaver ripped through the brown wrapping paper. Eddie took two more steps back and got ready to run.

I stared down at the box. Sound and light and air were sucked from the room. My gut dropped. I felt like I had been punched in the cock.

"What is it? Jack, what is it?"

My mouth opened but no words came out. I staggered sideways. Eddie craned his neck and whispered, "Oh shit."

There, neatly folded atop a bed of light-blue tissue paper, was The Chief's leather jacket, covered in dried blood.

CHAPTER 28

I thrust out my hand to Eddie. "Phone."

My first call was to Suzanne. She came on the line all sleepy and yawning. "This better be good. I was having the best dream."

"Get out of the apartment."

"What?"

"Listen carefully. Pack a bag and get out of town. Do you have friends you can stay with?"

"Well, yeah. My old roommate lives —"

"Don't tell me. Don't tell anyone. Just get your shit and go."

"What the fuck is this, Jack? You're scaring me."

"You're smart to be scared. Go now, okay? Right the fuck now. If you have any problems, you call me at this number. Day or night. And don't worry ... I'll take care of it."

The next call was to Grover. "We need to meet."

On the other end Grover's voice was full of good cheer and sunshine. "Jack! So good to hear from you. Can't do it today, old boy … the wife and I are going shopping for a new car."

"Fuck that. We're meeting."

Grover snapped to an understanding of the seriousness of the situation. "When and where?"

"The old place. You know the one I mean?"

"I know the one."

"See you in fifteen minutes."

The phone clicked off. I was standing in the basement with the phone pressed against my ear listening to the dial tone. Behind me was the box with The Chief's bloody jacket.

I closed my eyes. *Breathe, Jack, breathe.*

Eddie shuffled forward and reached for the phone. I shook my head. "I'm going to hang on to this one."

Eddie lowered his hand. "Yeah." He jerked his chin toward The Chief's jacket. "You … you think he's dead?"

My stomach was eating itself. "He never goes anywhere without that jacket."

"It was Joey Machine, wasn't it?"

"Joey Machine, Little Vito — it doesn't matter." I held up the butcher's cleaver. "They're all fucking dead."

Eddie nodded. His dark eyes flickered. I knew Eddie. In his head, logistics were pinwheeling. How many soldiers could he call? Weapons, vehicles, safe houses … Eddie was getting his ducks in a row.

I stared at him. "Now might be a good time for you to go on vacation."

Eddie didn't say anything. Finally, he frowned. "You know me better than that."

It's true. I did. "Whoever killed The Chief knows where I live. Where you live. They're coming. It's only a matter of time."

Eddie grinned, light from the storeroom's single bulb glinting off his gold tooth. "If I'm not safe here, I'm not safe anywhere." Eddie shuffled over to the door and threw it wide open. "Go get 'em, Jack."

Outside in the morning sun the streets were full of people going about their day — little old ladies picking through the fruit stalls, moms pushing strollers, grocers stacking vast heaps of leafy greens. I ignored them all. Time for one more call.

"Tommy. It's Jack."

"Jack! Where the fuck have you been?" Tommy didn't wait for an answer. He just steamrolled right ahead. "Jack, things here are all fucked up. Dad's dying. Little Vito's on the fucking warpath. He says he's going to have you killed."

"Tell him to get in line. Where's Joey Machine?"

"That prick? One of my guys saw him coming out of the King Eddie."

"Is he being watched?"

"Yeah, sure, sure. Don't worry about that prick, Jack. One word from me, my guys move in and it's all over."

Yeah. For them.

"Tell your guys to back the fuck off. This one's mine."

"Listen, Jack, this isn't a good time. I need you here. This thing with Little Vito ... there's gonna be a war."

"I hate to break it to you, Tommy: the war has begun."

Grover met me in a little dingy pub near Yonge and Wellesley. I was sitting in the back with my back to the wall. There was a pint of soda water bubbling in front of me.

Grover, impeccable as always in a white suit with a navy-blue shirt, slid into the booth across from me. No hellos — he'd heard my tone over the phone. He jumped right in. "What's up?"

"The Chief's dead."

Grover inhaled sharply, sucking through his teeth. "What happened?"

"Not sure. Someone sent me his jacket in a box."

"His jacket." Grover frowned. "You didn't see his body?"

"He never goes anywhere without that jacket. There was blood all over it."

Grover squinted. "Joey Machine."

"I think so."

"Sounds like his style." Grover sat stock-still, turning into a small white statue. Finally he blinked. "Where is he?"

"Tommy says he's at the King Eddie."

"Tommy's a fucking idiot."

I don't know why, but I suddenly felt protective toward Tommy. Yeah, he was a fucking idiot. He was a mean drunk who treated people like shit. But deep down, on some level, he was just like the rest of us. He was just trying to do the best he could with what he had.

Grover stood up. "I'll check it out."

The little man in the white suit turned and headed for the door.

"Grover!"

He turned.

"This one's mine."

A server edged past carrying a platter of chicken wings. Grover waited for her to pass, then stepped closer to me. "Fuck that. We're in this together, Jack. The Chief —" Grover broke off. I swear he was about to break into tears. "The Chief was my friend, too."

Then he was gone, marching through the pub and out the door.

How did it go down? My brain churned as I headed back to the office. If I knew The Chief, it was about Redemption. I could see him clear as day, rising in the morning in his destroyed motel room, the taste of cigarettes and beer still lingering on his tongue, heart and head pounding with regret. Seven years sober and then this.

The Chief is a man of action. I mean, he was. He'd have climbed out of that stinking motel bed, shoved his way through the empty bottles, and taken a shower. Then he'd have wanted to redeem himself. One grand action to make up for his drunken spree. He'd have shaved, thrown on his leather jacket, cleaned his guns, and then headed out to take down Joey Machine. To show the world he wasn't afraid.

Or maybe it didn't go down that way at all. Maybe The Chief was hunkered down on his bed sucking on a bottle of malt liquor when there was a knock on the door. And maybe The Chief had called an escort service, drunken fingers fumbling, drunk and horny and ready for some fresh pussy right off the boat. But that's not what he got when he opened the door. *BLAM BLAM*, two shots, head and heart. Game Over.

I liked the first story better. Stick to that. That's the Chief I know.

I mean, that's The Chief I knew.

CHAPTER 29

I spent a long night sitting at my desk playing blackjack with my potted plant. Strangely enough, the plant was winning.

Grover called me around 11:00 a.m., rousing me from a restless sleep. No pleasantries. He cut right to the chase. "Tommy's info is bullshit."

"I kind of figured it would be."

"Joey Machine has a country house up north. You know Orangeville?"

"Yeah, I know Orangeville."

"Joey's house is about an hour away. I'm getting the team back together. We leave tonight."

My brow wrinkled as I turned off the phone. I knew Grover, and Grover didn't move this fast. Usually he'd stake out the house for a few days, even weeks, watch the people come and go. Get a feel for their schedules. Then he'd go inside. Figure out the security systems and map the house, systematically, room by room. Then he'd come up with the best plan of attack. Then and only then would he assemble the team.

Grover was moving too fast. It worried me, but I couldn't blame him. We all loved The Chief.

The first time The Chief and I went on a run, I was scared shitless. Back then I was so green I didn't even have enough sense to know I was scared. The pounding heart, the dry mouth — I just chalked it up to excitement.

"It's like this," The Chief said, laying it out for me over beers and wings in a faceless pub in a Scarborough strip mall. He and I were still wearing our security blues from our last legit job. All that was about to change. "There's this guy I know named Grover."

"Grover? Like in the fucking *Muppet Show*?"

The Chief scowled. "You're thinking of *Sesame Street*. Yeah, like that. But don't you ever say that to his face. This motherfucker is deadly, boy. He'll snap out your spine and use it to pick his teeth." The Chief took another gulp of beer. He was already half in the bag and so was I. "Anyway, this guy Grover puts together jobs. Finds the target, assembles the team, the whole nine yards."

"Burglary? That's not my thing."

"Shut up and listen, Mr. Specialist. Remember the diamond heist from a few weeks back?"

"No."

"What are you, illiterate? It made all the papers."

My chair scraped back. I stood up scowling, wiping spicy wing sauce off my fingers with a lemon-scented Wet-Nap. "Fuck this. Go find some other sucker."

The Chief grinned as he beckoned me to sit back down. "Hey man, I'm sorry. The guys I hang out with, we insult each other all the time. It's nothing personal. Come on, sit down. Have another chicken wing."

I sat back down. I had another chicken wing.

The Chief nodded and smiled. "All right. You know, I'm glad you stuck up for yourself, kid. Tells me a lot about you. I think you and I are going to get along just fine."

"The diamond heist?"

"Yeah. Three million bucks in uncut gems. Anyway, the team got greedy. 'Why should we give Grover a share? He wasn't even there.'" The Chief snorted. "The little pricks. Grover only set the whole thing up."

"We're going up against an entire team?" My heart was pounding. Was this some kind of initiation? Throw the new guy into a pit of wolves and see if he comes out alive. With my youthful bravado, I knew I could do it.

Luckily for me, The Chief shook his head. "Nope. Just one. Lonnie Riggs. Long-time pro thief. Grover brought him in at the last minute. The original point man got stabbed in a whorehouse.

"Lonnie is the man holding Grover's share. The others ... well, they'll be dealt with. But for now Grover wants his diamonds."

"Where do we come in?"

"Right to the point. I like that, kid, I like that a lot. Lonnie's part of a floating poker game. Tough guys and high stakes. In three days that game is going to be in a warehouse down in the Port Lands. You and I are going to be at that game."

"I don't play poker."

The Chief grinned. "I'll teach you."

The Chief was as good as his word. He brought in his buddies and for the next three days we ate, slept, and breathed poker. It was intense. By the end of those three days guys were calling me Ace and slapping me on the back. The air was blue with cigar and cigarette smoke. Every night I'd go back to my hotel room and cough up huge gobs of gunk.

The day of the big game, The Chief showed up at my hotel and handed me a brand-new suit. Nothing too flashy — I wasn't going to waltz into the warehouse looking like a fucking clown — but it looked expensive. "Here, kid," The Chief said. "Put this on."

The suit fit like a fucking glove. In the mirror I looked lean and dangerous. The Chief nodded approval. "You got a piece?"

"A piece of what?"

"Kid, you kill me. A gun, man, a gun."

I shook my head no.

"That's okay. I know where we can get one."

It was my turn to shake my head. "I don't use 'em."

"What? Whaddaya mean you don't use 'em?"

"Like I said." I held out my hands, sinewy and strong, coiled like sleeping cobras. "These are all I need."

The Chief laughed admiringly. "Kid, you're fucking crazy. All right … let's saddle up."

It was dark by the time we got to the warehouse. Moonlight was shining on the oily black water. The Chief adjusted his shoulder holster and zipped up his leather jacket. "All right, kid, let's go."

I figured we'd be searched at the door, but I figured wrong. The guy guarding the door looked like a cross between Mr. T and a great white shark. He just nodded his huge head and let us walk on through. That meant one of three things: 1) the doorman had been paid off and was in on the scheme; 2) no one got searched and everyone at the poker table was packing heat; or 3) the doorman was just really bad at his job. The safe bet was number 2: everyone at the game had a gun, possibly even more than one.

Our footsteps echoed in the vast cavernous space as we walked toward the back, huge shelves jam-packed with boxes towering over us.

Something shifted in the darkness and I tensed, fists at the ready. The Chief didn't blink. He stepped forward and nodded to the darkness. "We're here for the game."

The shadow stepped aside. Another doorman, this one clad in all black. Once again we weren't searched. The doorman threw the door open wide and we stepped across the threshold.

Inside the air was already thick with cigar smoke. Five guys were hunched around a green felt table in what looked like a shipping/receiving office: the walls were covered in tacked-up invoices and bikini calendars. A circular fan was humming near a small dirty window.

A barrel-shaped man with curly hair and mutton-chop sideburns popped up from the table and grinned at The Chief. "'Bout fucking time you got here. I need some more fucking money to win."

A sour-faced man in a bright purple suit shook his head. "The night's young, you fat fuck."

The barrel-shaped man scowled. "Nice suit. Who are you, The Joker?"

The Chief held out his hands. "Gentlemen, gentlemen! Let's just play some fucking cards, all right?" The Chief clapped me on the shoulder. "This is Jack. He's a friend of mine. Anyone got a problem with him being here?"

Grunts and mutters. A crater-faced man in sunglasses exhaled smoke and stared me right in the eyes. The man in the purple suit shook his head. "Money is money."

The barrel-shaped man smiled at me and thrust out his hand. "Lonnie Riggs."

"Jack Palace."

"Nice to meet you."

"You, too." It was a strange feeling, shaking hands with a man who might be dead before the night was through.

I didn't like it.

The Chief handed me a tumbler full of whisky and straddled a chair. "All right, you fuckers. Let's play some fucking poker."

At first the cards were against me. Tens and deuces, sevens and fours — shit like that. I still came out betting but I was getting beaten like a second-hand gong. Then about halfway through the night my luck turned. I was holding two eights and caught a third on the river. I beat out Purple Suit for over half his stack. His sour face got even more sour. Then I was dealt pocket aces. Fuck it, I went All In. Lonnie Riggs called me. A bunch of junk came up on the turn. When Lonnie saw the aces, he hung his head. "Thought you were bluffing."

"I don't bluff," I said. I was bluffing.

The Chief ended up winning it all. He grinned as he raked in everyone's cash. "Well, gents … it's been real." Muttering curses, the others packed up to go.

The Chief turned to Lonnie. "Lonnie, what the fuck happened? You started out so strong and then you totally blew it."

Lonnie shrugged. "Some days you just don't get the cards."

Purple Suit and Crater Face made their goodbyes and left the room. The others shuffled out as well. Lonnie turned to follow, but The Chief caught his arm. "Hold up a sec. You still drive that blue car?"

"Blue car? The fuck you talking about?"

"You know. That car you used to have."

"What? I don't —"

The Chief hit him just above the right eye, a powerful punch that knocked Riggs back. Instantly I was there to catch Lonnie's arms as he went for his gun. The Chief hit him again, and again. He wasn't pulling any punches. I heard the bones breaking in Lonnie's face.

It was over in seconds. The Chief turned to me, his dark eyes flaring, Lonnie's blood splattered across his face. "Pull him up."

I heaved him up. The barrel-shaped man was heavier than he looked.

The Chief slapped his face. "Wake the fuck up."

Lonnie moaned through his broken mouth.

"You get Grover his motherfucking diamonds by noon tomorrow. You got that?"

Lonnie burbled something that might've been a yes. The Chief wiped his hands on the front of Lonnie's shirt.

"Let's go."

"Uh … what should I —"

"Just drop him."

I did.

Outside the door the shadowy doorman handed The Chief a towel. The Chief finished wiping off his hands and face. The doorman jerked his head toward the poker room. "We cool?"

"Yeah, we're cool." The Chief handed the doorman the bloody towel, then turned his back and walked away. I followed.

Back in the car The Chief grinned and pulled out his wad of winnings. "Welcome to The Game, kid. Here."

I shook my head. "That's too much."

"What did you do, swear a vow of poverty? Just take the fucking money."

I took the fucking money.

CHAPTER 30

rover drove in silence. It was fucking freezing; Grover had the AC blasting on full.

"Nice car."

"It's all right. I liked the Lexus better."

"Joey Machine's house. You ever been there before?"

"Sure, I go up there all the time. We play croquet, drink tea, and get fucking crumpet crumbs all over our fucking shirts."

"I'm just saying —"

"Let me stop you right there, Jack. I know what you're saying. You're saying it isn't smart to go charging in blind. You know what? You're absolutely right. But that's not what we're going to do."

I kept quiet. The car engine growled beneath us. A big rig passed us, its headlights slicing through the darkness.

Grover scowled. "Give me some credit, Jack. You know I'm not going to go charging in with all guns blazing."

"So what's the plan?"

"Open the glove box."

I reached in warily, half expecting a cobra to leap out and bite my face. Or maybe poison darts. Instead there was a folded-up blueprint.

"Is that —"

"Yep. Joey Economy's house."

I unfolded the blueprints. Fuckin' Grover had done it again.

"How did you get this?"

Grover stared straight ahead. The lights from the highway danced across his face. "I knew a guy who worked with Joey Economy years ago. He's the one who told me about this place. He's dead now. I went to the county clerk's office and bought the blueprints, just in case."

I smoothed out the blueprints across my lap. Without taking his eyes off the windshield Grover stabbed his finger at the top of the page. "You see this? That's the alarm system. You remember Paco? He's going to cut the wire. Then you and I are going in."

"What if the man's not at home?"

"Then we wait."

My mind tumbled as we drove north. Joey Economy, motherfucking Joey Economy. I was the one that brought The Chief with me when I went to see Joey. What if I had gone alone? Maybe I'd be dead, lying in a potato field with my throat slit, open eyes staring up at the sky. Hypothetical bullshit. I would've never even met Joey Economy if it wasn't for Tommy.

Tommy. He was a vicious son of a bitch, but that's what saved my life. I closed my eyes and shuddered. I didn't like thinking about it.

They came at me with mop handles, jumping me just outside my cell. The fucking guards had vanished like smoke. I broke the first one's leg and punched the second one right in the throat, but they kept coming. One of them took out my left arm with a massive swing, leaving it hanging, numb and useless. I kicked a guy in the crotch and threw another over the railing, but they kept coming, wooden blows raining down on my back, my shoulders. A mop handle bounced off my head. Everything went white and then red and then black. I fell to my knees coughing up blood. The assassins closed in. An eerie calm spread through my body. This was it. I was going to die.

"STOP! Step the fuck back. NOW!" It was Tommy. Big Earl Johnston, one of the jail orderlies, told me about it as I lay in the infirmary swaddled in bandages.

"Man, you should've seen that shit. You were all laid out on the ground, face all puffy, and those guys were closing in. One more blow to the back of the head, man ... *POW*! It would've been lights fucking out. And then Tommy marches up with his army behind him and it's all over. One word from him, man, and those fuckers froze like snowmen." Big Earl chuckled and shook his head. "You know what you are? You're a lucky motherfucker, that's what you are."

Yeah — lucky. I survived, I recovered, I got sprung back onto the streets right into Tommy's waiting arms. And now my best friend was dead and someone was going to pay.

Grover sailed the car up Highway 10, past auto dealerships and gas stations and little stone churches. The countryside started to unfold around us. Grover looked over at me and said, "You hungry? I'm hungry. Let's get a burger."

We stopped at this burger joint that had a converted streetcar as a dining room attached to the main building. We got our burgers and onion rings and fries and I headed for a table near the wall. Grover stopped me. "No. We're sitting in the streetcar."

"What?"

"I said we're sitting in the fucking streetcar."

We stepped into the streetcar and wedged ourselves into a tiny table. Grover looked around at the happy families surrounding us and smiled. "Didn't you ever used to go to restaurants like this when you were a kid?"

"No," I told him truthfully.

"I remember one restaurant we stopped at on a road trip had an entire airplane you could eat in. I must've been about seven or eight. I thought it was the coolest thing ever."

I'd never heard Grover talk about his childhood. Ever. Grover grinned and took a big bite of his cheeseburger. "See, Jack, this is what life's all about. Stopping to appreciate the little things. Sure, I like my boat and my fancy clothes and my gourmet food, but it hasn't gone to my head. You understand? On some level I'm still that little boy laughing his head off in a dining room made from an airplane."

I dragged an onion ring through ketchup. "I'm thinking of retiring."

"You should! You definitely should. You've got some money set aside?"

"Some. Not enough. But I've got some coming to me."

"From Tommy?"

"Yeah. From Tommy."

Grover chewed his burger and shook his head. "You need to get your hands on that money ASAP. The winds of change are blowing, Jack."

"Yeah." It was true. I needed to wrap up my work with Tommy, get paid, and get gone. Take Suzanne by the hand and head south into the sunshine.

On our way out I overheard a little girl, maybe two or three, ask her mom: "When does the train leave, Mommy?"

It's not leaving, sweetheart. There's no more track. This train's going to be sitting here forever.

CHAPTER 31

The gravel road crunched beneath our tires. Skeletal trees loomed from the darkness. Grover squinted through the windshield, peering through the murk. Without a moon these country nights were as dark as fuck.

"Jack, check the map."

I unfolded it and tried to figure out which squiggly line matched the near-complete darkness that surrounded us.

"Well? We going the right way?"

I folded up the map. "Yeah. Turn left at County Road 17."

Grover's head whipped around. "What was that? Was that it?"

"Yeah."

Grover slammed on the brakes. The car fishtailed in the gravel. "Fuck. Hold on." Grover reversed, engine roaring.

Back on track, Grover grinned. "I got a present for you, Jack. It's under your seat."

I reached under my seat and pulled out a long silver box.

"Go on, open it."

Inside the box was a knife that looked like it was carved from meteor rock: deadly and black and gleaming in the dashboard light.

"That blade is so sharp it'll cut through bone like butter."

"Thanks, Grover." The knife was perfectly balanced in my hand. I rotated the blade, watching moonlight bounce off its polished surface. I closed my eyes and thought of The Chief.

Ahead of us was a dark-blue van parked almost invisibly by the side of the road. Grover slowed the car to a crawl, then pulled in behind the van and cut the engine. The hush of country quiet filled the air.

The van door opened and a man wearing all black stepped out onto the road and began walking toward us. My fingers tightened around my new knife.

Grover jerked his chin toward the approaching man. "Be cool. That's Paco. He's been watching the house."

Grover climbed out of the car and I did the same, sliding the knife into its sheath. Our shoes crunched against the gravel. The air was cold and still. I swivelled my head but didn't see any houses.

Grover and Paco shook hands. "Anything to report?"

Paco shook his head. "Negative. The house is just down that hill. Two cars in the driveway. Lights are on."

"Joey inside?"

"Last I checked. That was about ten minutes ago. No one's been up or down this road since."

Up close I saw that Paco had a pair of night-vision goggles pushed up on his head like sunglasses. "Hey, Grover … do I get goggles, too?"

Grover grinned, walked back and and popped the trunk. Inside, arrayed on multilevel expandable racks, were nine silver briefcases. Grover opened up one brief-case and there were two pairs of night-vision goggles. "Yeah, you get goggles. What did you think, Jack? I was going to send you out into the desert with no water?"

"Fuck the water. I'll take the goggles."

"Take this, too." Grover cracked open another suit-case and pulled out a pistol.

I shook my head. "Don't need it."

"Just take it, Jack. For insurance purposes."

"No thanks."

Paco squinted. "What is it with you and guns?"

I held up my knife. The blade glittered in the moon-light. "You see this? One cut and you're done. Clean and precise. My hand controls it all. Now take that." I jerked my chin toward the gun sitting chunky and ugly in Grover's hand. "You squeeze the trigger. Bullets come out. Then it's up to physics and random luck. Sure, you can aim. But what happens if some citizen accidentally steps into the bullet's path? What happens if a car drives by, or the wind changes, or the gun misfires?" I leaned forward with my teeth clenched. "How many innocent people get caught in the crossfire and killed every year because some dumb fucking thug started spraying bullets at random?"

Paco shook his head. "You're crazy, man."

Grover grinned. "Paco's right, Jack. Didn't your mamma ever teach you not to bring a knife to a gunfight?"

Before I could answer, Grover cracked open another briefcase and pulled out an AK-47. He wasn't fucking around. Someone was going to die tonight.

The three of us stood by the side of the road, night wind rustling the tall grass. Grover slid down his goggles. "All right, let's do this."

Joey Machine's house was invisible from the road. We found a gated driveway and Grover pointed the tip of his AK-47 at the reflective green emergency number. "This is it. Come on."

We crept about a hundred feet away from the front gate. All around us huge trees were waving in the wind, their leaves rustling. Grover jerked his head. "We'll cut through here. Assume the fence is electrified. Assume there's cameras everywhere. Paco, you go that way. Jack, you go that way. We'll circle the house and close in. Move fast. Shoot anything that moves. Okay? GO."

I crouched down low, running downhill through the tall grass toward the house. Through my night-vision goggles the house was lit up like a jack-o'-lantern, red and orange and yellow. Two cars sat in the driveway, just like Paco said.

A shadow lunged, red and orange. In a split-second my new knife leapt from its sheath. The shadow hit my chest and we tumbled back. The knife did its work. I stood up, a dead dog bleeding at my feet. I crouched down and scanned the perimeter. Loud barks cut through the night. Suddenly I was blinded as massive spotlights flooded the yard.

Machine-gun fire. Barking and gunshots. So much for the element of surprise. I stood up, ripped off my goggles, and charged toward the house.

The sliding glass doors lay in pieces across the back porch. I glanced around the edges and slipped into the house.

Joey Economy was rich, there was no doubt about that. Paintings, bookshelves, piano — microsecond first impressions as I ran through the open-concept downstairs. Another burst of machine-gun fire shattered the huge living room window and I heard a woman scream. *Fuck.*

Paco ran past me, heading for a hallway. "Anything?" he shouted.

"No," I shouted back.

Gunfire punched into the piano, hammering sour notes into the air.

Through the shattered window I saw Grover approach, his AK-47 barking fire. He looked like a demon rising from the mouth of hell. He was shouting something but I couldn't hear him. He pointed up and I got it: upstairs.

I took the stairs two at a time. Paco stayed behind, covering me from the ground floor. At the top of the stairs was a short hallway leading to a closed door.

Eerie silence. I heard a woman whimper. *Fuck it,* I thought, and I kicked down the door.

Bedroom. A young, dark-haired woman crouched on the carpet. She was naked except for a black leather harness covered in metallic spikes. "I didn't mean to … I didn't mean to … wasn't my fault … don't … wasn't my fault …"

My knife hand, still sticky with dog blood, dropped to my side.

Behind the woman was a large wooden rack dripping with chains and manacles. Suspended from the rack was Joey Economy, naked, covered in welts and bruises, a red ball gag stuffed into his wrinkled mouth. He hung motionless, glassy eyes staring at nothing.

I stepped cautiously toward the rack, keeping my eye on the woman on the floor. Joey didn't move. I checked for a pulse.

Joey Machine was dead.

CHAPTER 32

In Orangeville we stopped for drinks and chicken wings. Grover was uncustomarily quiet, sitting straight-backed in the pub's booth, staring down at his beer.

Paco shook his head. "Man! That was some fucked-up shit right there."

Grover didn't look up. I nodded. *Yes indeed, fucked-up shit.*

Paco's face was a web of old scars twisting their way up into his jet-black hair. He picked up another wing and dragged it through the sauce. "Grover, I gotta admit, man, when you first contacted me for this gig I was a little worried. You ever watch *Star Trek*?"

Grover nodded. "Captain Picard."

"No, man — the original *Star Trek*. The one with all the fake rocks and shit."

Grover's face went sour. "I've seen it."

"You know how when they go down to the planet it's always the main cast, like Bones and Spock and Captain

Kirk, and then some poor sucker in a red shirt who you've never seen before? And then shit goes wrong and guess who gets killed: Mr. Red Shirt. Happens almost every episode, man."

I sipped my beer. It was cool and tangy on my tongue. I closed my eyes and there he was, Joey Machine, dangling dead on the rack.

Grover stared across the table. "What's your point, Paco?"

"When you called me up I thought I was the Red Shirt. The sacrificial lamb and shit."

Two tables over, a group of guys in flannel work-shirts and paint-splattered pants howled with laughter. Conversation mixed and matched in the air. A bored-looking server in a black miniskirt marched past with another platter of wings. My cellphone rang.

"I've got to take this."

I walked through the pub and into the outside air. "Yeah."

"Jack." It was Suzanne. "Are you okay?"

"I'm fine, babe. Don't you worry about me. How are you?"

"I'm staying in some bullshit motel. The couple in the room next to me fuck like beavers. Last night they were going at it so hard the painting above my bed fell off the wall."

"Rabbits."

"What?"

"Fuck like rabbits."

"Rabbits, beavers — it doesn't matter, Jack. I just wanted to let you know I'm going home."

Home.

Joey Machine was dead. Little Vito, Tommy, other unseen threats still circled like sharks.

"Not yet."

"That's bullshit. I miss my bed. I miss my books. I'm going home. If you want to come over, come on over."

"Where are you? I'm coming to see you."

"Right now?"

"Right the fuck now."

Paco and Grover looked up as I marched back to the table. I chugged the rest of my beer in one pull. "I've got to go."

Grover pointed to Paco. "Paco, give him your keys."

"What? Hey, man, I need that van for work!"

Grover got real still. His voice dropped to almost a whisper. "What did I just say?"

Nervousness flickered across Paco's scarred face. He dug into his pocket and produced the keys.

"Thanks." I nodded at Grover. "See you around."

"Jack."

"Yeah?"

"This isn't over."

"The man's dead, Grover. Seems pretty over to me."

Grover shook his head. "No. He doesn't get off that easily. He had friends. Colleagues. We're going to find them. All of them. That's what The Chief would've wanted."

I stood stock-still, breathing in chicken wing fumes. "I ... I've got to go."

Grover waved lazily as I left. "Be seeing you, Jack. Keep those knives sharpened."

Paco's van was a mess. The ashtray was overflowing with cigarette butts, and crumpled-up fast food bags covered the back seat like snowdrifts. I spun the radio dial until it landed on something soothing and classical. I started to pull out of the parking lot and then slammed on the brakes: Grover was standing in front of the van, Paco next to him.

I rolled down the window. "Yeah?"

"Hold up. Paco forgot something in the back."

Paco grinned. "I'll be just a second."

Slowly I pulled my new knife from its sheath and held it lightly against my leg. The old lessons came flooding back. *Don't let him get behind you. Keep staring at his hands. Keep Grover in sight at all times.* The van's back door rumbled open and Paco leaned in. He started to rummage through the fast food bags.

Grover stepped up behind Paco and shot him once in the back of the head.

"Jesus!"

The silencer on Grover's gun ate most of the noise. I craned my neck and scanned the parking lot: all clear.

In the back seat the white fast food bags were now splattered with blood. Grover shoved Paco's body into the van, slammed the door, and jumped into the passenger seat.

"Drive."

CHAPTER 33

After we dumped Paco in the woods Grover stood silently with his head bowed and his hands folded. "It's a shame. He was a good kid."

Then why did you shoot him, I wanted to say. But I knew Grover, and I knew enough to keep my big mouth shut.

A bird fluttered overhead, black wings beating against the nighttime canopy. Grover looked over at me. "He would've talked, Jack. He would've gone to his neighbourhood bar and gotten drunk and blabbed to all his buddies about his big adventure Up North. Do you understand?"

Hell no.

"Sure."

Grover put his arm around my shoulders and steered me back to the van. "He wasn't like you or me, Jack. He was impulsive. He didn't think things through. But he was a good kid. He had a daughter, did you know that? I'm going to send her some money. What do you think, ten grand?"

"Make it twenty."

Grover grinned in the moonlight. "That's one of the things I like about you, Jack. You're a generous guy. Now let's go back to the restaurant and pick up my car."

CHAPTER 34

I drove south in the dead man's van. After about half an hour the rolling hills and green fields of the Ontario countryside turned into concrete overpasses and squat, ugly warehouses. Welcome home.

I stopped at a gas station and then I pulled up behind a warehouse near the airport. The smell of the gas burned my nose as I doused the van. I lit a pack of matches and tossed it in. Behind me the van erupted as I walked away. Goodbye, Paco.

A bus carried me to Kipling Station and from there I jumped into a cab and headed south. Suzanne was waiting for me down by the lake in a motel that time forgot. This place was straight out of the early 1960s: a long concrete motor court with a sun-bleached sign. The motel sign was vintage and so was the carpet: the ghosts of a thousand cigarettes rose up as I walked along the corridor.

At Suzanne's door I paused, ran my hands through my hair and checked my shoes for blood. Good to go.

She answered on the fourth knock. "About time you got here." I leaned in to kiss her and she turned away. My lips grazed her cheek. She turned her back to me and hoisted up her luggage. "Come on, let's go."

"Let's have a drink first. It's been a long night."

She turned, slowly. "How do you think my night was, Jack? I'm sitting here in this shit-box, up all night listening to trucks honking and whores fucking and all the time I'm wondering if you're dead or alive. 'Oh, that Jack, he's such a swell guy, I wonder if I'll ever see him again.' You bastard!" Suzanne's fists battered my chest. I caught her wrists and tried to hold her tight but she jerked free. "We are not doing this shit again. Do you hear me?"

"Babe. Babe. Listen. I'm trying to keep you safe."

"I told you, I don't need you to keep me safe." Suzanne scowled. "I'm not some fucking princess you can keep locked away in a tower. And you're not a fucking knight in shining armour." Suzanne shook her head. "I can't take this shit, Jack."

I edged into the room and closed the door behind me. The paint on the door was scratched and the chain was busted. "Someone try to come in here last night?"

Suzanne wiped her nose and shook her head. "No. It was like that when I got here."

"We'll move you to another room. Just for a few more days. Maybe a week. And then —"

Suzanne laughed. "And then what? And then you'll have slain all the dragons? There's always going to be bad guys, Jack. In case you hadn't noticed, that's how the world works."

"Just another week. Week and a half, tops. I'll wrap up my business and then we'll hit the open road. Just the two of us."

Suzanne popped open her suitcase and knelt down. When she came up there was a gun in her hand.

"Suzanne … take it easy."

"Fuck you, Jack. I've had enough of your bullshit. You hear me?" She kept the gun barrel pointed up toward the ceiling. "If there's guys hassling you, I want to know about it. If we're really a team, then we're going to get through this shit together."

"No. It doesn't work like that. I work alone."

Suzanne shook her dark hair. "Bullshit. What about the guy who answers your phone? Or the guy you went up north with? I don't even know who else. How about the people who made your knives? No one works alone. It takes a fucking village, Jack."

"What are you, some kind of commie?"

"Yeah, yeah, laugh it up. But I'm serious." Suzanne pointed to the gun in her hand. "This isn't a fucking prop. I've used it before, Jack. I can do it again."

I shook my head. "I don't want you to."

"Why? Because that would ruin your perfect fantasy? Me in a hoop skirt and a frilly apron out in the backyard tending the fucking vegetables? This is reality, Jack. You and me. You and me against the world." Suzanne pointed to the cigarette-scarred wooden chair squatting by the window. "So you sit the fuck down and tell me."

"Tell you what?"

"Everything. Who's after you? And why?"

I shook my head. "It's too dangerous."

"You don't get it. You still think you're protecting me. Do you respect me?"

"Of course I do."

"Then respect me enough to tell me the truth."

So I told her. I told her about Tommy and prison. I told her about Tommy's dad sucking on a ventilator in the hospital. I told her about Little Vito and the gunmen on Spadina. I told her about Joey Machine and The Chief and The Chief's jacket.

I didn't tell her about Grover.

When I finished my throat was dry and scratchy. Suzanne's mouth was a thin grim line as she marched toward the door.

That's it, I thought. *I'll never see her again.*

At the door Suzanne turned. "Well?"

"Well what?"

"What are you waiting for?" Suzanne tucked her gun into her waistband. "Let's go see Tommy."

"Okay, stop. What are you going to do? March into Tommy's fortress with your guns blazing? Maybe you kill one guy, maybe two, and then you die in a hail of bullets. That's no good, babe."

"Or I take Tommy out. The element of surprise. He won't see me coming. Give me some credit here, Jack."

I took her hand in mine. "There's only one way out of this. I finish the job. Tommy gets his money. And you and I are free."

"And Little Vito?"

"Tommy will take care of him. Hell, for all we know Vito might be dead already." I grinned, trying to light up the room with my sunny optimism. Suzanne wavered. She had dark circles under her tired eyes.

I pulled her close. She buried her face in my chest. "Tell me a lie, Jack. Tell me everything's going to be okay."

I held her tight. "It is going to be okay," I murmured. "We're going to get through this."

Suzanne spoke into my shirt. "I'm not staying in this shithole another night."

"Okay." I held her closer. "Let's go home."

CHAPTER 35

Suzanne walked naked from the bathroom, her hair wrapped up in a towel, her normally pale skin now bright pink from the shower. I looked up from my giant gin and tonic and I couldn't stop staring.

Suzanne grinned, sauntering sexily across the carpet. She sat down on the black and chrome chair across from me and casually spread her legs. "That's more like it. The shower in the motel was the shits. No hot water. No water pressure at all."

Outside through the open window I heard the hustle and bustle of the Kensington shopping crowds. A bicycle bell dinged. Faint, tinny, Middle Eastern–sounding music was playing on a distant radio. I stared at Suzanne and adjusted the front of my trousers.

She cocked her head toward the open bathroom door. "Your turn."

The shower felt great. I closed my eyes and turned my face into the spray. Steaming hot water streamed down my body, coursing past the scars and bruises, soothing the aches and pains.

When I stepped out of the bathroom, Suzanne was still naked. She was standing in the kitchen mixing a martini. I came up behind her and grabbed her ass. She yelped and laughed and leapt away. I pushed her against the countertop and spread her ass with both hands. I was hard as a rock. My fingers dipped lower, into her folds. She moaned. She was soft and moist and warm.

She gasped as I entered her. No teasing, no bullshit — I wanted every inch of myself inside her NOW. I thrust in deeper, deeper. Suzanne grunted. "Go … slow …"

I slowed down, easing out and back in, my cock sliding inside her hot, slick pussy. My hand reached around and squeezed her breasts. I leaned down, thrusting in deep as she arched her back. Her wet hair flicked across my face.

"Jack. Oh, Jack."

I bit her neck, pushed her forward against the counter, held her hips and slammed into her, faster and faster, wet hot slick —

My legs shuddered as I came, pumping deep inside her, every bit of energy left in my body exploding from the tip of my cock. I collapsed on top of her, pinning her against the countertop. We breathed together, her body so warm beneath mine, our heartbeats in synch.

She moved beneath me and I knew she wanted up. I pulled out and stood up and stepped away, smiling. She smiled back, her eyes half-lidded.

"Nothing like makeup sex." She reached for her martini, took a big swig, and brushed her wet hair away from her face. "That was amazing."

"You're pretty damn amazing yourself, sweetheart."

She pointed to her martini. "You want one of these?"

"Yeah, sure."

She mixed me a martini and together we moved toward the bedroom. Light from outside was shining through the window, illuminating her fluffy white bed.

"Cheers." Our glasses clinked. The booze went down smooth.

She nuzzled up close. I put my arm around her and together we drifted off to sleep.

"Jack. JACK!"

I rose with a start, hand leaping to my knife on the nightstand. Outside it was dark. What time was it?

"What? What is it?"

Suzanne looked scared. Wide eyes and messy hair. "You were screaming."

I peered toward the window. "Is someone here? Did you see anything?"

"No."

"Are you okay?"

"I'm fine. Jack …"

"Yeah?"

"You were screaming. You wouldn't wake up. I tried to wake you but you wouldn't wake up."

"I'm okay." I managed a smile. "I'm fine."

"What were you screaming about?"

"I don't remember." It was the truth. "What time is it?"

"It's midnight."

I stood up, found my pants and pulled them on. "I've got to go."

Outside, the Kensington Market air was crisp and cold. I stopped at a street corner and took a deep breath, and then another, and another. My hands were shaking. A homeless man wearing three coats staggered by sideways. Loud music pumped from a punk bar's open door. I peered in as I passed: sullen forty-year-old men with mohawks perched at the bar nursing their pints. I flagged down a cab and headed for Tommy's.

Tommy's club was hopping, jam-packed to the rafters with girls in shiny silver halter tops and black micro-miniskirts and guys with shirts open to their navels — gold chains and hairy chests. A drunk guy with slicked-back hair and leather pants stumbled into me and snarled. I was sick of this shit. I punched him in the throat and didn't even stick around to watch him fall.

Tonight Tommy wasn't in his office. He was in the VIP booth overlooking the dance floor, a blonde on either side of him, a half-empty (or is it half-full?) bottle of Dom Perignon on the table. Tommy's bodyguard — *what was his name? Rocco?* — waved me closer. Tommy spotted me and smiled.

"Do my fucking eyes deceive me? Rocco, am I dreaming? Quick, somebody pinch me. Ow! You dizzy broad, not for real. Come on, Jack, have a seat. This is … what's your name again, sweetheart?"

"Elana."

Elana and her friend Sindi ("with an *S*!"): tonight they were models, but tomorrow it'd be back to the strip club.

The music throbbed. Below us on the dance floor an ocean of humanity rose and fell. Tommy leaned in close to my ear. His breath smelled like rotting oranges. "I set up a meeting for you. Tomorrow afternoon. You tell that shit stain Vito to pay me my money or I'm going to fucking cut off his head and piss down his neck."

"Ah, diplomacy."

"What?"

"Forget it."

Elana ran her fingertips along my arm. "I'm not wearing any panties. Want to see?"

"Sure, why not?"

She was telling the truth. Her pink slit winked out at me from beneath her miniskirt. "You want to go somewhere more private?"

"Sorry, darlin'." I grinned. "I can't afford it."

A cab blasting bossa nova tunes picked me up and carried me toward Chinatown. I leaned forward. "Hey, turn it down."

"This is happy music. Happy music."

"Yeah? Turn it down."

Back home, instead of heading directly up to my office, I passed through Eddie's restaurant, twisting sideways to avoid the lightning-quick waiters bearing huge trays of steamed dumplings and shredded pork. I ducked through a doorway at the back of the restaurant and walked through the kitchen. A skinny chef with a missing front tooth grinned at me and I grinned back. At the back of the kitchen a bored-looking teenager with spiky hair looked up from his comic book. "Yeah?"

"I'm Jack. Eddie inside?"

"Who wants to know?"

"I told you already. My name's Jack."

"Gambling?"

"What?"

The kid jerked his spiky head toward the closed door leading down to Eddie's illegal casino. "Gambling?"

"Yeah. Sure."

"Ten bucks."

I didn't protest and I didn't argue. I pulled a wad of bills from my pocket and peeled off a ten.

Inside Eddie's casino the air was choked with cigarette smoke. The tables were full. It was mostly Chinese men, but here and there were a few Westerners — old degenerate gamblers and a few young couples out for an illicit thrill. A young blond woman in giant sunglasses sat at one of the poker tables, a massive fortress of chips in front of her. There was a whole lotta gambling going on.

Eddie bellied up to me, shook my hand, and grinned. He was wearing a black suit, sunglasses, and a skinny tie.

"What's the good word, Jack? You want a drink?"

"Scotch. Put it in a big glass. No ice."

"One of those nights, eh?"

"They're all those nights."

Eddie turned, snapped his fingers, and pointed at me. Before I could blink, a tall glass full of Scotch was pressed into my hand. I said thanks but the waiter was already gone, swallowed up by the gambling crowd.

I raised my glass. "Cheers."

The Scotch burned down my throat. Warmth spread from my stomach. "You got a minute?"

"Sure, Jack. What's up?"

"Let's go up to the roof."

On the roof the night was getting colder. The lights from the CN Tower winked down at us. Eddie sparked up a cigarette. I kicked back in my lawn chair and stretched my legs.

"Christ, it feels good to sit down."

"Yeah."

Traffic roared and rumbled in the streets below. Music leaked from car windows, the dull idiot thud of too much bass. And then it was quiet once again.

I set my glass down and stared up at the sky. The city lights had eaten all the stars. "I've got a meeting with Vito tomorrow."

"Little Vito?"

"That's the one. I'm going to need backup." What did Suzanne say? No one works alone.

"No problem."

"I'm going to need guys I can trust. Guys who are calm, cool, and collected. No hotheads. No slack-jaws. Not like Manga Boy you've got working the door tonight."

Eddie frowned. "That's my nephew. He give you a hard time?"

I grinned. "Nothing I can't handle."

"He didn't make you pay the cover, did he?"

"Forget about it."

Eddie scowled, reached into his pocket, and passed me a ten-dollar bill.

"I said forget it."

"Come on, Jack, take the money. I'll talk to my nephew, straighten him out." Eddie shook his head. "Kids today."

"Think about it, Eddie. Were we any different?"

"I like to think so. But maybe not."

"So anyway, I don't want him. I need some folks who can be discrete. Fade into the background. Stay out of sight until needed. That sort of thing. I probably won't need them, but you never know."

"I've got you covered."

"Thanks, Eddie."

Eddie grinned. "That's what friends are for."

CHAPTER 36

Eddie insisted on driving me to the meeting himself. Tommy told me the address and I had it locked in my brain. The meeting was happening in the St. Clair–Vaughan Road area. Neighbourhood bars, Portuguese grocery stores, and Italian restaurants sat side-by-side with Jamaican barbershops and take-out restaurants. "Where Rasta Meets Pasta."

Eddie pulled his town car up to the curb and peered out the window. "You sure this is the place?"

We were in a residential neighbourhood surrounded by modest two-storey houses and carefully manicured lawns. A teenage girl walked by, being pulled along the sidewalk by a huge woolly dog. From somewhere down the street came the jingle of an ice cream truck.

I scanned the street name and the address. "It's the right address. Maybe Tommy fucked it up."

Eddie shook his head. "It's going to be hard for my guys to hide around here, Jack."

A little light went off. "Yeah. Maybe that's exactly what Vito was thinking."

"Or Tommy."

"You thinking ambush?"

Eddie nodded. "I'm always thinking ambush."

"Okay. Let's work this out. Worst case scenario, I walk into that house and it's empty except for a rug on the floor. Someone steps up behind me, *BAM BAM*, two shots to the head. I go down, they wrap me in the rug, and carry my body out the back door."

Eddie grinned. "That's worst case, all right."

"I don't see any of Vito's guys around. Do you?"

Eddie craned his neck. "There's a guy cutting his grass. Another guy polishing his car. And there on the corner is a telephone repair man. His rig looks real enough."

"Sometimes a telephone repair man is just a telephone repair man."

"Exactly."

"Where are your guys now?"

"Two of them are at the coffee shop down the street. There's one guy in the park up ahead. Two more in the video store around the block. They're waiting for my word."

"They're going to have to get closer."

"I know. It's gonna be tough."

I sat back. "All right. Here's what we do. We hang back. Tell your guys to cool their heels. You and I are going to sit right here and watch the house."

"You mind if I shut off the AC? I'm concerned about my carbon footprint."

Eddie shut off the AC and we rolled down the windows. Eddie watched the house while I scanned the street. Then we switched. No one went in, no one came out. After about ten minutes I was starting to sweat.

"Fuck it — I'm going in."

"I'm going with you."

"Uh-uh. No you're not. I'm going in alone."

"Come on, Jack. You might need me."

"That's what your crew is for. Give 'em a call, tell 'em to head on down. You see this?" I held up the cellphone Eddie gave me a few days ago. "I'm calling you right now. What do they say in the movies? 'We'll keep an open channel.' You hear anything alarming, you send in the fucking cavalry."

"Just one question. When they frisk you and take away your phone, then what?"

"It's a phone. They're not going to take away my phone."

Eddie smirked. "Jack, you really are clueless, aren't you? That, my friend, is not just a phone. It's a GPS, it's a camera, it's a computer."

"So you're saying this meeting is pointless. Little Vito and I could just sit in different cafés and text each other threats. 'U R ded d00d LOL.' Is that it?"

"Yeah, that's it. That's it exactly." Eddie snorted. "Come on, Jack. Of course they're going to take your phone. Cut the lines of communication. Isn't that the first thing that happens in a war?"

I shook my head. "His war is with Tommy, not me."

"Does Little Vito know that?"

"That's what I'm about to find out."

I stepped out of the car into the bright sunlight. The air smelled like fresh grass and dryer sheets. Somewhere down the street a baby was crying.

The curtains were drawn and the blinds were down. I knocked on the door and waited. My hand tensed around the knife in my pocket.

A bead of sweat trickled down the back of my neck. The door opened, slowly.

Standing in the doorway was a little old woman in a frilly yellow apron. She was brown and wrinkled like a walnut. "Yes? You have reservation?"

"Uh … maybe. The name's Jack. I'm here to see Vito."

The woman's face brightened. "Vito! Come on in, come on in."

Inside I smelled cumin and onions and sizzling beef. I was standing in the middle of what looked like an old woman's house: dried flowers in a vase in the hallway, religious knick-knacks lining the walls.

"This way."

We stepped around the corner into what at one time might've been the living room. Now it was a dining room complete with three tiny tables. All the tables were empty except one near the wall: a huge man in a grey suit stood as I entered the room.

"You must be Jack." The big man smiled. "Come on in, take a load off. Rosie, how 'bout a couple of beers? Jack, I hope you like Mexican food. Rosie makes the best in the city."

The old woman blushed, turning a deeper walnut. She said, "You're a nice man, a nice man," as she scampered toward the kitchen.

I pulled back a chair but remained standing. Little Vito held out his hand. I shook it.

"Really glad you could make it, Jack. We've got to clear the air, you and I."

Vito gestured to my chair. I remained standing. He smiled and took his seat. Then I sat down.

Rosie brought the beers. Ice-cold Coronas. For a split second I wondered about poison, then I decided it wasn't Vito's style.

The beer was cold and delicious. I stopped myself from draining the bottle in one pull and then stared across the table at Vito.

"I figure you know why Tommy called this meeting."

Little Vito laughed. He sounded like a mule caught in a cement mixer. "Tommy called this meeting? I called this meeting. As I said, we've got to clear the air."

I nodded. "I'm listening."

"First off, I want to apologize for my guy on Spadina. I wanted to meet you so I sent him to extend an invitation. You broke his nose, you know."

I shrugged. "He pulled a gun on me. He's lucky he's still alive."

"Yeah. Anyway, it was a mistake and I'm sorry." Vito drained his beer. "Let's not get off on the wrong foot. I've asked around about you, Jack. Everyone says you're the best."

"I'm just a guy trying to make a living."

The mule-in-cement-mixer laugh again. "Aren't we all. You realize, of course, there's better career opportunities than working for Tommy."

"Like, say … working for you?"

"Seems to me that a man of your talents would only be happy working for the boss."

"Tommy's dad *is* the boss."

"Come on, Jack. You and I both know The Old Man is hanging by a thread. When he dies, God forbid, there's going to be an organizational shift. Tommy knows this. Why do you think he's got you running all over the city? He's trying to collect as much cash as he can. Not for the organization, but for himself. You watch. He's going to get that cash and do a quick fade."

"I don't think so. Tommy wants more than that."

Vito ignored that sentence. He rumbled on. "Now, I wouldn't be against Tommy taking an extended vacation. He's had some hard knocks in this life. Maybe he's earned the right to sit on a faraway beach with a book and a beer."

"Books aren't really his thing."

"Oh no? When he was a teenager he always had his nose buried in a book. Fantasy-type stuff. Elves and flying dragons. Quests for the princess. It was better than another beatdown from The Old Man."

"You knew about that."

Vito nodded. "Everyone knew. You didn't have to be Kojak to follow the bruises straight back to The Old Man's fist." Little Vito shrugged his massive bear-like shoulders. "Don't get me wrong, my old man smacked me around, too. We were all raised like that. Our dads, they knew the world is a hard place. They wanted to prepare us. But Tommy's dad … well, I don't want to say too much. It's not my place to get between a father and a son."

"The way Tommy sees it, this is a family business."

"Tommy sees it right. Did you know I'm The Old Man's cousin? Yeah, we used to pal around at Easter time. My dad would roast an entire lamb on the spit in our backyard. Tommy's dad and I, we would sneak under the tables, trying to steal glasses of wine and look up all the women's dresses. Kid stuff, you know? Man, we had some good times."

Little Vito looked hazily off into dreamland. Rosie appeared with a platter of chiles rellenos. Little Vito smiled. "I hope you're hungry, Jack. This is just the tip of the iceberg."

I speared a chile with my fork. Drops of red grease splattered across my white plate. The chiles were damn delicious: meaty, cheesy, spicy.

Little Vito raised his napkin and wiped cheese from his chin. "Tommy's a good kid, but he's not a leader. Do you understand? This organization … it's a heavy thing, Jack. The weight of the world gets dumped on your shoulders. Tommy … I'm not saying he couldn't do it. I'm just saying there's better people for the job."

"Like you."

Vito nodded slowly. "Yeah. Like me."

My knife scraped across my plate as I cut my chile into little pieces. "Tommy says you owe him money."

An amused half smile tweaked the edge of Vito's lips. "Is that what he says? How much?"

"A lot."

"So let me ask you this, Jack. Say I was to give Tommy this money he says I owe him. Call it a bon voyage present. Would he do the right thing?"

"The right thing being giving you the keys to the kingdom."

"I'm not thinking about myself here, Jack. This is a big organization. A lot of families with a lot of mouths to feed."

My plate was empty. I looked at Vito. "Now let me ask you a question. Say Tommy does decide to head down to some faraway beach. Could you rest easy? Could you run The Empire with an untroubled mind?"

Vito shrugged. "That's entirely up to Tommy. He wants to leave peacefully, I got no problems with that."

Rosie brought in a deep dish of chicken enchiladas swimming in green sauce. I kept staring into Vito's eyes. He smiled. That's when I knew there was no way in hell he was going to let Tommy leave.

We sat and we spouted more bullshit and we ate enchiladas. We talked about horse racing and baseball. We talked about inflation, how the price of shit is on the rise. We talked about the state of the world (fucked) and politics (fucked) and global warming (we're all fucked). I finished my enchiladas and stood up.

"You're leaving already? Don't you want dessert? Rosie makes a mean sopaipilla."

"I've got to get going. You've given me a lot to think about."

"Hey, I understand. You're a busy guy. Well, you tell Tommy to think it over. I hear Costa Rica is nice this time of year."

CHAPTER 37

"**F**uck no!" Tommy was on the warpath, snarling across his office while his minions cringed. "This is bullshit, Jack, and you know it's bullshit."

"Yeah. It's bullshit."

"That little prick thinks he can muscle me out of my own organization. Fuck that! And fuck him!" Tommy turned and hurled his heavy crystal Scotch glass at the mirror running the length of his office bar. Glass shattered.

"Seven years of bad luck," Tommy's bodyguard muttered.

"Shut the fuck up, Rocco! You superstitious fuck."

Tommy stumbled over to the bar and splashed Scotch into a fresh glass. "That prick. That motherfucking, cocksucking prick. What has he ever done? He'd be nothing without my dad. Without my dad that stupid fucker would be dead ten times over. Fuck him. Costa Rica? Fuck that. This is my life we're talking about here.

My motherfucking life. You don't even know how patient I've been, Jack. I've done some shit you can't even imagine. I've been helping my dad build up this organization for years. What's that fuck Vito ever done? He sat back and let me and my dad do all the dirty work. Fuck him. You think he's ever gotten his hands dirty? I oughta slit open his soft white belly and choke him with his own intestines. Ha! Now that would be fucking funny. You think you can muscle me, you little prick? I'm going to kill you. KILL YOU!"

Tommy staggered back and threw a phantom punch. His drunken fist sailed through the air. I stepped forward to catch him before he fell.

Snarling, Tommy shook me off. "Get your fucking hands off me."

Up close, Tommy was in bad shape. He was unshaven and his eyes were bloodshot. His red and black Hawaiian shirt was encrusted with filth. He stank: B.O. and stale sweat and sour milk.

"Tommy … maybe you should get some sleep."

"Sleep? Fuck that. No time. They're coming for me. Man the fucking barricades, Jack. We're going to pour some boiling oil on their motherfucking heads." A sly, ugly smile broke across Tommy's face. "See, Jack, I know something they don't know. I know how it all works. I'm the motherfucking puppet master. My dad trusts me. He's always trusted me. Right before he went into the hospital he called me into his office and he said, 'Tommy, you're my only son. If anything happens to me, I want you to run the family business.' You hear that? Me. He picked ME. Not some overstuffed fucking useless old fuck. Me. Costa Rica? I'll send him to Costa Rica. I'll mail his head to Costa Rica in a motherfucking box. I'll rip open his chest and sew it back up with a howler monkey inside. There's your motherfucking Costa Rica! How 'bout a banana, you stupid fuck? I'll shove a banana up your ass!"

Tommy clawed into his pocket and came up with a handful of shiny black pills. He shovelled the pills into his mouth and washed them down with the rest of the Scotch. Then he absently tossed the empty glass over his shoulder, almost hitting Rocco in the head. The bodyguard dodged at the last second and the glass bounced harmlessly off the white shag carpet.

Tommy blinked and stared over at me. He suddenly looked so sad, so tired. There were huge dark circles under his eyes. He was lost. "Jack." His voice was pale and distant. "It's good to see you. I … I'm going to lie down now."

Tommy's body crumpled. Rocco and I caught him before he hit the shag. Together we steered his unconscious body over to the black leather couch.

Rocco gazed down at his passed-out boss and shook his head. "He's been like this for days. Won't even go see his old man in the hospital. I keep tellin' him, 'Tommy, this looks bad.' It's not winning him any points with the boys, you know what I'm saying?"

"Yeah. I know what you're saying."

"Hey, you want a drink or something? A sandwich?"

"No thanks."

"A girl? Tommy was talking about you earlier. Said to get you whatever you wanted. Said you were his only friend."

Tommy's only friend. Goddamn it.

"You're tugging on my heart strings, Rocco. What are you going to do next, start playing the violin?"

"I played the piccolo in junior high."

"Forget it."

"So, uh … he's going to be out for awhile. You want to wait, or —"

"Nah. I'll give him a call later."

"Yeah."

With a sigh, Rocco plopped down into a leather easy chair across from his boss and pulled a folded *Archie Double Digest* out of his back pocket.

I was halfway home when my phone rang.

"Yeah."

"It's Rocco. You gotta get back here."

"What's going on?"

Silence on the other end. "Rocco?"

"Tommy's dad just died."

CHAPTER 38

The cab I flagged down got me back to the club in under ten minutes. The driver was a skinny, grinning dude in a straw hat who drove like he was being chased by the devil himself. I gave him a big tip.

On the first floor of the club it was business as usual. Skinny girls with pouting lips gyrating to the booming beat. Upstairs it was a different story. Guys in dark suits were rushing back and forth, mumbling into cellphones. Big guys in track pants and gold chains lumbered after the guys in the suits. A guy with blue track pants pressed his huge mitt against my chest. "Sorry. Members only."

I was sensitive to the situation, so I decided not to throw him down the stairs. Luckily for both of us, Rocco appeared in the doorway of Tommy's office. "It's okay. He's with us."

Blue Track Pants removed his hand. "Oh yeah?" He turned to me and nodded. "You'll have to forgive me. It's … an emotional time. For all of us."

I nodded sympathetically. "I understand."

Rocco was gesturing to me frantically. I walked over and he pulled me inside Tommy's office.

"We got a problem," Rocco said. Tommy was still passed out on the couch. His cellphone was vibrating along the length of the coffee table. Rocco pointed to Tommy's stretched-out body. "We gotta get him up."

I shook my head. "It's not happening. Answer the phone. Tell whoever it is that Tommy is grief-struck. He's not going to be going anywhere or doing anything."

"That's not gonna fly. The lieutenants are meeting at the hospital. Tommy's expected to be there."

"What can I tell you, Rocco? You saw how many pills he took."

"Look, it doesn't matter what kind of shape he's in. He's expected to look a little fucked up. His dad just died." Rocco lowered his massive head. Then he looked up at me. "I've got to get him to the hospital, and you've got to help me."

I knew he was right. In Tommy's absence the jackals would start baying. Guys in shiny suits would start jostling each other, trying to fill the void left by Tommy's dad. Tommy needed to be at the hospital as a show of strength.

"Tommy ... wake up." A thin tendril of drool dribbled out of his mouth onto the black leather couch. He snored. So much for strength. I looked over at Rocco. "Make some coffee."

"I'm on it."

I scanned the room. "You know what we really need ... do you know if Tommy keeps any adrenalin around here? An adrenalin shot straight to the heart should get him up and about."

Rocco eyeballed me like I'd lost my brain. Maybe I had.

"Adrenalin? No. How 'bout some cold water?"

I splashed a glass across Tommy's face. Nothing.

Rocco shook his head. "This ain't good."

No, it wasn't. "Relax. We can deal with this. You ever see that movie *Weekend at Bernie's*? All we need to do is get him into a suit, slap on some dark glasses, and prop him up on a hospital couch. Then the lieutenants can shuffle in, pay their respects, and get out. They'll see that Tommy is large and in charge. Problem solved."

"There's no time for jokes."

Rocco was right. Tommy was going to have to wake up. "Do you know Tommy's doctor?"

"Tommy hates doctors."

"Look, you guys must have a doctor or two on the payroll. Get them down here ASAP. Something in the doc's little black bag will get Tommy up and motivated. In the meantime, send someone down to the hospital to stall for time."

"You go."

I shook my head. "Those guys don't know me. It wouldn't work. Call the doc."

Rocco pulled out his phone and made the call.

While Rocco was on the phone the office door opened and a little man with a pencil-thin moustache and a grey suit slipped inside. The dapper man glanced at me and Rocco and then stared at Tommy on the couch.

"What the fuck is this?"

I stepped forward. "He's resting. Overcome with grief."

"Grief my ass. Look at him. He's drooling."

"It's been a long day."

The dapper man squinted at me. "Who the fuck are you?"

I smiled and held out my hand. "Jack Palace. And you are …?"

The man glanced at my hand like it was crawling with spiders. Rocco jerked his chin toward the new-comer. "That's Mickey 'The Mouse' Santiago. He worked with The Old Man."

Mickey hung his head. "God rest his soul."

Yeah. The Old Man was slicing throats in heaven now.

"I came down here to get Tommy. The others are getting restless. There's decisions to be made."

Rocco rumbled forward. "You want a drink, Mickey?"

"Fuck that. Grab his arms. Let's get him up."

I shook my head. "The doc's on his way."

"The doc? He can't cure what Tommy's got. Come on, get him up."

"No."

"No? What the fuck do you mean no? Who the fuck are you?"

"I told you who I am."

Mickey "The Mouse" stepped forward, his black eyes flashing hate. "I'm taking Tommy to the hospital. Clear a fucking path."

"No."

The Mouse turned slightly and nodded. "All right. Then we'll do this right here." A flash of silver: a tiny gun leapt into The Mouse's hand.

My body moved before my brain caught up. My leg swept forward and connected with Mickey's gun arm. Two shots: one plowed into the couch inches from Tommy's head. The other shot went wide, slamming into the ceiling. I had Mickey on the floor before Rocco could blink.

"My arm! You broke my fucking arm!"

"You tried to kill Tommy. Who sent you?"

"Go fuck yourself."

With a sickening snap I broke his other arm. The Mouse screamed.

"Who sent you? WHO SENT YOU?"

Rocco lumbered forward and kicked Mickey in the face. An explosion of blood splattered the white shag.

The office door burst open and an army of track-suited gorillas, guns at the ready, thundered into the room.

I started shouting, "He tried to kill Tommy! He tried to kill Tommy!" There were guns pointed everywhere: at me, at Rocco, at the man on the ground. I was trying to clear up any confusion before the gorillas began blasting. I said it one more time for emphasis. "This prick tried to kill Tommy."

Rocco nodded his massive head. "It's true." He glared down at the man on the shag. "What the fuck, Mickey?"

Blue Track Pants stepped forward. I shouted, "No, wait!" but it was too late. Two shots and Mickey's head exploded. I stood up and staggered back, my face dripping with blood and brains.

Blue Track Pants spat on the dead man's corpse. "That's what you get, you murdering fuck."

I backed away toward the bar. *Vodka, yes, lots of vodka.*

The man in the blue track pants swivelled his gaze toward me. His eyes narrowed suspiciously. "Whaddaya mean, 'wait'? Rocco, who is this guy? You sure he's with us?"

Rocco nodded. I knocked back four fingers of vodka and stepped forward. "Yeah, I'm with you. Maybe you didn't notice, but I just saved Tommy's life. But thanks to you we'll never know who sent Mickey to kill him."

The big man shrugged. "Who gives a fuck?"

The vodka warmed my soul. I stepped closer to the big man. "You think this was a one-time thing? Whoever sent Mickey is going to send someone else. If we knew who sent Mickey …"

A light dinged in the big man's eyes. "We could find him and fuck him up."

"Yeah, exactly."

Blue Track Pants shook his head. "I wasn't thinking. Usually I'm more together, you know … more on the ball. Here I am, acting like a dumb shit. Tommy's dad, he was like an uncle to me. The Old Man did everything for my family. Everything. My sister Gloria, she got sick with the lupus. The Old Man paid to send her to the States to a private clinic. He got Ma a job with the payroll department at his trucking company. He was … he was a good guy."

The big man's voice cracked. His troops milled around and looked away uncomfortably. For a second I thought he was going to break into tears, but the moment passed. He looked up at me. "You think I'm dumb, right?"

"I don't even know you."

"Come on, don't lie. You think I'm just a big muscle-bound gorilla who shoots first and asks questions later. I mean, I know that's what just happened, but you got to believe me, today I'm not myself. Ask Rocco. He knows me. He'll tell you I'm a smart guy. I mean, I was never that great in school, but that's because it didn't hold my interest. But The Old Man, he used to ask my opinion about things. He'd say, 'Nemo, what do you think about this or that?' He valued my advice. You know why? I'm good with people. They underestimate me. To them I'm like furniture. Might as well be a couch or a coat rack. People say stuff in front of me they wouldn't say otherwise. The Old Man would excuse himself and go out into the hall and people would talk. They would forget I was there. Then they'd leave and The Old Man would say, 'Nemo, what do you think?' And I'd say, 'you gotta watch that guy,' or 'that guy is your friend.' He listened to me, you know? I mean *really listened*. I'm not … there's not … it's like no one's gonna treat me that way again." Nemo hung his head. He blinked rapidly, holding back tears, gun held lightly at his side.

I walked back to the bar and poured him a vodka. "Here."

Nemo shuddered. "Man! What is that, turpentine? That shit burns!"

"That's quality vodka."

"Vodka, huh? I'm not much of a drinker."

One of Nemo's troops stepped forward. "You need us here?"

Nemo turned. His shadow fell across his troops. "Here's what I need you to do. You and you, guard the stairs. No one comes up. You got that? You, you, and you, go downstairs. Rocco, how you holding up?"

"There's a doc on his way. We gotta get Tommy up."

"Fuck the doc. Let him rest."

"There's people waiting for him at the hospital."

"Let them wait. Maybe you haven't heard. Tommy's the boss now."

CHAPTER 39

When Tommy passed out, he was The Black Sheep. When he woke up he'd be The Boss. Boss in name only, though, as the lieutenants jostled for position. To be the Real Boss, Tommy was going to have to slap down the jackals and slap them down hard.

Nemo's army had shut down the club. The doors were locked and the dance floor was empty. Inside Tommy's office it was eerily quiet. Rocco played solitaire, flipping each card up with a flourish. I paced across the carpet. I was in deep and it was just getting deeper. Tommy kept snoring. Right here, right now, this was the eye of the hurricane. But the storm was coming.

Nemo knocked and stuck his head through the door. "Everything okay?"

Rocco nodded. Tommy snored. "Just fine," I muttered. There was a crimson stain fading to brown on the white shag carpet. Nemo's guys had carried the body of Mickey "The Mouse" Santiago out about three hours ago.

I was dying for a drink, but I had to stay sharp. Like I said, the storm was coming.

"Ow, fuck! My fucking head!" All eyes turned toward Tommy. The new boss was sitting up on the black leather couch rubbing his temples. He squinted up at me and scowled. "Don't just stand there, Jack — get me a fucking drink."

Behind me in a flurry of cards Rocco leapt toward the bar. Tommy squinted again. "Nemo? What the fuck are you doing … here …?" Tommy trailed off as it hit him. "My dad. He … is he …?"

Nemo bit his lip and looked away. I nodded solemnly. "It's true, Tommy. Your dad died a few hours ago."

"Hours? HOURS?" Tommy leapt up, all wild hair and rumpled half-buttoned Hawaiian shirt. "What the fuck? Why didn't any of you fuckers wake me up? Rocco!" Tommy snapped his fingers. "Cellphone!"

"It's dead, Boss."

"What? Plug that shit in! Jack, give me your cell."

I passed it over. In my head, I heard Eddie's voice: *Another one for the lake.*

"Yeah, operator? Get me Mount Sinai. What? No, the hospital. Yeah. Hello, Mount Sinai? Put me through to my dad. I mean, my dad's room. Room number? Oh shit." Tommy covered the receiver with his palm and looked over at Nemo.

"Four-O-three."

"Room 403. Yeah, that's right. Put me through. I know. I know he's deceased. There's someone there, right? A doctor or some shit? This is his son. I don't give a damn how sorry you are. Put me through to my dad's doctor right the fuck now."

Diplomatic as always.

Tommy paced, clutching the cellphone. His other hand was shaking. Rocco looked worried. Nemo stood with his head down and his arms folded, awaiting instruction.

Tommy jabbed his thumb at Rocco and Nemo. "You and you — Rocco, bring the car around. Nemo, you keep your guys in line. Keep 'em focused. There could be trouble." Tommy stopped dead in his tracks and stared down at the crimson stain on his white shag carpet. "What the fuck is this? Rocco, did you spill your juice?"

"No, Boss. It was The Mouse. He tried to kill you. Jack stopped him. Saved your life."

"Jack saved my life? Then what the fuck am I paying you for?"

Rocco looked sheepish. I opened my mouth to defend him but Tommy plowed ahead. "Ah, I'm just fucking with you. You're a good guy, Rocco. You and Nemo both. Now go on, get outta here."

The two men left. Tommy was still on hold with the hospital. An uncomfortable silence descended.

"So … is it true?"

"Is what true, Tommy?"

"Rocco says you saved my life. Is that true?"

"I stopped Mickey from shooting you. Maybe he would've killed you, maybe not." In my head I was doing cartwheels and jumping up and down like a little kid. Tommy saved my life and now I've saved his. Nothing like repaying a Blood Debt to put you in a good mood.

Tommy grinned. "So I guess we're even now."

I grinned back. "Yeah. I guess so."

"You know what that means, don't you, Jack?"

I sure hoped so. "Tell me."

"It means that as soon as you've finished this job for me, you're free to go."

My heart sank and my stomach followed. "This job."

"Yeah, that's right. You still haven't ... Hold on. Yeah, Doc? That's right, I'm his son. So what happens now? Oh yeah? No, I haven't made any arrangements with any fucking funeral home. What am I, a mortician? What? Look, I'll look into it and call you back."

Tommy slammed my phone closed and idly stuffed it into his pants pocket. "You didn't hear Nemo say anything about funeral arrangements, did you?"

"Nope."

"Man, I hate funerals. When I was a kid we'd have to go to funerals all the time. Get dressed up in a starchy suit, sit for hours on uncomfortable wooden pews, stand up sit down stand up kneel. Then we'd have to go out to the grave and it's all these old women in black just wailing away and being carried off to the limos and everyone would be shaking my dad's hand like he was the fucking Mayor of the Cemetery, you know — and he's there in his five-thousand-dollar suit giving envelopes with like a hundred bucks in them to these grieving widows and they're slobbering all over his hand like he's the fucking pope. When I got older I just wanted to scream, 'Lady, don't you know your husband died because of my dad? Who do you think put out the contract, you dizzy broad?' And my dad just ate that shit up. Standing there in the boneyard in his shiny shoes, waving his hand at all the peons bowing and scraping, lackeys like Nemo draping a coat over his shoulders."

Darkness twisted across Tommy's face. "Do you realize The Old Man had more time for Nemo than he did for me? Always a kind, encouraging word, some helpful advice. You think he ever helped me do A GODDAMN THING? HUH? DO YOU?"

Tommy was screaming now, tears running down his face. "FUCK NO! FUCK NO! FUCK YOU, OLD MAN! FUUUUUUUUCK YOOOOOOOU!"

"Jesus Christ, Tommy." My eyes flickered toward the door. "Keep your voice down."

Tommy stared at me and through his tears he smiled a shark-like smile. "You can't tell me what to do, Jack. No one can tell me what to do. Not now. Not anymore. Do you know why? I'll tell you why. Because now I'm the fucking boss, that's why. Stick with me, Jack. I'll make you my right-hand man."

"I, uh … I'm flattered, Tommy. But you should probably pick someone from within The Organization. One of your dad's guys."

"My dad's guys. Yeah, right. Someone like Little Vito? He's sworn to kill us, Jack. We've got to kill him first. Don't you see?" A manic light gleamed in Tommy's eyes. "We've got to kill them all."

"Tommy … earlier you said something about me not finishing the job. You know I always finish the job."

"I know you do, Jack. That's why I like you so much. But I'm telling the truth. I sent you to collect my money.

I still don't have it all. You know what you need to do. You need to get out there and get me my fucking money."

"Who's left? I collected from everyone except Joey Machine and Little Vito."

Tommy shook his head. "There's someone who owes me more than both of them put together." Tommy leaned forward. His breath smelled like rotting garbage. "My dad."

"Your dad is dead."

"The fucking money he owed me didn't die. Money doesn't die, Jack. At his house there's a vault. It's my money inside that vault. My inheritance. You get me? If we don't get it out, Little Vito will steal it all. That fucking prick. By the time we're done with him he's going to be begging to die. Fucking begging. Now get out of here. I've got a funeral to plan."

CHAPTER 40

My legs were heavy as I walked to Suzanne's bar. My brain was tumbling like laundry in a dryer. I'd thought I was free. Now I had to collect a debt from a dead man. According to Tommy, there was a contract out on my life. I didn't know if that was true or not. Here's something I did know: I needed a fucking drink.

Suzanne lit up like a Christmas tree as I stumped through the door. The usual assortment of boozehounds and barflies were clustered together in the murk, old men with gravelly voices muttering into their bottles of Labatt Blue.

I swung onto a stool and pointed to a bottle. "Vodka. Keep 'em coming."

Suzanne filled a glass with ice and poured. I took a sip and my nose went numb. It was a start.

"Tommy's dad died."

Suzanne frowned. "How's Tommy?"

"Tommy?" I shrugged. "Hard to say. He never really got along with his old man."

"Still … that can't be easy."

I pushed my empty glass across the bar. Suzanne topped me up. "Tommy is sending me after a dead man's money."

"What are you going to do, rent a shovel?"

"I'm supposed to go after his estate. It's bullshit." The vodka went down smooth. The numbness spread.

Suzanne cocked her eyebrow at me. "If Tommy's dad is dead … does that mean Tommy's in charge?"

"Yeah. Sort of. He's the boss by blood, but the troops are uneasy."

"So say Tommy gets bumped off. That cancels your debt, right?"

"Tommy staying alive is the best insurance we've got. Whoever kills Tommy will come gunning for me. If Tommy lives, I can finish this job and we can walk away clean."

"Just waltz into the sunset, huh?"

"That's right. You and me, babe. You ever been to Costa Rica? I hear they have monkeys."

Suzanne's eyes crinkled as she smiled. "I've never really been big on beaches. I'm more of a city gal."

"So we go to Rio. I can dig it."

Damn, she looked so good. Soft and diffuse. She smelled like cookies. "When are you done here?"

"Whenever I want. Charlie will cover for me."

"Let's go back to your place."

"No."

"No?"

"Let's go to your place."

"Ah … it's pretty small."

"So you live in a shoebox. I don't care."

"I'm not set up for entertaining."

"Do you have a bed?"

"No."

"No? What do you mean, 'No?'"

"I've got a couch."

Suzanne smiled. "Good enough."

We walked hand in hand through Chinatown. I pulled her through the crowds, past the piles of garbage, the smell of rotting produce mixing with sweet and sour pork. A street vendor set a wind-up dog down on the sidewalk and the dog did flips. Speakers outside a clothing store (RETAIL AND WHOLESALE) played a sour warbling version of the Chinese national anthem. A group of drunken street kids staggered by, their skin and their clothes the same dusty grey.

We stopped outside Eddie's restaurant. "This is it."

"You live in a restaurant?"

"That's right." I pointed to the window display: a barbecued pig, a cuttlefish, and a rack of ducks. "You see that rack? That's where I sleep." I took Suzanne by the hand and led her toward the door. "Come on. I want you to meet someone."

The last woman I brought home to Eddie was Cassandra. That was five years ago. It didn't end well.

It was different this time. Suzanne and I sat down at one of the plastic-covered tables and a server brought us menus and a pot of tea. I made eye contact with the server and asked, "Is Eddie working today? Tell him Jack's here."

The server nodded and hustled off. Minutes later Eddie appeared in his black suit, grinning from ear to ear.

"Jack! What's new?"

"Eddie, this is Suzanne."

"Nice to meet you. This guy here …" Eddie's hand landed on my shoulder, "this guy here is a hell of a guy."

Suzanne turned to me and grinned. "Now I know why you wanted me to meet him."

I shrugged in mock protest. "What can I say? He's right. I'm a hell of a guy."

Eddie swept the menus from our hands. "Forget these. I'm going to have the chef take care of you right."

Eddie was as good as his word. Platters of food began to emerge from the kitchen: hot and sour soup, barbecued pork, dumplings, fried chicken, noodles, steamed vegetables. I didn't even know some of the things I was eating, but it was all damn delicious.

Suzanne pushed away her plate and clutched her stomach. "Ohhhh. I couldn't eat another bite."

"How about a fortune cookie?"

Suzanne shook her head. "I hate those things."

"You hate fortune cookies? How can you hate fortune cookies?"

"When I was younger I got a fortune cookie that was empty. No fortune. No future. Freaked me right the fuck out."

"'No future?' That's not what the cookie was telling you."

"Oh no?"

"Nope. It was saying, it's up to you to write your own fortune. Create your own future. And you did."

"Yeah. I did, didn't I?"

Beneath the table, our hands met.

After dinner I borrowed a bottle of wine from Eddie and took Suzanne up to the roof. She walked to the edge and stared out at the city lights. I came up behind her and wrapped her in my arms.

"Welcome to the asphalt beach."

"Are there sharks?"

"Not up here."

Suzanne smiled and reached for me. "Then I love it. I love you."

"I love you, too." The words floated in the air, as gentle as clouds.

"Jack ..."

"Yeah?"

"Take me downstairs."

My hands fumbled with my keys. I was drunker than I thought. Suzanne laughed as the keys tumbled from the lock.

"Don't worry, I'll get it." I stabbed the key into the lock again and gave it a twist. I was praying for no roaches, rats, or mice. *Welcome to my vermin farm. Rats? No, honey, those aren't rats. Those are my champion miniature Schnauzers. Yeah, I enjoy breeding tiny dogs in my spare time. Everyone needs a hobby.*

The door swung open and I flicked on the lights. No roaches, rats, or mice.

Suzanne stepped inside. "Well ... you weren't kidding."

"Small, huh?"

"I'd call it … minimal." Suzanne laughed. "It's small, all right." She gestured to the walls. "No pictures?"

"No. I've got a plant, though."

"Does your plant have a name?"

"If it does, it's never told me."

Suzanne sashayed over to the couch. "And here is the famous couch I've heard so much about."

"That's the one."

Suzanne plopped down and patted the cushion next to her. "Come on over here."

"Don't mind if I do."

Our lips met, and then our tongues. I started to pull off her shirt. She reached over and ripped open mine: buttons flew across the room.

"My shirt —!"

"Shh." She pulled me toward her tits. She moaned as I bit her nipple. My hand found her crotch. Her hand was already there, rubbing herself through the fabric of her jeans. She unbuttoned her jeans and I grabbed the waistband of her panties and yanked them down. My penis sprung free, jutting out into the cool office air. Suzanne lowered herself down and took me in her mouth. So soft, so wet, so hot.

I pulled away. "On your knees." She obeyed, sliding off the couch onto the linoleum. I grabbed her head and brought her forward. She slid her mouth around me and plunged her head into my lap. My eyes slammed closed and my back arched. Pure pleasure rattled my frame. *It's just like when Cassandra —*

My eyes flipped open. I tried to banish the thought, but it was too late. It was like the old impossible exercise:

"Do not think of a white horse." The memory of Cassandra swept unbidden into the room.

Suzanne looked up. "What is it? What's wrong?"

"Nothing," I lied. "I mean … it's just … this couch."

"Is it broken? Is there a spring poking you?"

It would be easy to say yes. "It's not that. It's … too many bad memories."

Suzanne stood up, arched her eyebrow, and appraised the couch. "So throw it out. Shitcan it, Jack, straight to the curb."

"Yeah. I should."

Suzanne plopped down next to me with a sigh and reached for my damaged shirt. "You want some safety pins?"

"I've got another shirt." My hand brushed her bare leg. "We could go to your place …"

"I don't think so." Suzanne stood up. "The moment has passed."

"We can get it back. I know we can."

Suzanne smiled sadly. "Another time, all right? I'm going home."

Drunk and horny, I watched her leave.

There was a bottle of vodka in my desk. I walked over and fished it out. "Well, plant — looks like it's just you and me." My shoes thumped onto the desktop. The vodka seared my throat. For a brief second I thought about going downstairs to see if Eddie could set me up with a girl. A girl with pale skin and jet black hair. A girl like … Cassandra.

"Fuck it," I said to the plant. "We'll sit right here and wait for morning."

CHAPTER 41

I woke with a start to the sound of jackhammers pounding the pavement right below my window. The red digital numbers on my clock radio told me I'd been asleep for almost five hours. It was 10:45 a.m.

Downstairs I found Eddie in the restaurant, eating bacon and eggs and reading the *Globe and Mail*. I sat down at the table and the server poured me a steaming cup of hot black coffee.

Eddie grinned. "So … your new gal. What was her name again?"

"Suzanne."

"She seems nice."

"She is nice." I sipped my coffee and looked away. Eddie took the hint and dropped it. The newspaper rustled as he turned the page.

"Eddie. I need another phone."

"You throw the old one in the lake?"

"That can't be good for the environment."

"What?"

"Throwing phones in the lake. All those electronics can't be good for the fish."

Eddie speared a bite of egg. "I never really thought about it."

"Yeah, well … there's got to be a better way to get rid of those things. Sledgehammer, maybe. Reduce them to dust."

"Yeah, maybe."

"In any case, I need a new phone."

Eddie grinned, reached into his pocket, and slid a fresh cellphone across the plastic-topped table. "You want some breakfast, Jack? This bacon is freakin' fantastic. Heirloom. The pig got shoulder massages while watching *Masterpiece Theatre*. You know. Fancy."

The floorboards cracked as I stood up. Or was that my knees? "Another time. I've got to go. I'll grab something on the way."

"Where you headed?"

"You really want to know?"

Eddie snorted. "Maybe not. You need any help? My guys are still itching for action."

"You tell your guys to be careful what they wish for."

Eddie laughed. "Too true. Be careful out there, Jack."

"Always."

Down by the lake it was a beautiful day. Sunlight danced across the water. Gulls circled and dove. Grover's boat rocked gently beneath my feet. Grover, glowing in his white suit, grinned and shook my hand.

"Nice of you to drop by, Jack. It gets a little lonesome out here on this tub all by myself."

"Where's your wife?"

"She's on vacation. Down in the Florida Keys visiting her mother. I'm supposed to be retired, remember? I didn't want her to see this."

Grover strode across the deck and threw open the door to The War Room. Inside, corkboards covered the walls. Pinned to the cork were pictures of houses, cars, people. Black arrows slashed across the photos. In the middle was a blurry black and white picture of Joey Machine. Beneath that was a picture of a sunken ship with a big black question mark drawn over it.

I glanced over at Grover. "You've been busy."

Grover grinned. "Joey Machine was good at covering his tracks but I'm a tracker from way back. You see this? That's Joey Machine's brother. Some nobody living in Kansas. That's his wife and kids. This is their dog, Sparky."

The golden retriever stared stupidly at the camera.

"Grover ... these people, they didn't know The Chief."

"So?"

"So they didn't have anything to do with his death."

"Jack, Jack ... you can be so naive. You see this?" Grover stabbed his finger at a photo of a splashy, expensive McMansion. "That's where Joey Machine's brother lives. Do you know what his job is? He sits on the school board. How did he afford a house like this? I'll tell you how: his brother's dirty money."

Beneath my feet the boat shifted and groaned. "You don't know that."

"I know more about Joey Machine and his family than you'll ever know. They're all weeds, Jack. Poisonous plants choking the dirt."

Grover had a mad gleam in his eye. He unlatched a polished wooden box and pulled out a huge silver .357 Magnum. "You and me, Jack. It's up to us."

"Grover."

"The Chief was a good man. A good, good man."

"Grover."

"Yes?"

"What can you tell me about Tommy's dad's house?"

"Which one?"

"The one with the vault."

Grover grinned. "Adding to your nest egg, eh? Good for you. I tell you, Jack, retirement will add years to your life. I'm looking forward to getting back to it. Now let's see … the vault, the vault. That would be the Wychwood house. Near Bathurst and Davenport. Up near Casa Loma."

"Tommy's dad lived in Wychwood Park?"

"He had a house there. He liked the quiet. That was his enclave, his Fortress of Solitude. Did you know Marshall McLuhan lived just up the street?"

"What about the house?"

"I don't have blueprints for it, if that's what you're asking. Standard two-storey with a few alterations. Bulletproof glass in the windows. Security system updated every few years. It's a very solid stone house."

Grover walked me through the floor plan. I closed my eyes and tried to visualize. Overhead, gulls circled and cried. The boat heaved beneath my feet.

"The vault is on the ground floor near the kitchen. It's a converted pantry. Do you have the combination?"

I shook my head. "No." Tommy's old man didn't even trust him with that.

"It's going to be tough."

My face stretched into a smile. "That's why I came to you."

"I would love to help you out, my boy. You know that. But ..." Grover's gaze fell on the photos pinned to his wall. "I've got to catch a flight to Kansas City."

"The Chief's dead. Joey Machine is dead. An eye for an eye. It's over."

Grover sprung forward, hissing like a cobra. "It's ... not ... over. It's not over until my foot is on his brother's throat."

"For all you know, Joey Machine and his brother weren't even close."

"'For all I know?' You don't know what I know. You think I don't know?"

"It's not that. It's just — look at you. You've got it made. You got out of The Life at the right time. You've got money in the bank and a roof over your head. You've got a beautiful wife. Just let it go."

For a minute the cabin went silent. Waves slapped the boat. Grover stared at me with his ice-blue eyes. Then he smiled and shook my hand. "Thanks again for dropping by, Jack. I'll give you a call when I get back from Kansas. The wife and I are planning a dinner party. Bring your gal around — I'd love to meet her."

———

Sirens rose into the air as I walked along the lakefront. Dirty water and rusted tubs and goose shit. My hands trembled and my neck was stiff. Too much tension — time to unwind. There was an all-night gym not far from here. I passed beneath an overpass. Swirls of electric-blue graffiti on the cracked concrete. Dead squirrels and dog shit. A sad old shopping cart piled high with the contents of a human being's life.

Inside the gym I shoved a ten dollar bill through the cage. The bored attendant had two different-coloured eyes. He gave me a locker key and a more-or-less clean towel, then went back to watching his tiny black-and-white TV.

A huge man with greased-up muscles was bouncing around the ring. I watched for a while. His right hook was all right but his jab was lousy. He wasn't as fast as he thought he was. You could tell by the smug look on his face that he'd never been knocked out.

"Hey," I called out to him. "You looking for a sparring partner?"

"Yeah, right." Muscleman turned his back to me and kept throwing phantom punches.

I turned to the ring man and held out my hands. "Lace me up."

The ring man was a little hunched-over dude. He looked like he had always been here, like the gym had been built around him decades ago. He started to fumble with the laces on my boxing gloves. "You don' wan' to fight him, mister. That's Carlos. He kill you, man."

"You let me worry about Carlos. Tie those gloves tighter. Tight!"

I stood below the ring and held out my hands. "Hey, Carlos! What's the matter? You chickenshit?"

Carlos reeled back like he just smelled something rotten. "You crazy, old man?"

"Yeah, maybe. It's just that I was watching you, and frankly, you suck. I could give you a few pointers."

Carlos grinned and turned to the ring man. "This dude IS crazy." He turned back toward me. "Look, old man, I don't need you in here acting all crazy and biting my ear off and shit. You dig?"

I shrugged. "So you're scared. I understand."

A dark cloud settled over Carlos's face. "Man, fuck you! I'm not scared of anything. You think I'm stupid, old man? I know you. I know your type. You're a pervert, man. A stone cold freak. You want a big beautiful man like me to fuck up your shit. Well, I'll fuck you up good, but it'll cost you. A hundred bucks."

"Tell you what. You win, I'll pay you five hundred."

"Oh, I'm gonna win. Get in the ring, motherfucker!"

Ding went the bell. Carlos pranced from his corner like a fucking matador. I stepped back and his fists sailed past me. I laughed. This pissed him off to no end. He came in swinging. I stood there and took it.

His first punch hit my jaw and pushed my teeth through my cheek. Blood flooded my mouth. I grinned as red rivulets trickled down my chin. The copper taste of blood. Took me right back to the days of my sunny childhood. Mom's boyfriend winding up again as I crawled backward across the dusty floor. Two nickels and a bottlecap under the couch. I stood up and Mom's boyfriend knocked me down. Which one was he? The ugly one. They were all ugly. Snaggletooth. Raccoon Mullet. That dude with one arm shorter than the other. That didn't make him ugly, but the drinking sure did. He threw a beer bottle at me from across the room and I laughed right in his fucking face. Push those buttons. Send them over the edge. Red-faced screaming, face all twisted. Turn them into monsters. Watch as they rip off their human faces and their true selves scream into the air. I stood there, human, grinning through the blood. I'm no masochist. The pain was like a river and the river carried me away. They tried to hurt me but they couldn't. Fuck them. I'm still standing.

Drops of sweat and blood hit the ring. Someone shouting — clapping — feet pounding the floor. Mob frenzy, out for blood. Carlos wound up his Sunday Punch. It might impress the ladies, but I ducked it with ease. Carlos was pissed off. His red face was bunched up like a rubber Halloween mask. I grinned and dropped my guard. The blows rained down.

Apartments that smelled like dead mice and stale beer. Moving at midnight to Beat The Clock. Landlords shrieking as the truck pulled out. Mom and Boyfriend (faceless now, just big hands and hair) cackling like evil geniuses, thinking they'd just pulled off The Crime Of The Century. Siphoning gas in shopping centre parking lots. Off to another city, another province. Leaving trails of fast-food wrappers flapping in our wake. The Deadbeat Parade. A new apartment, a new school. Another drop-down drag-out fight in the high noon schoolyard. A Problem Child. "I don't have a problem," I spat at the guidance counsellor with a frilly white shirt and hands that crawled across my legs like ants. "You're the one with the fucking problem." Suspended. Expelled. What the fuck did it matter? Pack up your shit, it's time to go. Hustling across a frozen motel parking lot at midnight, clutching all my clothes stuffed inside a garbage bag, moonlight glancing off the truck's broken bumper. Weaving drunk all over the road. I would fix my eyes on an obstacle ahead and bear down hard with my mind and think, "Crash. Crash." In my mind Mom and Boyfriend would be dead, their bodies crumpled up like paper, their faces wiped clean by the windshield. I would walk across their bodies and emerge from the upside-down truck (one wheel still spinning) and I would be free.

Blows rained down onto my face, my chest, my back. Did I feel it? Oh yeah, I felt the fucking burn. I was in The Zone. I was ready.

My first real punch sent Carlos plummeting to the mat like a fucking anvil dropped from a Zeppelin. The *KABOOM* when he hit shocked the crowd into silence.

"Get up. Come on, get up."

"Lucky punch, old man." Carlos still didn't get it. Good. He bounced back up and I waded in close.

Head wounds bleed plenty. I worked a spot above Carlos's left eye until blood covered his face like a curtain. His other eye puffed up nice and purple. Out of the goodness of my heart I decided to give Carlos's dentist some work. His teeth skittered across the canvas like cockroaches exposed to sunlight.

The kidneys. Hit the right spot and pain shoots up your back. A deep-down ache that cannot be denied. I could rupture something if I hit hard enough, but fuck it, he knew the risks. If you get in the ring, you could die in the ring. That's the risk you take.

My fists tingled inside the gloves. They streaked forward as fast as lightning. The Avenging Hammer of Thor.

I could have killed this guy, but I didn't. I wanted to taste blood, but I'm no killer. They call this "The Sweet Science," but there's too many rules. Regulations. Referees. Bells. Corner men. Gloves. It's not fighting. The Chief taught me that. It's too abstract. That was always my problem with sports. Too much ritual, not enough warfare.

Two more punches and Carlos sprawled out backward on the mat. I stepped back to see if he would do anything, but the kid was done. I spit out my mouth guard and a mouthful of blood splattered the canvas. I stood over the fallen kid, waiting for that old thrill of victory to come flooding through my body. All I felt was sick.

Silence in the cheap seats. One old man shook his head, dumbfounded. I swung down from the ring and thrust my bloody gloves toward the ring man. "Unlace 'em."

My hands throbbed. I grabbed my towel and hit the showers.

In the shower my blood washed pale pink across the tiles. Steam gathered. I wanted this water as hot as it would get. Hotter. I wanted scalding fucking lava pouring down my back. Throw me into the volcano and I will climb out laughing. Do you hear me? You cannot stop me.

My hands were already swelling as I laced up my shoes. No one looked at me in the locker room, but I could feel it: the air was heavy and sullen. Shadowy shapes hung back, waiting to follow me outside.

Outside the gym I turned the corner and stepped into the alley to wait.

I didn't have to wait long. They moved in a pack, like wolves. Six of them. Shaved heads, tank tops, and tattoos. Their leader was a long, lanky lad with a goatee and a scar slashed across his left cheek. He stepped toward me as his followers closed the circle.

"You think you're tough, old man? I think you're lucky."

A short and squat man with a blue bandana over his head stepped forward. "Yeah! If Carlos wasn't hungover, man, he would've killed you."

Scarface grinned. "We're not hungover." There's a metal flash in Scarface's hand. His switchblade sprung open. Man, that sound took me back. Scarface bobbed from side to side, fixing me with his cold fish eyes. "Come on, old man. Let's see how tough you really are."

Scarface lunged. Silently, the wolves moved in for the kill. I grinned. In a split-second I was holding a knife in both hands. Scarface blinked, but it was too late. His own momentum carried him straight into my waiting blade. The gang leader gurgled as my knife sank deep into his throat. I twisted the handle and then yanked it out. Scarface tumbled back, painting the alley with his red arterial spray.

I stood in the alley with my feet firmly planted, my knives at the ready. "Who's next?"

The gangsters hesitated. Fear flickered on their faces. Then two of them charged forward, their knives swinging wildly. The hilt of my knife slammed into one of the gangsters' noses with a satisfying crunch. A tall, skinny gangster with huge black pants tried to get behind me to slit my throat. I slammed my knife right into his eye and gave it a twist. His scream set dogs barking up and down the block. Three down. Three left.

Blue bandana hesitated, blinking down at his fallen comrades. Then he turned tail and ran, his switchblade clattering onto the concrete, his buddy, Hairnet, pounding the pavement right behind him.

In the alley, I rose from my fighter's crouch, blood dripping from my knives. There was one gangster left: A young kid, sixteen, maybe seventeen. Shaved head and a bad teenage moustache. There was an angry-gangster Mickey Mouse airbrushed onto the front of the kid's black T-shirt. The kid stood frozen in the alley, staring at me while his buddies bled around his feet.

I grinned. A dark stain spread across the kid's crotch. "What're you going to do, Mickey?"

The kid turned and fled so fast it was like he was shot from a cannon.

Sirens rose and sirens fell.

Time to get gone.

CHAPTER 42

Eddie was waiting for me when I got back to my office. The big man sat stuffed behind my desk. He was impeccably dressed, as always: black suit, black shirt, white tie. My plant was bobbing and swaying in the breeze blasting from a rotary fan on my desk. I pointed to the fan. "That's new. Housewarming present?"

"More like house cooling. Remind me … I've got to get you some AC in this place." Eddie Yao mopped his brow. "Tommy's been calling nonstop. He's angry as fuck, Jack. You better call him back quick."

I ignored the phone in Eddie's outstretched hand and stumped over toward the bathroom. Eddie frowned at my bruised and battered face. "Hey, are you okay?"

"I went to the gym."

"Oh Jesus. Is the other guy okay?"

"He'll live. Can't say the same about his friends."

Eddie gave his head a shake. "I don't want to know."

"No, you don't."

With a groan Eddie heaved his bulk from behind my desk. "You really should call Tommy."

"Yeah. I will. But first I'm going to take another shower."

"Good idea. You want me to send your suit out for cleaning?"

"Burn it." I had two more identical black suits hanging in my tiny closet.

Eddie scooped up my suit. At the door he stopped and turned. "You sure you're okay?"

"Don't you worry about me."

"Gotcha. I left my phone on your desk."

"I hope you buy those things in bulk."

Eddie grinned. "I know a guy. See you on the roof?"

"Yeah, maybe." I wanted to sit on the roof for a million years. Forget Tommy, forget the punks from the gym, forget everything. Future alien archaeologists would find me fossilized in a lawn chair, one hand clutching a petrified beer.

My office shower was tiny but the water pressure was fantastic. Scalding hot water buffeted my body. I closed my eyes and turned my face to the spray. I didn't even think about the gangbangers bleeding in the alley. They'd had a choice and they chose poorly. They attacked me and I defended myself. Reap the whirlwind, boys.

My eyes snapped open. I blinked rapidly, but it was no use. Every time I closed my eyes all I could see was that damn photo on Grover's corkboard. That goddamn golden retriever staring stupidly at the camera.

I shut off the water and reached for a towel. Fuck it … Tommy could wait.

Moonlight bounced off the greasy water. Crickets chirped in the weeds poking up through the cracked concrete. Grover's boat was tied up at the end of the pier.

Grover was standing on the deck waiting for me. His white suit gleamed in the moonlight. "Glad you changed your mind, Jack. You're going to love Kansas City. They make the best smoked brisket sandwich you've ever tasted."

I tilted my chin at his suit. "How do you keep those things so clean?"

"My suits stay clean because I'm careful. You know that. The key is being aware of your environment at all times. Some dumb shit might wear white pants and sit in ice cream. Not me." Grover spotted the suitcase in my hand. "You're travelling light."

My suitcase was empty. "Yeah. You know me."

Grover chuckled. "That I do. Come aboard, I'll pour us some drinks."

Inside the cabin there was no trace of the corkboards or the photographs. Everything was freshly cleaned.

"Spic and span in here."

Grover nodded. "Yep. The Wife comes home in two days. We'll be back by then."

"In and out."

"Exactly. *Salud.*" Grover passed me a vodka and we clinked glasses. The boat rocked gently with the waves. Outside the window, red lights winked from a distant harbour.

Grover shook his head. "The Chief was a good man."

"He was. But he was human. He had his faults."

Grover frowned. "Careful, Jack. Don't speak ill of the dead."

"I didn't figure you were superstitious."

"Superstitious? No. But I don't tempt fate." Grover's lips twisted into a grin. "Let's face it, Jack. People like us … we need all the luck we can get."

"We make our own luck."

Grover leaned back. His empty shot glass dangled from his hand. "I used to think like that. I thought skill and hard work would always win in the end. But it doesn't work that way. The world is full of billions of hardworking people who bust their asses every single day and never catch a break. No … it's not all about working hard. There's another realm, Jack. I'm fully convinced. The universe is a complex place. Sometimes things just happen. If you're in the right place at the right time, you stand to reap the benefits."

"I don't follow."

"I'm saying luck is real."

"Maybe. But the problem with luck is it can run out. Like what happened to The Chief."

"The Chief was murdered, Jack. Cut down in cold blood by a fucking psychopath. Luck had nothing to do with it."

"That's what I'm saying. The Chief got drunk, got sloppy, and got murdered. He made his choices and he made his own luck — bad luck."

The boat creaked and bumped against the pier. Grover stood up, set his shot glass down on the table, and stared out the window. "Do you know why we called him The Chief?"

I shook my head no. "I always figured he was part First Nations."

Grover's grin was reflected in the glass. "He might've been. But that's not why we called him The Chief." Grover turned away from the porthole and set his hand down on the back of a leather armchair. "He was a volunteer firefighter. That's right. He grew up in a small town and he was the chief of the volunteer firefighters."

"I didn't know that."

"He saved lives, Jack. He was a good man."

"The Chief told me something once. He said everyone is organized into some kind of gang. Therefore everyone is a gangster."

Grover grinned. He looked like a tiny wolf revealing his fangs. "The Chief was a wise man. Do you doubt him? That's exactly the way the world works."

"I thought about it for a long time. I don't buy it. These people in Kansas City. Joey Machine's family. They're not gangsters. They're just people trying to get by."

"Listen to The Chief, Jack. Joey Machine's brother is a gangster. His wife, his kids, his dog — they're all fucking gangsters."

"His dog is a gangster?"

"Living off the proceeds of crime. That mutt is a gangster, just like you or me."

"The dog's not a gangster. And I'm not a gangster."

Grover laughed, short, dry little barks. "Oh no? Let me guess. You're just a person trying to get by."

"That's right."

YARD DOG

"I've got a news flash for you, Jack. You work for Tommy. That makes you a gangster."

"And Tommy's barber? His mechanic? The guy who bags his groceries?"

"Gangsters, every last one of them. The Chief was right."

I shook my head. "I don't buy it."

"Drink your vodka, Jack."

I ignored the shot glass. The boat bumped against the dock. In the distance, a trawler churned the water.

Grover poured himself more vodka. "Let me ask you a question. Why did you come here tonight?"

"You know why."

"You've had some moral epiphany. You're trying to stop me from going to Kansas City."

"This isn't you, Grover."

"Then who the fuck is it, Jack? Am I my Evil Twin?"

Grover took a step backward. I stood up.

Grover laughed again, dry and cold and joyless. "You're unbelievable, Jack. You really are. I've never met anyone as self-deluded as you. 'Not a gangster.'" Grover took another step backward, toward the shadows. "It's a good thing The Chief can't see you now. You never disappointed me, Jack. Not until today. I'll send you a postcard from Kansas City."

I ducked just in time. With a flash of silver a knife flew from Grover's hand and buried itself in the wall inches above my head. I sent one of my own knives flying back into the shadows, but Grover was gone.

Shit, shit, shit. Another knife leapt into my hand. Cautiously I edged toward the cabin door and kicked it open. A hail of gunfire lit up the night. I pressed my back flat against the cabin wall as wood splintered all around me. Bullets punched into the table, the walls, the carpet. My ears were ringing. The air smelled like smoke and cedar.

The gunfire stopped. Silence came rushing through the bullet holes. I ducked through the splintered doorway and rolled onto the deck. The moon hung full over the greasy water. Spent shells rolled and clattered against the rail. Grover was gone.

I ran for the railing as fast as I could. I was up and over in seconds, diving toward the water below. I was in midair when the boat blew up. The fireball propelled me forward. It felt like there was a dragon breathing down my neck.

The moon greeted me as I bobbed to the surface. Pieces of burning wood floated all around me. I swam under the pier, not wanting to give Grover a clear shot. Chances were he was long gone but you know what they say: safety first. In the distance I heard sirens. I kicked off my shoes and swam for shore.

CHAPTER 43

I did my best drunk act with the cabbie, and I'm pretty sure it worked. I couldn't be the first person who drank too much and fell into the lake. The cabbie didn't want to stop, but I leapt in front of his car. He was cursing as he slammed on the brakes. "No, no, no," he kept saying as I opened the back door and wedged myself inside. "No, no, no." The wet hundred dollar bill I pressed into his palm helped him change his mind. After all, it's only water.

If there wasn't a contract out on me before, there was now. I leaned back and closed my eyes. I was tired, so tired. Adrenalin surge depleted. Cold and wet seeped into my bones. I should've killed Grover when I had the chance.

But I'm no killer. Soon Grover would come for me. Would I be ready? The knock on the door. The crocodile smile. The gun held behind the back. Would it be quick or slow?

Stop that. Pull it together. Maintain, maintain. There's always a solution. There's always a way out.

The cab dropped me off at a downtown hotel. In my room I double-bolted the door, pulled on a fluffy white robe, and hung my wet clothes from the shower rod. I called down and had the concierge send up some dry clothes from the gift shop. Room service sent up two bacon cheeseburgers, a Caesar salad, and a platter of onion rings. After the boat explosion I wasn't so worried about my cholesterol. Who was I trying to impress, the autopsy doctors? "Half his head was blown away, but get a load of this liver. Smooth, subtle, and spotless."

There's that fatalism again. Is this what happened to The Chief? Did he look around his tiny trailer one night and just say "Fuck it"? The Chief went out riding a tidal wave of sex and booze and drugs. There's worse ways to go.

I sat crosslegged on the bed in my gift shop sweatpants and red sweatshirt with a white maple leaf emblazoned on the front. My eyes closed. My breathing slowed. Grover's corkboard appeared, shimmering in my mind's eye. Black marker scrawled maniacally over everything. Photos, arrows, names, addresses, phone numbers.

My eyes snapped open. I reached for the phone.

"Hello?"

"Is this William Mezell?"

"Who's calling, please?"

"Mr. Mezell, I knew your brother."

"I don't have a brother."

Oh Christ. "Listen to me carefully. There's no time for the song and dance. You had a brother named Joey. He's dead. There's a man who wanted to kill him. He never had the chance. Now he's pissed off and crazy. He's coming to kill you."

"What? Who is this?"

"Here's what you need to do. Gather up your family and head for the hills. You hear me? Go someplace you've never been before. Call it a vacation."

"You're serious."

"I am."

"I'll call the police. They'll —"

"They'll call in the cleaners to mop up your blood. This man is coming and he will kill you all. Get out. NOW."

Silence on the other end. I could picture Willy Mezell standing in his kitchen, designer copper pans hanging spotless from a rack above the stove. Maybe he was holding a glass of Scotch. For sure he was wearing a sweater vest and tan slacks.

"How … how will I know when it's safe?"

"Someone will call and leave a message. Check your messages remotely. Do you understand?"

"I … yes."

"Good. Now, GO."

I hung up. I wasn't worried about someone tracing the call. I'd checked in with a fake name and a fake ID. Time for two more calls.

"Eddie. I won't be home for a while. Grover is on the warpath."

"That's not good."

"No, it's not."

"What can I do?"

"Close up shop."

"I can't do that."

"You can and you will. Go to the fucking mattresses. You hear me? This is not a drill."

"This isn't good for business, Jack."

"Neither is getting killed."

"Be careful."

"I always am."

One more call.

"Hi, Suzanne?"

"Jack."

"We've got a problem. You need to get out of town for a few days."

"This shit again?" Her voice was exasperated.

"Afraid so. But listen, this time —"

"No."

"No is not an option. Get out and get out now."

There was a pause on the other end. "Some women like that, don't they, Jack?"

"Like what?"

"When guys bark orders. Not me, though."

"I …" I closed my eyes tight. Breathe in, breathe out. "You're in danger. Get out of town and call me in a couple of days. Everything is going to be fine, I promise."

"Oh really? You promise? Everything's going to be hunky-dory? I can't do this, Jack."

"What?"

"This. Us. I can't do it."

"Suzanne. I'm sorry. I'm really sorry. Things got fucked up. But I can make this right. I just need some time. We're almost there, babe. I can see the light at the end of the tunnel."

"Jack —"

"Just go out of town. Anywhere. I'll pay you back. Two, three days, tops. Just do this one last thing. Do this and then we're done. I'll be out of your hair forever. I'm not happy about it, but if that's what you want then that's what you'll get. Okay?"

"Goodbye, Jack."

Shit, shit, shit. Numb, I hung up the phone, wiped my prints off it, and stared out the window. Blue skies and sunshine. It was a beautiful fucking day.

CHAPTER 44

Tommy's club was closed. Someone had put a concrete barricade in front of the front door. I circled around and headed for the back. In the alley two guys in blue sweatsuits saw me coming and peeled themselves off the wall.

"We're closed."

"I need to see Tommy."

One of the guys was wearing an obvious hairpiece, sandy brown as opposed to his real black hair flecked with grey. He was older than Tommy's usual crew. He pulled up his shirt to reveal the butt of a gun. "I said we're fucking closed."

"My name's Jack. Tommy called me. He wants to see me."

"You're Jack?" Hairpiece gave me the once-over. "I've heard of you. You don't look so tough."

I managed a crooked smile. "It's an illusion. It's done with mirrors."

Hairpiece looked like he just bit a lemon. "You're not so funny, either."

"Look. Tommy wants to see me. So we can stand out here jawing or I can go in there and get shit done."

Hairpiece turned and grinned at his buddy. His buddy looked bored out of his fucking mind. "You know who Tommy is? Tommy is a scared little bitch."

The other guy's laughter rang cruelly through the alley. Hairpiece stepped aside. His buddy knocked twice and the door opened.

Inside, the club was dark and quiet. Like a tomb. Nemo pushed the door shut behind me and bolted it.

"What's happening, Nemo?"

There were big dark circles under the huge man's eyes. He hadn't slept and he hadn't shaved. He looked at me with big sad eyes and he shook his head. "It's not good, Jack. No one's returning Tommy's calls. The wheels have come off this train."

"Those guys outside?"

"Murray and Mike. They work for Little Vito."

"And you?"

Nemo shrugged. "I work for The Boss."

Nemo led me upstairs. Our footsteps echoed in the darkness. Tommy's bodyguard Rocco was sitting slumped in a folding chair outside Tommy's office. He looked rumpled and beaten down. Hopeless.

"Rocco."

"Jack."

"The Man inside?"

"Yep." Rocco sighed. "They're not letting him leave."

"What? What do you mean?" At my side Nemo squirmed uncomfortably.

"They got us trapped in here like rats. Tommy got a call from his Uncle Gus. He said sit tight, don't worry, they're gonna work it all out. That was yesterday. Then those two fuckers show up outside. Laughing their heads off, pissing in the alley. Our alley. Tommy, he's furious. He starts calling everyone he knows. But here's the thing: no one is calling him back."

Nemo shook his head. "That's not good."

Rocco frowned. "No, it's not. They're letting us twist in the wind." Rocco glared at Nemo.

The big man shifted again, moving from side to side. "Rocco. You know I'd help if I could. It's out of my hands. I'm just a soldier, like you."

"Yeah. Sure. Just like me. Except you can come and go and I'm trapped in here with Tommy."

Nemo held out his ham-sized hand. "No one's trapped, all right? This right here is what you call a temporary situation. It's for Tommy's own protection. And your own protection."

Rocco turned his mournful eyes toward me. "You hear that, Jack? My own protection." Rocco leapt up and Nemo stepped back, his hand darting toward the waistband of his track pants. "Why the fuck do I need protection, Nemo? Huh? I've worked my ass off for this family. Now they're going to turn their back?"

In a quiet, calm voice Nemo said, "Rocco. Sit down."

Rocco blinked. I stepped away, removing myself from the line of fire. Without taking his eyes off Nemo, Rocco slowly shook his head. "What's the matter with you, man? We go fishing together. I held your son in my arms."

"You leave my son out of this."

"In my arms! How many times have I eaten at your table? How many times?"

Nemo glanced away. "You know that shit doesn't matter."

"We're friends! We're fucking friends!"

The muffled gunshot sounded like a kid's toy. Rocco's mouth hung open as he looked down at the red hole in his chest. Wordlessly he slumped back and slid down the hallway wall.

Nemo loomed over Rocco's body and shouted, "THAT SHIT DOESN'T MATTER!" Then Nemo turned to me. With a sheepish look in his eyes, he said, "Sorry you had to see that, Jack."

I didn't say anything. In less than half a second I could have a knife in my hand. In another half a second the big man could have a second mouth slashed across his throat.

Nemo lowered the gun. He shook his head. "Things ... things are a little fucked up. I've been under a lot of pressure recently. A lot of stress. Sleep is important, you know? You don't realize how important it is until you don't get enough. You know what I mean?"

Rocco's blood seeped into the carpet. I nodded at Nemo. "Sure. You got to get enough sleep."

"Oh yeah. And it's got to be quality. You can't just toss and turn and wake up every five minutes. You got to get down into it, you know?"

"Yep." I wondered if Nemo ever woke up screaming. "Sometimes when I'm travelling I bring my own pillow."

"Oh yeah? Hey, that's a good idea."

I took a step away from the seeping puddle of blood. "You bet. It's like a little piece of home wherever you go."

"Yeah. Yeah. You know what, Jack? I'm gonna try that. Next time I go out of town, I'm going to bring my own pillow." Nemo shook his head again. "I really am sorry about that. He deserved better, you know?"

I felt the air change and I braced myself. Nemo's shot punched into the wall behind me but I was no longer there. Slow down the film: there I was kicking the gun from Nemo's hand. That's me spinning, the knife in my fist. The blade dipped into Nemo's throat. My momentum carried me forward and pulled the knife free. There's Nemo, a startled look on his face. His shattered trigger finger jerked, trying to fire the gun that was no longer in his hand. He stumbled back. With a lunge I stabbed the big man in his heart. The look of surprise turned into a look of agony. Nemo fell back dead.

I was standing in the hallway of the abandoned nightclub with two bodies on the floor and a bloody knife in my fist. Breathe in, breathe out. Slowly I stepped around the blood, squared my shoulders, and knocked on Tommy's office door.

No answer.

"Tommy. It's Jack."

Strange whimpering sounds came from behind the door.

"It's Jack. I'm here to help you."

Tommy's muffled voice. "Jack?"

"Yeah, Tommy. It's me."

"Rocco?"

"Nemo shot him. He's dead."

"Nemo?"

"He's dead, too."

The door opened a crack. A shaft of light sliced across the hallway. Tommy peered through the crack and blinked.

He looked horrible. Unshaven, dark circles, greasy hair. But something more than that. He looked haggard, as if wolves had been chasing him for weeks through abandoned frontier towns. For the first time that I could remember, Tommy looked afraid.

"Jack." Tommy's voice was hoarse, raspy, almost gone. "I'm a dead man."

"Tommy."

"They're going to kill me."

"No one's going to kill you. I'm going to get us out of here."

Cautiously, I moved forward. "I'm going to come into the office now. Okay? You're going to be okay."

Inside, the office smelled like fear: sweat and salt and urine. In the far corner Tommy had made a make-shift fort out of black leather sofa cushions.

Tommy had a gun in his hand. I took a step toward him, moving slowly, carefully. "Give me the gun, Tommy."

Tommy scowled and shook his head. "Yeah, right. No fucking way."

"Listen to me very carefully. Do you want to live? I can get you out of here, but we're going to do it my way. Do you understand?"

Tommy's eyes narrowed. "How do I know you're not here to kill me?"

"You know me, Tommy. I'm not a killer." Behind me, Nemo's blood pooled in the hallway. "Now give me the gun."

He did. For a split second an image flashed through my brain: me, turning the gun on Tommy and squeezing the trigger. Who would complain? One shot and I'd be free of Tommy forever. But I couldn't do that. I checked the gun for bullets. It was fully loaded.

Tommy stumped across the carpet to the safe embedded above the bar. "I'm not leaving without my money."

The money, the money. It was always about the fucking money. I felt like grabbing Tommy by his stinking shirtfront and shaking him like a dog with a chew toy. "FORGET THE FUCKING MONEY!" Tommy was the sort who would drown in a shipwreck, plummeting down into his watery grave still clutching a chest full of treasure. Let go and live. It's that fucking simple.

Inside the safe were stacks and stacks of banded twenties. Tommy scooped them into a black leather bag and then turned to me. "All right, Jack. Get me the fuck out of here."

Tommy headed for the door, but I stopped him. My palm thudded against his chest. "Here's how this is going to work. You follow me. Stick close. Do whatever I say when I say it. No, don't say anything. I know you don't like it, but this is how it has to be. When I say jump, you fucking jump. You listen to me and you'll live. You got that?"

Tommy clutched his money bag and sulked. "You wouldn't talk to me like that if my dad was alive."

Maybe he was right. "This has nothing do with your dad. This is about you and me staying alive. You ready? Come on, let's go."

In the hallway I led Tommy past the corpses of Rocco and Nemo. As he passed Nemo's body Tommy kicked the big man's corpse in the head and spat. "That's what you get, you fucking prick."

"Quiet."

"I was just —"

"I said BE QUIET!"

Slowly I moved across the second floor toward a window overlooking the street. Two black SUVS were parked outside, drivers with sunglasses at the wheel. Four men in suits lounged against the cars. Another man in a suit was talking to the gangster with the hairpiece. Looked like for once Tommy was right. Little Vito's crew was coming to kill him.

I doubled back.

"Hey, where the fuck are you going?"

"Your office. Come on."

"Are you fucking crazy? We'll be sitting ducks!"

I didn't answer. Tommy shut his trap and followed me back down the hallway.

My fingers got sticky with blood as I lifted Rocco's and Nemo's guns. I don't like guns, but sometimes you don't have a choice. What had Grover said? "Don't bring a knife to a gunfight." I don't like guns, but I do like living. I wasn't going to let them carve "He Didn't Like Guns" onto my tombstone.

I stuck Tommy's gun in my waistband and checked the other guns for bullets. Other than the bullet Nemo had shot at me and the one bullet now lodged in Rocco's chest, the guns were full. Good.

Inside Tommy's office I made a beeline for the bar. Tommy opened his mouth and I shot him a look that could wilt flowers. Wisely he shut the fuck up. Amber liquid sloshed as I grabbed two big bottles of 150-proof rum. Tommy trembled as I strode over to him. Before he could protest, I ripped two strips from his dirty shirt.

"Hey! What the fuck?"

"Shut up." The rum smelled like a doctor's office in the Caribbean: pure alcohol with just a hint of cane sugar. I splashed the overproof booze onto the strips of Tommy's shirt. Then I stuffed the booze-soaked strips into the now three-quarters-full bottles.

Tommy caught wise. His eyes lit up. I passed him one of the Molotov cocktails. "You still have your lighter?"

Tommy's eyes gleamed as he held up his silver Zippo. "Check it."

Using his thumb, Tommy flipped the top. A butane flame leapt from the lighter.

"Good. No, don't light it yet. Let's go."

Back into the hallway. With a grunt I heaved Rocco's body onto my shoulder in a fireman's hold. Lift with your legs, not your back. My teeth ground together as I struggled down the stairs. I was wishing anyone but Tommy was bringing up the rear. I wished The Chief were here, silently smiling, an AK-47 cradled lovingly in his arms. Or Grover. No, don't think about Grover. What kind of madman blows up his own boat?

Downstairs I dropped Rocco's body onto a chair. His blood had soaked through my shirt. I smelled copper and rum and Tommy's sweat. The legs of Rocco's chair scraped against the dance floor as I dragged it toward the door.

Tommy's voice hissed in my ear. His breath could curdle milk. "What the fuck are you doing?"

"Shh. Wait."

Rocco's head slumped to the left. I positioned the chair about fifty feet away from the front door and pulled Rocco's head upright. From a distance it looked like the dead man was guarding the door. At least, that's what I was hoping. *It won't fool anyone for long, but it doesn't have to.*

I tilted my head close to Tommy's ear. "They're coming in the front. We're going out the back. Hang on to that Molotov until we get outside. Got it?"

"Yeah. Yeah."

"Good."

I strode over to the bar and pulled down another bottle of overproof rum. Liquid amber splashed all over the floor in front of the front door. I saved the last swallow for myself. It was like drinking fire.

Tommy was a bundle of jittery nerves. I closed my eyes. If this didn't work we were both dead.

Outside the door I heard voices, talking and laughing. Here they came.

I pointed toward the back door and Tommy ran, the Molotov sloshing in his hand. I raised my gun. The door opened and all hell broke loose.

Rapid-fire gunshots: the first two gangsters fell to the floor. Shouts and screams. More gunfire: bullets flew across the room and slammed into Rocco's body.

Rocco and his chair went tumbling backward. I dropped Tommy's now-empty gun, sparked the Molotov with my lighter, and threw it overhand toward the gangsters storming through the door. More screams as the gangsters went up. Orange flames leapt toward the ceiling. My heart jackhammered in my chest as I ran for the back, unloading Rocco's gun behind me.

Tommy was bug-eyed by the back door. From the alley I heard shouting and the revving of a car engine. Not much time. I chucked Rocco's gun, pulled out Nemo's revolver, and kicked down the back door. The door caught a gangster in the face. A hairpiece went flying. Nemo's gun barked and two gangsters in suits spun and fell into the trash.

"Light and throw! LIGHT AND THROW!"

Behind me Tommy fumbled with his lighter. A black SUV pulled into the alley and rumbled straight toward us. A bullet whined, ricocheting off the brick wall, and I whirled and returned fire. A gangster in track pants clutched his throat and dropped to the ground. I grabbed Tommy's Molotov, lit it, and hurled it at the oncoming car. Flames flickered against the windshield.

I shoved Tommy back into the club as the burning SUV hurtled by, missing us by inches. I grabbed Tommy's arm and yanked him toward the street. "COME ON!"

Smoke alarms started to scream. How many left? I'd lost count. We pounded down the street and ducked into another alley. My chest heaved. It felt like my lungs had been packed full of broken glass. I flattened out against the brick alley wall and steadied my gun. No one was following.

We staggered through a maze of alleys, past bricks and graffiti and garbage. I ditched Nemo's gun. It clattered into a Dumpster as we ran.

"Jack!" Over my shoulder I saw Tommy, legs wobbling, staggering over to a graffiti-covered wall. His face was as pink as a boiled lobster. Tommy braced himself against the wall, vomited all over his shoes, staggered a few feet and then collapsed in a doorway. "That's it … I can't … no more. No —" Tommy's whole body shuddered. He turned and threw up again, a sickly green trickle.

I knew how he felt. I scanned the alley, trying to crane my neck toward the street beyond. "Wait here."

The coast was clear. At the mouth of the alley I put my hands on my knees and lowered my head, trying to steady my breathing. Sweat dripped from my forehead to the dirty concrete. Cars passed by, the hush of tires on asphalt. From a window far above me I heard a girl singing. I'd heard that song before. Cassandra used to sing it, a million years ago. Leonard Cohen's "Anthem." The girl's voice floated down into the alley, so sad, so sweet. I pulled myself upright, brushed sweat from my face, slicked back my hair, and casually sauntered across the street to a payphone. Men and women dressed in business casual gave me a wide berth. One blond woman in sunglasses saw me coming and crossed to the other side of the street. *Hey lady, I may be sweaty, dishevelled, and covered in a dead man's blood, but don't judge a book by its cover. Really, I'm one hell of a fellow.*

Quarters rattled into the payphone. "Eddie. It's me."

"Are you okay?"

"Just peachy. You?"

"I took your advice. Packed up and left."

"Good man. Listen, we need a pickup."

"How many?"

"Counting me, two."

"You got it."

Back in the alley I found Tommy wandering around in shock. I cracked him one across the face and that seemed to do the trick. His eyes flashed as he raised his fist. "Don't you ever fucking hit me again. You hear me? I will fucking kill you. I will —"

"Yeah, yeah. I know. You'll rip off my face and fry it in a pan with some garlic and onions."

"Is that some sort of slur? Are you putting down my fucking heritage? I know people in the Anti-Defamation League. Don't make me get litigious on your ass."

Ignoring Tommy, I bent down and scooped up a fistful of garbage. Tommy watched incredulously as I smeared the garbage across my shirt front.

"What the fuck?"

"You ever hear of Urban Camouflage? Right now you look like a gangster. A fucked-up gangster, but still a gangster. Here."

I threw a handful of muck at Tommy. He side-stepped. "What the fuck?"

"The Chief taught me this. Not every homeless person is dirty and smelly, but that's what a lot of people think. If we look 'homeless' enough, people will look the other way. Now come on … we've got some walking to do."

Tommy grumbled, but he followed my lead. Together we staggered from the alley, heading south. We weren't that far from my office but we were heading in the opposite direction, toward the lake.

My office. The couch. My desk, my plant. I might not ever go back. Thinking about my plant dying slowly on my desk made my stomach hurt. Soil drying up, leaves curling and turning brown. Fuck Grover. He could be waiting in my office with a fucking machete for all I cared. I wasn't going to let him kill my plant.

Tommy and I collapsed onto a park bench and sat there waiting. At our feet pigeons clucked and cooed. Cars went by. A young woman in yoga pants jogged past with her German shepherd. She glanced toward us and quickly looked away.

"Whaddaya know," said Tommy. "It fucking works."

Suddenly my mouth was the Sierra Desert. There were cacti and cattle skulls on my tongue. I wanted a beer the size of the Empire State Building. I wanted to dunk my face into a river of ice-cold beer and drink until my stomach hit my knees.

A nondescript black car pulled up and idled in front of the park. The passenger window rolled down and there was Eddie, masked behind his giant sunglasses. Salvation.

Inside the car the air conditioning felt like God himself was blowing me kisses. I grinned like a fool as I clapped Eddie on the shoulder. Beside Eddie, his driver muttered something in Cantonese.

"What'd he say?"

Eddie laughed. "He says you smell like shit."

Tommy stiffened. I put my hand against his chest. "Relax, relax.... Say, Eddie?"

"Yeah?"

"You don't have any beer in that glove box, do you?"

"Nope. But we've got plenty of beer back at the safe house."

The Safe House. Such beautiful words. In my mind's eye I saw billowing white sheets and fountains and swimming pools and bikini girls. *The Safe House.* Kebabs sizzling on the grill. Floating around the pool with an ice-cold beer in a styrofoam beer cooler. Waking up well-rested and stepping out onto the balcony to greet the sunrise. No worries. No hassles. *The Safe House.*

Needless to say, when we pulled up to the safe house it didn't quite live up to my expectations. It was a plain old bungalow in Scarborough, all concrete and aluminum siding. Eddie's driver pulled the car around into the garage and the garage door rumbled closed. Eddie turned to me and grinned. "Home sweet home."

At the back door we kicked off our shoes. Tommy was asleep almost before we stepped inside. Eddie barked an order and two of his guys leapt up from the kitchen table and manoeuvred Tommy toward a bedroom. Without asking, Eddie opened the fridge and passed me an ice-cold beer. I knocked it back in about three-fifths of a second. Eddie smiled and passed me another.

I put my feet up on one of the avocado-green kitchen chairs. Eddie tilted his head. "There's a hole in your sock."

"That's where the light gets in."

"What?"

"Forget it."

My head buzzed with beer. *When did I last eat?*

As if reading my mind, Eddie stood up and walked over to the fridge. "You hungry? We've got shrimp."

The shrimp were cold, garlicky and delicious. I tucked in until they were gone and then I leaned back in my chair.

Eddie sat down across from me. "The boys weren't happy about closing up shop."

"It's a temporary thing."

"Level with me, Jack."

"I'm telling you straight up. It's temporary. Grover ... let's just say he's taking The Chief's death pretty hard."

"He's coming to kill you."

"Yeah. I think so."

Eddie jerked his head toward the hall and the bedrooms beyond. "And Tommy?"

"I couldn't leave him there. They were going to kill him."

"Little Vito's guys."

"That's right."

"So now Little Vito is after you, too."

"Yeah." I shot Eddie a crooked grin. "It never rains, but it pours."

Eddie tilted back his beer. "You got that right." Eddie slammed the beer bottle down on the table. "We'll get this shit worked out, Jack. We always do."

"That's what I like about you, Eddie. You're an optimist."

"Work it out or die trying."

Suddenly the Sandman walloped me with a fifty-pound sack. My legs got rubbery and my chin bobbed toward the table.

"Get some rest, Jack. Tomorrow's another day."

"Don't remind me."

CHAPTER 45

I woke up before dawn. My joints were aching and my muscles were screaming. I was getting too old for this shit.

Eddie had courteously left a cellphone for me on the kitchen table. I clenched my teeth and punched in her number.

Suzanne answered, voice heavy with sleep. "Hello?"

"Sorry to wake you."

"Jack?" There was a thunk as Suzanne fumbled the phone. "You okay?"

"I'm fine. I'm somewhere safe. Where are you?"

"What time is it?"

"It's early. I'm sorry. Where are you?"

"Where do you think I am? I'm at home."

I closed my eyes. My teeth clenched.

"Jack?"

"I'm here. Suzanne … I've never lied to you. There's

some seriously bad guys coming for me. They might try to get to me through you."

"I'm in danger."

"That's right."

"Because of you."

"It's not me. It's the people who are after me. I'll send a car. They'll take you someplace safe."

"I told you, Jack. I can't get sucked into all of this. Not again."

"It's almost over, baby. I swear it. Eddie and I, we'll deal with this. And then that's it. I'm done. You and I, we'll live out the rest of our lives in peace and harmony."

"Peace and harmony. Right after you kill everybody."

"I'm not a killer, babe. But I will fight to defend myself and the people I love."

"And so will I. Goodbye, Jack."

The phone went dead. *Fuck. That didn't go well.*

Outside the kitchen window the sky was changing from black to grey to shimmering silver. In another half hour birds would be chirping and tugging worms from dew-fresh lawns.

Eddie stumped into the kitchen rubbing his eyes and wearing a ridiculous powder-blue bathrobe about five sizes too short. "Mornin', Jack."

"Morning, Sunshine. Looking good." I stood up and headed for the door.

"Where are you going?"

I grinned. "You know the drill. The earliest bird gets the fattest worm."

Residential neighbourhoods unfolded around me as I walked past joggers and dog-walkers. Up ahead two teenagers were staggering down the sidewalk, laughing loudly, heading home to bed. I could smell the booze wafting off of them from here. Lucky kids.

Residential faded into commercial. Strip malls, Chinese food, used car sales. I found a payphone and made a call.

"Yeah." The voice on the other end was groggy.

"This is Jack Palace."

"Jack." Silence on the other end. "I heard we had a visit from you the other day."

"I'm not going to bullshit you, Vito."

On the other end of the phone, Little Vito chuckled. "You know, it's been my experience that whenever someone says they're not going to bullshit me, the next thing to come out of their mouth is pure bullshit."

"I was there. At Tommy's club."

"You know, Jack, there's a lot of very pissed-off people over here."

"I did what had to be done."

"I can appreciate that. But you have to understand: my guys, they're howling for blood."

"I understand."

"Who was with you?"

"I was alone. Just me and Tommy."

"Bullshit!" Little Vito growled. "I've got eight dead. A torched SUV. A club that almost burned to the fucking ground."

"You don't have to tell me. I was there, remember?"

"I look forward to our next meeting, Jack."

"Vito … this shit's got to end."

"Oh, it will. Don't you fret about that."

"War's not good for business. Well, it's good for some businesses. But not yours."

Again, silence. I pictured my words seeping into Vito's brain like water in a freshly watered flower pot.

"Listen to me very carefully, Jack. You had your chance. Remember our dinner? I spelled it all out. You made your choice. Now you're stuck with it. Give my regards to Tommy's dad."

The phone went dead.

Shit, shit, shit. I grabbed the receiver and bashed it to fucking pieces. Then I turned and slowly walked back toward the house.

In the kitchen Tommy was up and eating, shovelling eggs into his mouth like he had a gun to his head. Behind him two of Eddie's guys stood with their arms folded. Eddie, eyes hidden behind his sunglasses, sat across from Tommy. Tommy saw me coming and his eyes lit up.

"Jack! Tell these guys to lighten the fuck up, will you? They're following me around like they're fucking glued to my ass cheeks."

There's an image I could've lived without.

"Tommy ... this is bad. This is very bad."

Tommy waved it off. A piece of egg yolk was dangling from his chin. "Nah. You'll take care of it. I believe in you, Jack."

Eddie cleared his throat. "Jack's saved your life twice now. You realize that?"

"Hey, I'm grateful. Don't think I'm not grateful.

You …" Tommy pointed to Eddie and then to the other two guys, "and you and you … you'll be taken care of. You know who my father was? He was a rich fucking bastard, that's who he was."

Tommy pushed away his empty plate and patted his belly. "Good eggs."

"Tommy. Tell me something. Little Vito must have enemies."

"You're damn right. Me. I'm his fucking enemy."

"Yeah. Who else?"

"Who am I, his secretary? How the fuck should I know?"

I shut my eyes.

I've got a headache THIS BIG.

Tommy jerked his head at Eddie's two guys looming behind him. "Let's talk in the other room."

I tilted my chin at Eddie. "That okay?"

Eddie shrugged. "Fine by me."

Tommy's bedroom was on the smallish side. Yellow wallpaper flowers wound around the walls. A hand-made quilt was folded at the foot of the bed.

Tommy sat down on the bed and sighed. "Jack. It was a fucking miracle we got out of that club. No, don't say anything. You saved my life and I'm not going to forget it. I could've died in there. That's what I woke up thinking this morning: I should be dead. I should be fucking dead. And then that rat Little Vito would get everything." Tommy leapt to his feet. "Fuck him! He's stealing my hard-earned money, Jack."

"Tommy … maybe it's time you walked away. Forget the money. Forget The Empire. You've got your life, your health —"

Tommy broke down coughing.

"You've got your life. You could move away, start fresh."

"Yeah, right. What am I going to do? I never went to school. I've never done anything."

"You managed a nightclub. You've got some cash. Take your money and split to the Caribbean. Open up a little bar on the beach. Sit in your hammock and drink rum all day."

Tommy smiled sadly and slowly shook his head. "It sounds nice, doesn't it? But it's not for me. The beach? Come on, Jack. I'm a city boy."

"So move to Montreal. Vancouver. There are other cities."

"Yeah. But this is my city."

"Not anymore it's not."

Tommy stood up and paced across the wooden boards. "You and me, Jack. We can set things right. Little Vito won't know what hit him."

"No."

"No? What do you mean, no? We can take these guys. I'm going to cut off Little Vito's head and mount it on a pike. That's what you fucking get! You mess with me, I'll saw off your fucking head."

"Forget the head-sawing for a minute. Listen to me. You need to grab your cash and get gone. Little Vito isn't about to forget what happened yesterday. He's going to come gunning for both of us."

"Not if we get him first. Come on, Jack. You and me. We go over to Little Vito's house and we wait. He comes outside, *BAM BAM BAM*! We fuck him up. Leave him lying there bleeding in the driveway."

"And then what? We go waltzing off into the sunset? Free as fucking birds? You know it doesn't work that way. You cut down Vito, Vito's friends come gunning for you."

"Fuck Vito's friends!"

"Tommy." I stared at the mobster's son. "It's over."

"Jack. Jack. What are you saying?"

"I'm saying that in about five minutes, I'm walking out that door. Five minutes after that, Eddie's guys will drive you anywhere you want to go. They'll drop you off and then they'll drive away. Have a nice life."

"WAIT! For fuck's sake, just wait a minute." Tommy's hands shook as he pushed back his hair. "Let's think about this. Let's work something out. Okay, okay, so we're even. I saved your life, you saved mine."

"Twice. But who's counting?"

"Right, right. Look, I wasn't bullshitting back in the kitchen. My father has cash stashed all over this city. You and me, Jack … help me get the cash and you'll get your cut. A hundred grand. How's that sound?"

It sounded like bullshit. "Make it two hundred."

"Two! Who am I, Scrooge McDuck?"

"Two hundred." Enough to buy a little house out in the country. Vegetable garden out back. Sunflowers. Tire swing. Pies cooling on the windowsill. Suzanne, laughing in a pale-blue dress. Kids shovelling sand in the sandbox. Fluffy orange and white cat stretched out sleeping in a sunbeam.

Tommy held out his hands. "All right, all right. What can I say? You've got me over a barrel. Two it is. But before we get the money, we've got to deal with this Vito situation. There's this guy, friend of my father's. His name's Lou. We need to talk to him."

I pulled out Eddie's cellphone and flipped it open. "Set it up."

Lou looked like a younger and tougher version of Ed McMahon. He was sitting spread out in an oak-panelled booth at the back of the bar like an overfed housecat on a velvet cushion. Lou's hair was silver and carefully brushed back. Half his face was hidden by enormous smoky sunglasses. A huge man standing next to the booth was either a horse in a human suit or Lou's bodyguard. The human horse beckoned us closer. Lou hefted his massive bulk from the booth and kissed Tommy on both cheeks.

"Tommy, Tommy. How are you holding up?"

"You know how it is. We're all just hanging on."

"That's all you can do." Lou turned his smoky lenses to me.

"Jack Palace."

Lou nodded, then tilted his chin toward Horse Man. "That's Yanni."

Yanni cocked his eyebrow and gave me the once over. I was supposed to be intimidated.

I wasn't.

"Sit, sit." Lou wedged himself back in the booth and gestured to the waiter, a tall, bald man in all black. The waiter slid forward. "How 'bout another Scotch. Tommy, what are you drinking?"

"Club soda."

"Club soda?" Lou and I exclaimed at the same time.

Tommy nodded. "Yeah, that's right. I got a lot of work to do."

Lou smiled approvingly. "Good man. Your father would be proud."

Tommy beamed. His cheeks turned bright pink.

Lou pulled out a gold cigarette case and flipped it open. "Smoke?"

"No thanks."

Lou lit up, right beneath the no smoking sign. The big man followed my eyes and laughed. "What are they going to do, kick me out of my own club?"

Tommy and Horse Man joined in laughing. I chortled along. The Workplace Laugh. Too loud, too fake.

Lou's gold rings gleamed as he spread his hands across the table. "All right. So what's the situation?"

"It's like this. The situation is all fucked up."

"It usually is."

"You got that right."

More guffaws. I shifted from foot to foot.

"Jack and me, we had a run-in with some of Little Vito's crew."

"I heard about it." Lou blew smoke. "So why come to me?"

"I respect you, Lou. My father respected you. Little Vito … well, I don't know about Vito."

"Tommy … you know I love you like a son. No one would've been happier than me to see you take over the family business. But …" Lou shrugged.

Tommy's face went black. "That prick Vito stole it all. He stole the shoes off my fucking feet."

"Whoa, whoa. I'm going to pretend I didn't hear that."

"Sorry. I'm sorry. I'm just a little upset."

"Sure, I understand. These are difficult times."

"Vito tried to kill me. You hear what I'm saying? Me, the boss's son."

Lou shook his head. "Vito is boss now."

"Yeah, whatever. Look, you know me. I only want what's best for this family."

"As do we."

"Good. So we're all on the same page. Vito isn't the boss … you got that? I'm the fucking boss."

"Tommy, Tommy. I know how you feel. These are emotional times. But it's been decided. Vito is in."

"This is bullshit. BULLSHIT!"

Lou shrugged. "That's life. Someone moved your fucking cheese."

I leaned down and whispered "be cool" in Tommy's ear. Tommy nodded and said to Lou, "If that's the way it is, that's the way it is. Fuck it. I'm going to retire. I don't want any more blood on my hands."

Lou nodded. He looked like a slug on a leaf. "Good, good. I'll talk to Vito."

"The family's got to get past all this bullshit, you know?"

"I hear ya."

"Get back to making some fucking money."

"I hear that."

"Good. Talk to Vito. Let's work something out."

———————

Eddie's guy Willie was leaning against the car smoking a cigarette, watching the girls go by. Willie saw us coming, ground out the cigarette with the heel of his shoe, and then got behind the wheel.

Beside me Tommy's shoulders slumped. "You see that, Jack? He didn't even open the door for us."

"We don't sign his paycheques."

"Just last month I had it all. Now I've got … what?"

I turned to Tommy and grinned. "Your life."

CHAPTER 46

Back to the safe house. Willie zigzagged through traffic, shaking off any tails. Tommy was uncustomarily quiet as we walked into the kitchen.

Eddie looked up from the *Globe and Mail*. "How'd it go?"

I shrugged. "Time will tell."

Tommy was shaking his head. "It's bullshit. Fucking bullshit."

"Be cool, Tommy."

"What am I supposed to do, just sit here with my thumb up my ass waiting for Lou's call? Fuck that. We've got to get proactive. Come on, Jack … let's go get my fucking money."

I laughed. "You know what I like about you, Tommy? You're focused."

"Damn right I'm focused."

"You're like a laser beam."

"Damn right! Now come on. Do you want to get paid or not?"

I closed my eyes and the house in the country was right there. I could smell the lilacs and the freshly cut grass.

Eddie folded his newspaper. "You need any help?"

Tommy scowled. "No, we don't need any fucking help! Just get us a fast car and a bag of guns. Jack can do the rest."

Eddie stared at me over the top of his sunglasses. He raised his eyebrow. I shot him a smile. "No worries, Eddie. We can handle it."

"You know, the whole point of having a safe house is that you hunker down and sit tight." Eddie turned and rattled off rapid-fire Cantonese. Willie The Driver leapt for the stove and stirred the simmering sauce.

Tommy nodded. "Yeah. What can I say? When you're right, you're right. But that rat-ass Vito is out there pilfering my daddy's lockboxes right this instant. If Jack and I don't get out there, all my money is going to be long gone." Tommy grinned at me. "And who knows? Maybe we'll run into Vito. Kill two birds with one stone."

Yeah. Or maybe Vito will run into us.

Eddie, without saying a word, tossed me the car keys.

Tommy slid into the passenger seat. I adjusted the rear-view mirror and fired the engine. "Where to? Your dad's Wychwood House?"

"Nope. Lou says that place is off limits. He claims my dad left that house to some out-of-town bigwig. Some guy from New Jersey. That's fine by me. I'm not fucking bitter. Jersey Boy can have it all. When did I ever spend any time there? That was my dad's hideaway, his refuge from the rest of us. I was never allowed to go anywhere near that house. FUCK THAT HOUSE! FUCK! FUCK!" Tommy punched the dashboard and then shook his hand, wincing.

"Tommy ... you can't beat up a car."

"Fuck you, Jack. I'll beat up whatever the fuck I want."

That attitude is going to get you killed. That's what I wanted to say. Instead I kept my big mouth shut and cranked the wheel. The car slid smoothly into traffic.

The car slipped through quiet residential streets, past tiny 1940s bungalows. Tommy pointed. "Turn left here. Left! Yeah, that's it. Now up ahead take another left."

I turned the wheel. Tommy peered through the window. "My dad bought a little house in this neighbourhood just after the war. When he moved out, he rented the place. Never could bring himself to sell ..." Tommy trailed off. Ahead of us was a construction site, filling the windshield.

"Is that the place?"

"FUCK ME!"

Before I could stop him, Tommy was out of the car and running toward the construction site.

"WHAT THE FUCK? WHAT THE FUCK IS THIS?"

A burly man with a wraparound moustache and a hard hat stepped in front of Tommy. "Sir ... you can't be here."

"Can't be here? Can't be here? This was my father's house! What the fuck did you do?" Tommy ducked and dodged around the construction worker, ran into the wooden frame and fell to his knees on the freshly-hardened concrete. "No, no, no!"

The construction worker had one hand on his cell-phone. I took a step forward, a dopey smile plastered across my face. "Sorry about this, sir. My name is Steve and that's Earl. I'm Earl's social worker. He ... well, a few years ago his childhood home burned down. He's had a problem with construction sites ever since."

The construction worker was none too impressed. "He can't be here, and neither can you. It's not safe."

"Understood. Sorry again. I'll get him out of here. Sorry."

Tommy was scratching his nails across the concrete. I hauled him up by the scruff of his neck like a momma cat. "We've got to go."

"It's under there, Jack! I swear to God!"

"Forget it. It's gone."

I led Tommy back to the car. I gave the construction worker another dopey smile and a wave before I slammed the door and fired up the engine. Beside me Tommy straightened up and smiled. "All right. So that didn't work out. Don't you worry, Jack. There's plenty of money out there."

"Right." Somewhere out there was an Early Bird hopping and whistling down the sidewalk, a jaunty top hat perched upon his head, a bag of Tommy's money thrown carelessly over his shoulder. Did the Early Bird get it all?

"No, seriously. I'm telling you, Jack. My dad had cash stashed all over this city. What I said to Lou about retiring ... I was serious. I've seen the light, Jack. Help me get out of here and I'll make it worth your while."

"Sure, Tommy."

Did I believe him? I wanted to believe, but the man was making it difficult. Did Tommy's dad stash cash? Of that I had no doubt. Was any of that money left? Possibly. More likely it had all been hoovered up by Vito and the rest of the jackals.

Still, Tommy's dad had connections. Say the money was gone. Maybe, just maybe, Tommy could get one of his dad's old friends to loan him some Escape Cash. And then there was the matter of that canvas bag Tommy took from the club. There was money in there, huge wads of it, tied up in rubber bands. How much? Enough for a down payment on my place in the country. Rocking chair on the porch. Drinking lemonade and watching the world go by. Red, red robins going bob bob bobbin' along.

What would The Chief have done? I'll tell you what The Chief would have done. He'd have said, "Enough is enough." He'd turn to Tommy and demand his cash up front. If Tommy said no, he'd walk. That's it. Just turn his back and walk away. In fact, that's exactly what The Chief did.

Yeah, and where was he now? Dead, that's where. Cut down by Joey Economy, a.k.a. Joey Machine. Right? No one ever found The Chief's body. Maybe he faked the whole thing. Maybe he was sitting on a beach far, far away. It was crazy to think so, but these were crazy times. Deep down, though, I had a feeling The Chief was dead.

What would Grover do? There was no telling. Grover was unpredictable. The Random X Factor. He might work for Tommy just for the fun of it. Or he might shoot Tommy in the back of his head, take his money, and give it all to a homeless man. There was no way to know for sure.

Tommy settled back in the leather seat as traffic rushed past. "Well, let's head back to the house. What do you think Eddie's making for lunch?"

"He's not your personal chef, you know."

"Hey … I know that. Don't you think I'm grateful? I'm crazy grateful. I've got gratitude busting out all over. I owe you … I know that."

"You owe Eddie, too." Even as I said it my stomach sank a little. Five percent, ten percent, fifty percent — if there's no cake, it doesn't matter how you slice it.

"Hey, I'm good for it." Tommy grinned crookedly. "That was something else back at the club. Did you see those fuckers run after I threw that Molotov? Whooo-EE!"

I shook my head slightly and ground my teeth. My hands tightened around the steering wheel. What a fucking liar. I threw the Molotov, not him. Tommy had learned nothing. He was still lost in fantasy, playing cops and robbers.

Back at the house Eddie didn't look too pleased to see us. "Any luck?"

Tommy shook his head. "Nah. The entire house was gone. Someone tore it down. Don't worry … there's more out there. Do I smell spare ribs?"

Eddie looked over at me and I gave him a slight shrug. Eddie shuffled past me and muttered, "I can't stay closed down much longer, Jack. We're bleeding money."

At the stove Eddie served up BBQ pork spare ribs, white rice, and broccoli with black bean sauce. Tommy dove into the food like a man who's just been rescued from the desert. Eddie scowled and looked away.

I went up to the stove and served myself. I ate slower than Tommy, scraping every last scrap of meat from the bones. My fingers were sticky with sauce. I closed my eyes, and for a split-second, all was right in the world.

Tommy pushed away his plate, patted his belly, and groaned. "Goddamn, that was good. Eddie, you're some kind of genius."

I stood up and opened the refrigerator. "Anyone want a beer?"

Tommy shook his head. "Uh-uh. Not me. Got to stay focused. Well, maybe one beer."

Three beers later Tommy had a big smile on his face. Now was the time.

"Tommy … this house, this food, these beers … they're not free."

Tommy looked shocked. Or was that mock shock? "Jack! What are you saying? You know I'm good for it! I'm the man with the golden plan! There's cash stashed —"

"All over the city, yeah, I know. So here's what we're going to do. You pay Eddie and me now. Then you can replenish your supply from one of your dad's hidey-holes. Okay?"

"Well, I … see, the thing is … I don't have that much on me. We left the club so fast. I didn't have enough time to grab that much cash."

"How much did you grab, Tommy?"

Tommy opened his mouth but Eddie answered for him. "Fifty-one thousand, four hundred and eighty-three dollars."

A black cloud passed over Tommy's face. "You counted my money? You counted my fucking money?"

Eddie stood up and loomed over Tommy. "That's right." Eddie turned and shouted something in Cantonese. Willie The Driver ambled forward, opened a drawer and pulled out Tommy's money bag.

Tommy sat there, incredulous. "What the fuck? You fucking STOLE MY MONEY?"

I shook my head. "No one stole anything, Tommy."

Eddie nodded. "It's all there. You want to count it? Go ahead and count."

Tommy's chair scraped the linoleum as he jerked to his feet. "This is bullshit. BULLSHIT! I see your little shakedown scheme now, Jack. How could I have been so blind?"

"Shakedown?" *You little prick. I should've left you to die at the night club.* "No one's shaking you down, Tommy. We're working for you. But we don't work for free."

"Yeah, yeah. I know how it is. You're businessmen, right? Just like my father. Fucking businessmen." Tommy spat words like a cobra spitting venom.

Eddie pointed to Tommy. "Put the money on the table. My price is one hundred thousand. I'll need a twenty percent retainer."

"One hun! That's outrageous. That's highway robbery."

Tommy's twitching face was reflected in the cool gaze of Eddie's sunglasses. "You don't have to pay. You could just walk out that door. I won't stop you. Jack, will you stop him?"

"Eddie's right, Tommy. We won't stop you."

"A hundred thousand. A hundred thousand dollars."

"For Eddie. Plus the two hundred thousand for me."

Tommy groaned like he was just punched in the gut. "You're killing me. You're killing me, Jack."

"No. What we're doing is keeping you alive. If you want to walk, walk. Maybe your buddy Lou would take you in."

"That fat slug would slit my throat while I slept."

"Then I suggest you stay here. Good food, cable T.V., no throat slitting. How much is that worth to you?"

Tommy said nothing.

"Is your life worth three hundred thousand dollars?"

"You're a fucker, Jack. You know that? You guys are fucking me all the way to the bank."

Eddie pointed to the bag. "Put the money on the table."

Grumbling, Tommy did as he was told, stacking the cash in neat bundles. Eddie got twenty thousand. I got another twenty thousand. Tommy folded the last wad of cash into his front pocket.

"There! You happy now? Thanks to you clowns I'm down to my last eleven thou."

"Don't forget the four eighty-three."

"Fuck you."

CHAPTER 47

Walking around with twenty thousand bucks in your pocket could put a smile on your face, but it could also make you paranoid as fuck. I passed my stack across the kitchen table to Eddie.

"Hang onto this for me, will you?"

Eddie nodded. I didn't even see his hands move, but when I blinked the money was gone.

Twenty grand. Plus what was left from the money Eddie kept for me while I was in jail. That's enough for now, but I sure as shit can't retire on it.

Tommy had stormed off down the hallway and slammed the bedroom door. The only thing missing from his teenage-style sulk scene was heavy metal music blasting through the walls.

Eddie cocked his head. "Should I bring him back?"

"Nah. Leave him be. He feels ripped off now but after he's thought about it he'll realize it's a bargain."

Eddie grinned. "You think we'll ever see the rest of it?"

"Hard to say. Tommy's a born bullshitter."

"I don't like him, Jack."

"I don't blame you."

Eddie scraped back his chair. "You know, when I was just starting out in the business I met a guy like Tommy. He was full of sound and fury, all bluster and bullshit. I didn't want to work with him but he was connected, so there you go. 'Yeah, yeah, I'll pay you next week. Don't worry about it.' Then the next week would roll around and my wallet stayed empty. I expressed my concerns to my boss one day and he said not to worry, I'd get my money."

"Is this story going anywhere?"

"Point is, I got my money. But no one will ever see that guy again." Eddie's chair creaked. "What's the next move, Jack? We can't just sit here and wait for Grover or Little Vito to come gunning for us."

If I was a real smart guy I'd have a plan. Not just any plan, but a plan so intricate and fiendish it would make angels fall to their knees and weep. I'd arrange it so Little Vito would drive to an abandoned warehouse thinking Tommy and I were inside. Grover would be in the warehouse waiting for me. Then in a hail of bullets and confusion Little Vito and Grover would kill each other. Tommy would crack open one of his dad's treasure chests and pull out wads of loot and Eddie would clap me on the back and say, "Good job." Then Suzanne and I would ride off into the sunset on the back of a fucking unicorn.

"It's under control," I told Eddie. It was a small lie, teeny tiny and oh so lily white. I looked at Eddie smiling, how relieved he was. Poor bastard was losing tens of thousands a day as dust gathered on his gaming tables. Grover or no Grover, Little Vito or no Little Vito, Eddie was going to have to reopen his casino soon. He wasn't sitting in that dingy house for Tommy; he was doing it for me. Oh, I knew it. That creaking sound? That was my back buckling beneath all the responsibility. Save Tommy. Stop Grover. Stop Vito. Get Eddie back in business. Win back Suzanne's heart. "On second thought, let me hold that twenty grand after all."

Eddie squinted at me over his sunglasses. "You're not going to do something stupid, are you, Jack?"

"Who, me? Nah. I'm going to invest it wisely. Do they still sell Beanie Babies?"

Eddie grinned wryly and handed over my money.

I tilted my head toward Tommy's bedroom. "Keep an eye on our Problem Child. I might not be back tonight."

"You need any help? I could send Willie …"

"Tell Willie to go home and play with his kids or his model trains or whatever the fuck Willie does on his days off. Tonight I'm flying solo."

"Be careful, Jack."

I grinned. "Always."

Birds were singing as I strolled down the street. Marking territory, looking for mates. *I hear ya, birds.*

On the subway a bored-looking young woman was cutting her fingernails. The subway doors pinged open and she got up, leaving a pile of fingernail clippings on the seat next to her. I felt like grabbing her shoulders and slapping her, hard. "What the fuck is wrong with you? Do you think someone wants to sit down in a pile of your scrapings?" But no, she wasn't thinking about other people AT ALL. Selfish and stupid. Totally oblivious. As soon as she got off the subway, to her the subway no longer existed.

I went to school with people like her. Gum-smacking idiots. I overheard my ninth grade teacher, Mr. Mackintosh (what a putz that guy was — creases in his brand-new jeans, a blue pen stain on his shirtfront, and a heavy dusting of dandruff on his shoulders), explaining proudly to another teacher (Mrs. Judy, everyone called her — a big woman who wore dresses shaped like horse blankets) that he arranged his seating chart so the dumbest kids would be closest to his precious plants. That way, he explained, the kids would breathe out CO_2 for the plants and at least they'd be good for something.

My desk was next to the biggest plant in the classroom.

Man, fuck that prick. Fuckers like that shouldn't be teaching kids.

Back in Chinatown. Back to the hustle and bustle of the crowds and the drunks and the neon signs glowing against the sky. A drunk in a dirty coat shambled past me and puked in the gutter. I smiled. It was good to be home.

Suzanne's bar was a block away. My feet tingled as I walked closer. I knew how this should play out. I should have slicked back my hair and put on my best suit and bought a bouquet of flowers and a box of candy. I should compose achingly beautiful love songs on a fucking lute and play them outside her bedroom window. I should get down on one knee and pull out a box containing a diamond big enough to choke a horse.

I didn't have a diamond, flowers, a lute, or a suit. Luckily for me the liquor store was still open.

Outside Suzanne's bar I squared my shoulders and took a deep breath. *All right, boyo. This is it. Once more unto the breach.*

Inside I squinted through the murk. It was the usual crowd: stumblebums and drunks and hipsters. A tall man wearing serious glasses stared intently at the jukebox. A table full of girls broke out into shrieks of laughter. An old man with a face like discarded lunch meat lurched by, a piss stain running down his leg. I walked by two fresh-faced university guys who looked like they were about twelve years old. "I love this place," one of them said to the other. "It's so Authentic."

Ah, well. In another year or so the students and hipsters would be gone, roaming the streets searching for their next Authentic Fix.

Where the hell was Suzanne? Chris, the other bartender, was right where he should be: behind the bar pouring out a shot of Jack. Suzanne was nowhere to be seen, so fuck it, might as well flee this scene and … oh wait, there she was, walking back to the bar with a tray full of empty glasses.

She scowled when she saw me. My fucking heart dropped into my boot. *Dangerous, Jack. She has her hooks in you.*

Yeah, yeah. I know. I should be a lone samurai on a mountaintop, practising my sword moves as the sun comes up. Totally alone. Forever.

Screw that action. I used to think that way, back when I was younger, but I didn't anymore. It's all about connection. You think you're alone? There are billions of people on this rock orbiting the sun. Billions and billions. Like it or not, we're all connected. We're All In This Together.

"Suzanne."

"What are you doing here?"

"I need to talk to you."

"I'm working."

"This will only take a minute."

Suzanne glared into my eyes, and she must have seen something there, because her anger drained away and she sighed.

"All right. Just for a minute."

I followed her into the back office. Stacks of empties lined the walls. A sad scarred desk sat in the corner, piled with papers and one of those giant calculators that old people use when they start to go blind.

"I brought you this." I handed Suzanne the bottle of red wine.

"Thanks."

She let me take her hand. "Suzanne, I'm sorry. I didn't mean for you to be dragged into all of this. I'm not going to stand here and bullshit you. I'm not going to pretend everything is hunky-dory, peaches and cream. It's not. Things are fucked up, but the end is in sight. No, wait … I know, I know, I've been saying that for weeks.

But it's true. Tommy paid me off. Look." Suzanne cocked her eyebrow as I pulled out the thick wad of bills. "Soon Tommy will be on a plane heading south. Beaches and hammocks, bikinis and rum punch. As soon as that plane takes off, you and I are free. We'll leave all the crap behind us. A fresh start. You and me, together."

Suzanne didn't say anything. She leaned against the desk and stared past me toward the door. "Jack. Remember back on the roof? You said you loved me. Is that still true? Do you really love me?"

"I want to be with you. I want to wake up every morning and have you next to me."

"But do you love me?"

I stared down at the floor. "I don't know what love is."

Suzanne stepped closer. "It would have been easy to lie. To say, 'Yes, Suzanne, I love you more than anything. I love you like the river loves the sea.' But you told the truth."

"Yeah. As horrifying and sad as that is."

Suzanne smiled and wrapped her arms around me. She smelled so good, like warm vanilla cookies. "I don't know what love is, either."

We stared into each other's eyes. I smiled. "Maybe together we can figure it out."

CHAPTER 48

Outside the bar I was grinning like a fool. Suzanne's words were ringing in my ears: "Come back when I get off work. You can walk me home." It was tempting to stay and wait at the bar. Have a few drinks, a few laughs, and watch Suzanne work. Her cheeks getting flushed as she rushed back and forth, stopping to exhale and push a stray piece of hair off her sweaty forehead. Instead I borrowed a page from the comedians and left on a high note.

Were they waiting for me here in the old neighbourhood? Were there assassins lurking in every alley, behind every trash can? I shouldn't have been walking these streets, but it felt so good to be back. I had only been away a few days, but it felt like forever. My feet took me home, tromping along the gum-encrusted sidewalks to suddenly stop and stand across the street from Eddie's restaurant. My eyes gravitated toward the roof. The asphalt beach. How many nights had Eddie and I sat up there, beers in hand, chewing the fat and solving the problems of the world? Plenty of nights spent smiling under the stars, high above the hustle and bustle of the city. *Don't worry, Eddie. I'll work this out. You'll be home soon.*

A shadow flickered alongside me and I tensed — this is it — but no, no assassin, just two young lovers out for an evening stroll. *Don't walk up behind me like that, kids.*

I had about six hours to kill. I got back on the streetcar and zipped up Spadina to the subway station. The subway rumbled westward and I emerged into the open air of High Park — flowers and squirrels and trees. Two flight attendants strolled by laughing, the wheels on their rollie bags click-clacking along the sidewalk. I shot them a smile as they passed and they smiled back. Yessir, love was in the air.

My stomach rumbled. I ducked into a burger joint that had thatched beach-style umbrellas over the patio out front and perused the menu. This place had about thirty-six different burgers, and right now I felt like I could eat them all. Exotic burgers weren't really my scene — Mango? Peanut butter? Chutney? — so when the ponytailed server came to take my order, I told her "straight up burger — beef, mustard, pickle, onion."

"You want sweet potato fries with that?"

"Onion rings."

The burger was fucking delicious. No one knew me in this part of the city. I was just another solitary man eating a burger, safe from the hit men and assassins prowling outside my usual haunts. Still, I sat facing the door with my back to the wall. Old habits die hard.

After dinner I found a bar, ordered a beer, and drank it slow. Two tables over, a group of grizzled old men in thick plaid shirts were arguing, their voices hoarse and booze-cracked. That would be me someday. If I made it that far. Shuffling from rented room to the bar and back again. Staring at cracks in the wall, waiting for the phone to ring.

Or maybe not. Hey, you never know. Maybe I'd be sitting sprawled out on an overstuffed easy chair before a roaring fire, grey-haired Suzanne knitting next to me, grandkids and cats tumbling together at our feet. Why the hell not? It could happen.

Hours flew by. Time to head back. *Don't blow it, Jack.*

Chris, the other bartender, blocked the door as I tried to enter. "Sorry — we're closed."

Behind him Suzanne saw me and smiled. "It's okay, Chris. He's with me."

Chris squinted at me and then the slow dawning of recognition spread across his face. "Jack! Sorry, man. It's been a long night."

"Don't worry about it." I stepped into the bar, breathing in the stench of stale beer and smoke. Even though smoking was no longer allowed, the place still smelled like cigarettes.

Chris buttoned up his coat. "You okay to finish closing up?"

Suzanne smiled and nodded. "No problem. See you tomorrow."

Then Chris headed out, the door clicking shut, and Suzanne and I were together again.

Lips met lips. Bodies slammed together. Hungry hands roamed. Suzanne bit my lip and I bit hers. I slammed her against the bar and started to yank down her pants.

"Not here." She took me by the hand and led me to the back room. My pants were gone in two seconds, hers in three. My eyes roamed across her milky-white body. My penis jutted up in my boxers like an exclamation point.

"Goddamn, I've missed you."

"Shut up and fuck me."

Don't have to tell me twice.

I pushed her onto the desk, peeled off her lacy red panties, and spread her legs apart. She was hot and wet and ready. I entered her quickly, pushing all the way in. She gasped and bit her lip. She felt good, so good.

"Do it … do it …"

Yes. I plowed into her, fast and hard, trying to jam every inch of myself deep into her body. She writhed across the desk, shrieking with pleasure. More — faster — harder — yes. Yes. YES!

I came so hard I saw stars. Everything went white and then black and then I was lying across her body, our chests heaving, our sweat mingling. At the same time we both broke out laughing, laughing, laughing and we couldn't stop.

CHAPTER 49

We disentangled our limbs and Suzanne pulled up her red panties. Grinning, we gathered up our clothes and got dressed.

"Are you coming over to my place tonight?"

"Is that an invitation?"

Suzanne gave me a playful swat. "You know it is."

"In that case, I accept."

The country house, the grandkids, the roaring fire. Yes. Smiling, we left the back room and stepped back into the bar.

"Hello, Jack."

I froze. There at the end of the bar was Grover, his white suit glowing beneath the bar's yellow lights.

I stepped in front of Suzanne. "Suzanne. Back door. NOW."

Grover smiled and gave his head a shake. "Stick around, Suzanne. Pour Jack a drink." In front of Grover was a glass of Scotch. His left hand was on the bar next to his drink. His right hand was hidden beneath the bar.

I took two quick steps forward and Grover held up his left hand. "That's close enough, Jack. Have a seat right over there."

"No thanks."

"I really think you should. Come on, Jack. Grab a seat and have a drink with me." Grover smiled his crocodile smile at Suzanne and I almost threw up. Slowly I lowered myself into a chair.

"Good! Now what'll it be?"

I nodded to Suzanne. "I'll have what he's having."

Grover grinned. "Excellent choice."

Suzanne poured me a Scotch. Grover kept grinning. "Let's all relax. We're all friends here."

I didn't buy it for a minute. *What's he got under the bar?* A gun. Some kind of gun.

I tilted my chin toward Grover's face. "How'd you get that cut over your eye?"

Grover nodded. "I'm glad you asked. Funny thing … Joey Machine's brother was waiting for me in Kansas City. He had a whole crew. Sure, they were old, but you have to respect the old-timers. They put up one hell of a fight." Grover stopped talking and stared over at me. "It's almost as if they knew I was coming."

The bar's overhead light shimmered in my Scotch. The ice tumbled and began to melt, golden and beautiful. "I called the brother. I told him to run."

Grover smiled crookedly. "He should have listened."

"So he was a gangster?"

"What did I tell you, Jack? The Chief was right. We're all gangsters."

Grover started to raise his right hand above the bar. I tensed, ready to charge.

His hand was empty. "Jack, relax! Relax. As soon as I got down there I knew you had tipped them off. I don't blame you. You were trying to do the right thing. I love you for that."

"You didn't love me so much back on the boat."

A shrug of his white-suited shoulders. "That was a little misunderstanding. Could've happened to anyone."

"Sure, Grover. What's a little machine-gunning between friends?"

"Look, Jack. You were right."

"What?"

"Back at the boat. You were right. The Chief is dead. Joey Machine is dead. I should've let it go."

"What?"

Grover laughed. "You sound like a broken record, Jack. I came here tonight to apologize. You were right and I was wrong." The little man shrugged again. "These things happen."

Suzanne's hand was slowly drifting toward an icepick. I glanced over at her and shook my head no.

Grover followed my gaze and chuckled. "She's feisty, Jack. Gotta love that."

Suzanne's face went dark. For a split second I was convinced she was about to jab the icepick right through Grover's eye. Instead she said, "Feisty? That's something you say about a Jack Russell terrier. Also, I'm right fucking here. Don't talk to Jack about me like I'm not even in the room."

Grover blinked. *Oh shit*, I thought. Grover sipped

his Scotch and nodded. "You know what? You're right. That was rude. I'm sorry, Suzanne." Grover tilted his chin toward the icepick. "You're protecting your friend. I can relate. Still … let's keep things friendly, shall we?" Grover grinned. Suzanne swallowed hard and stepped back, away from the icepick.

Grover turned back toward me. "You didn't disappoint me after all, Jack. You told the truth. Killing Joey Machine's brother didn't bring back The Chief. It didn't make me feel any better. Well … it might've made me feel a *little* better. Those old guys, boy, I tell ya. It's been a while since I've had a workout like that."

Grover stood up and drained his Scotch. He approached me slowly, his hands in plain sight. "Jack. I forgive you. Do you forgive me?"

I stood up, too. "Sure."

Grover shook his head. "You're just saying that. You're not buying what I'm selling, but I'm serious over here. Look, let me make it up to you. You still working for Tommy?"

"For now, yeah."

"All right. I can help you with that. Little Vito is furious, Jack. Word is he's going to have you killed."

"Yeah. I've heard that."

"Well, let me work something out. I know these guys, Jack. I'll make a few calls. Don't you worry about a thing."

And just like that Grover spun on his heel and marched out the door.

Suzanne grabbed hold of the bar. I rushed over and wrapped her in my arms. Her heart was thumping hummingbird-fast. She pressed her body next to mine and we held each other tight, tight, tight.

CHAPTER 50

Outside the safe house Willie The Driver was sitting on the concrete porch smoking a cigarette and reading the *Toronto Sun*. He glanced up, saw me coming, and smiled.

"How are you doing, Willie?"

Willie shrugged. I knew how he felt.

Inside the house Eddie and Tommy were playing Xbox. They both looked up from their controllers as I came grinning into the room. "Good news, Eddie. Your long exile is over."

"Are you saying I can go back to work?"

"Yep. That's exactly what I'm saying."

Tommy leapt to his feet. "That's fucking great! You shot him, right? You shot Vito right in his fat motherfucking head!"

"Nope." I laid it all out for Eddie and Tommy: Grover, the bar, Grover's offer. By the time I was finished Tommy was glowering and shaking his head.

"I don't like it. It's a set-up."

Eddie looked over at me and frowned. "You think Grover's legit?"

"Maybe. We'll see. But here's something I do know: he's not going to come gunning for you to try to hurt me." I grinned. "So it looks like you're back in business."

Eddie grinned and clapped me on the shoulder. "This calls for a beer. Want one?"

Tommy shouted after us as we headed toward the kitchen. "Wait a sec, wait a sec! What about me?"

"What about you?"

"You think Little Vito is just going to let me skate? Uh-uh. No fucking way."

"Look. Give Grover a chance. He says he can work something out. Maybe it's true."

"Maybe? Fucking maybe? This is my neck on the chopping block here! There's only one way out of this, Jack. You find Little Vito and you put a bullet in his brain."

I shook my head. "You know I don't work like that."

"Yeah, well … maybe you should. Because if you think Vito's gonna let you just waltz away into the sunset, you're sadly mistaken."

Maybe Tommy was right. Maybe I was living in a fool's paradise. Did I trust Grover? Hell no. But right now he was my best bet.

"Let Grover do his thing. Who knows? This time next week you could be sitting on a beach in Costa Rica, drinking a margarita and working on your tan."

Tommy shut up. Behind his eyes I could see his mind spinning with possibilities.

Eddie handed out the beer. I started to raise the bottle to my lips but Eddie caught my hand. "We need a toast."

"Oh yeah? What to?"

Eddie grinned. "To freedom."

The three of us clinked bottles. "Freedom!"

Laughing, we drank our beers.

CHAPTER 51

Damn, it felt so good to relax. Eddie and I were kicking back on the roof of his building, sipping Scotch and shooting the shit. Returned to the asphalt beach. Above us a handful of stars were shining bright enough to cut through the haze of the city lights. I leaned back in my lawn chair and smiled. Little Vito was still out there somewhere sharpening his knives, but I'd put my own knives against his any day of the week.

I threw twenty grand into Eddie's lap.

"Put that back in the bank for me."

Eddie's hand flickered and the money was gone.

"Hey, Jack."

"Yeah?"

"You think we'll see any of the rest Tommy owes us?"

Tommy was still hunkered down at the safe house. At least, that was where he was supposed to be. Knowing Tommy, he was out on the town, drunk out of his mind and looking to get laid.

"Hard to say."

Eddie raised his glass to his lips and took a sip. "I had a thought the other day."

"Keep drinking. That'll fix it."

"Seriously, Jack. Tommy's caused us nothing but grief. I was thinking — just hear me out, now — say we hand him over to Vito."

I shook my head. "Not going to happen."

"Just hear me out. We hand him over to Vito in exchange for a big chunk of cash. Then it's over — really over. Vito's got what he wants, we get paid, and Tommy's out of your hair forever."

"Eddie. You know we can't do that."

Eddie nodded and grinned ruefully. "Yeah. I know. But wouldn't it be sweet?"

Behind us, gravel crunched. We both leapt to our feet, Eddie's hand ducking into his jacket, the knife already in my hand. Grover stood grinning over by the door leading downstairs.

"Evening, gentlemen. Sorry to startle you. Jack, I've got good news."

Eddie frowned. "How the hell did you get up here?"

Grover kept grinning. "Magic. Jack, how much has Tommy paid you?"

"Twenty grand."

"That's peanuts. He's holding out on you."

"I know it."

"He's got money stashed all over the city."

"That's what he says."

"It's true. You think he was going to pop open his treasure chest for you? He's planning to disappear."

"I know that, too. It was my idea."

"Oh yeah? Your idea, huh? You think so? I say he's been planning this from the start."

Eddie shook his head. "You think he's smart enough for something like that?"

"I watched Tommy grow up. Every day I saw someone underestimate him. Most of them are dead now. I'd hate to see you two make that same mistake."

The cool nighttime breeze ruffled my hair. In the distance the lights of the CN Tower winked and blinked. "Grover. You said you've got good news."

"Yep. It's all worked out."

"Say what?"

"I had dinner with some guys last night and we worked it out. Little Vito's not happy, but if he wants to keep his bosses happy, he'll do as he's told."

"So what's the plan?"

Grover, Eddie, and I huddled together like football players. Up close Grover smelled like talcum powder and old leather. "All right. It's your basic payoff. Little Vito's agreed to eight hundred thousand."

"That's a lot of lettuce."

"Lou talked him down from a million. Tommy brings the money to Lou and then continues on to parts unknown. Lou takes his cut and gives the money to Vito. Vito gives some of the money to the families of the men killed when Tommy's club burned down and pockets the rest. Vito's the boss, Tommy's out of the picture, everyone's happy. Do you forgive me now, Jack?"

My brow wrinkled. "So where do I come in?"

"Simple. You help Tommy get the money."

"And then Little Vito and I are square?"

"That's right."

"And Eddie and I … what's our cut?"

"You get no cut. I know, I know. But you get to live."

I looked over at Eddie. He nodded. I nodded back. "We'll take it."

I walked up Spadina toward Kensington Market. There was a light on in Suzanne's window. I called her from a payphone, walked back to her place, and rang the buzzer.

She opened the door and she looked beautiful. Dark hair sleep-tousled, one hand holding closed a short white robe. We hugged, kissed, and headed upstairs.

I padded across the living room shag in my stocking feet while I filled Suzanne in.

"So that's the situation. We've got twenty grand, but that's all we've got."

Suzanne shook her head and smiled. "I don't care about the money. What's money? As long as we're alive, we can make more money." She leaned toward me. I went in for the kiss.

The windows exploded. I grabbed Suzanne and dove for the floor as bullets whined through the air and punched into the walls.

"Stay down."

"Jack —"

"STAY DOWN!"

I army-crawled toward the shattered windows. A black Cadillac roared off down the street and squealed around a corner. I leapt to my feet and brushed glass from my pants.

Then I stopped dead in my tracks.

Suzanne was lying on the floor clutching her arm, her blood soaking the shag.

"Jack …"

"You're going to be okay, you're going to be okay." I willed my voice to be calm as I tied the tourniquet. Inside I was raging.

Suzanne's teeth chattered as she went into shock.

I tossed a paisley blanket on top of her. "I'll be right back."

"Don't go.

"Just sit tight. Don't move. You're going to be okay."

"They could come back."

"No. Whoever was in that car, they won't be back tonight."

"But they could come back." Suzanne thrust out her jaw. "Get me my gun."

"I'll be back, okay? Just sit tight."

Suzanne reached out and caught my leg with her good hand. "My gun."

I didn't want to argue. I gave her the gun. She cradled it to her chest like a teddy bear.

I left her there wrapped in a blanket clutching her gun. I plowed through Kensington Market, pushing past shocked hippies with guitars and Jamaican fishmongers. A crowd was gathering, pointing up toward Suzanne's shot-out windows.

On College Street I stopped at a payphone in front of a convenience store.

"Eddie. I need your help. NOW."

———

Grim-faced, Eddie drove us to Doc Warner's. She was a good doctor and she didn't ask questions. She had a modern sterilized office on Bloor Street atop a travel agency and next door to a massage parlour. Doc had a legitimate practice: botox mostly. Getting rich by feeding off other women's insecurities. She didn't see it that way. "I'm helping people look their best. A little confidence goes a long way."

Who knew there'd be big bucks in pumping would-be socialites' lips full of botulism toxin?

Doc found a vein and set up her morphine bag. Suzanne was sweating, her eyes rolling back. "She's in shock, Doc."

"Here." Doc Warner threw me another blanket. I wrapped it around Suzanne's trembling body.

Suzanne's hand clenched mine. I sat grimly staring as Doc Warner cut into Suzanne's flesh and probed for the bullet. Blood bubbled around the wound. Suzanne gasped. "You're doing great, baby." In my mind I had Suzanne's shooter cornered in an alley. He whimpered like a dog as I closed in.

We took Suzanne to Eddie's aunt's, and then Eddie drove me back to the safe house. Along the way I told him what I knew, and after that we didn't say anything.

At the safe house I practically kicked down the door. In the hallway Willie leapt to his feet, a gun in his hand. He saw me and looked wary. Then he spotted Eddie, smiled, and holstered his gun.

"Where's Tommy?"

Willie pointed down the hallway toward the bedroom. I stomped down the hallway and smashed open the bedroom door.

Tommy jerked awake and lunged for the gun on the nightstand. I swept the gun onto the floor and yanked Tommy, screaming, out of bed. I slapped him twice, hard. "Shut the fuck up!"

"Jack?"

"No, it's the fucking Tooth Fairy. Get dressed."

"What the fuck? What's going on?"

"You and I are going fishing."

"What?"

"Eight hundred thousand, Tommy. We're going to get that money right fucking now."

"Eight —? What?"

I slapped him again, hard. "I said GET FUCKING DRESSED!"

Tommy sulkily scooped up his pants. "So that's it, Jack. You're ripping me off. And after all I've done for you."

My fists clenched. It took every ounce of willpower I had not to shove Tommy's head right through the fucking wall.

"It's not for me, it's for Vito. It's your fucking exit fee. Don't say anything. That's the price, end of story."

"This is bullshit."

I punched Tommy in the face and he went down, sprawled across the bed. He looked up at me towering over him, blood dripping from his mouth, eyes wide with fear.

"You think that's bullshit? Do you? I'll tell you what's fucking bullshit. Having to bail you out, again and again. Because of you Suzanne almost died. That's right, she got shot tonight. She almost fucking died." I hauled Tommy up and shoved him toward the door. "Let's go."

———

In the passenger seat Tommy touched his swollen lip. "You shouldn't have hit me, Jack."

In the back seat I didn't say anything. He was right. I lost my cool. In my line of work, if you lose your temper, you could end up dead.

Eddie stared through his sunglasses straight ahead, through the windshield. "Where to?"

Tommy sulked. "I don't know. Why should I trust you guys? You've been trying to shake money out of me all week."

For fuck's sake. I leaned forward and hissed, "I'm through playing games. From now on we're playing by my rules. Here's how it works: you tell us where the money is. We go get the money. We give the money to Little Vito, then you hop on a plane to parts unknown. That's it — end of story."

Tommy twisted and fidgeted. "Yeah, well … it's not that easy, you know? All that money … it's invested, you know? It's tied up. Operating capital and what-not. That cash greases the skids of a lot of operations. There's going to be plenty of people pissed off to see that money disappear."

"You let me worry about that." I wanted to reach forward and slice Tommy's throat. I wanted to push his bleeding, bleating body out of this moving car and into a trash-strewn ravine. "As you might recall, I'm pretty shit-hot when it comes to collections. Now answer Eddie's question."

Tommy tried another tack. "Jack. Jack. I'm sorry. Why are you talking to me like this? I didn't shoot your girlfriend. Come on, man ... I thought we were friends."

"Answer Eddie's question."

Tommy slumped back in his seat. "Turn left."

We drove and kept driving, heading north and then west. Portuguese bakeries appeared outside my window. A group of kids loitered outside a KFC. A stumpy old woman dressed all in black limped along the sidewalk.

Tommy pointed. "Stop here."

"Here?" Eddie pulled over and reached for the ignition. I reached forward and stopped his hand.

"Keep it running."

I stepped out of the car and stood in front of a rundown pool hall with blacked-out windows. A hand-lettered sign pinned to the door read MEMBERS ONLY. I popped open Tommy's door. "Come on ... get out."

Tommy looked nervous. "Yeah, uh ... you know, Jack, maybe you should handle this."

"Don't you worry. I'm going to fucking handle it. Now quit dicking around and get out of the car."

At the door I knocked three times. The peephole slid open.

"Yeah?"

I pushed Tommy forward. "Talk."

"It's Tommy. Come on, open up."

The eye in the peephole darted left and right. Deadbolts clanked and the door creaked open.

Inside, the pool hall was murky and dark. Shapes came into focus as my eyes adjusted. Directly in front of us was a long, tall man with a fedora and a trim goatee. Behind him were three pool tables and a long mahogany bar. A group of three men holding pool cues stood mutely around one of the tables.

Goatee jerked his chin at me. "Who's this guy?"

"That's Jack. He's my bodyguard."

Goatee leaned closer, staring at Tommy's busted lip. "Doesn't look like he's doing a very good job."

"This? Naw, naw. It's fine, it's nothing. I fell down. Don't worry about it. Tomasso around?"

Goatee nodded and tilted his head. "In the back."

Tommy and I walked into the murk. The three toughs playing pool stared at us as we passed.

At the back of the club was a brown door. Tommy knocked twice and then twice more. A muffled voice shouted out, "Come on in!"

This place was a study of contrasts. The pool hall was murky and grim, but this room was well-lit and comfortable. Framed prints hung on the red-orange walls. A plush black leather couch sat facing two black leather easy chairs. Classical music was playing from hidden speakers. A big man with silver hair rose smiling from behind a massive oak desk.

"Tommy! How are you, my friend?" The big man was wearing a charcoal-grey sport jacket and slacks. His shoes were buffed to a fine sheen. His fingernails were manicured. Impeccable. Probably had a humidor full of imported cigars and a cellar full of vintage wine.

Tommy and the big man kissed each other's cheeks. Tommy gestured to me. "Tomasso, this is my bodyguard Jack."

The big man's hand squeezed mine like he was crushing walnuts. "Jack. So good to meet you." Tomasso turned back toward Tommy. "Enrique didn't offer you a drink?" Tomasso tsk-tsked. "A glass of wine? A nice port?"

"Forget it, T. This is a business call."

"Of course, of course." Tomasso ushered us toward the easy chairs and then took a seat on the couch. "What can we do for you today?"

Tommy hunkered down in one of the easy chairs and then leaned forward intently. "T, you know me. I've never been a bullshitter. Am I right?"

"This is true."

"Well, I'm not going to bullshit you now. I need money, and lots of it."

Tomasso laughed. "A common problem."

"Yeah, well … it's your problem now."

The big man frowned. "Forgive me. I'm not sure I understand."

"We've sunk a lot of dough into your operation over the years. Now it's time to pay us back."

Tomasso shook his head. "Tommy, Tommy … this is highly unorthodox. Your father —"

"Never mind my father. My father is dead."

"And we were sorry to hear about your loss. Still, there are ways of doing business."

Tommy nodded. "Yeah." Suddenly there was a gun in his hand. "Here's one of them."

Tomasso sat in shock, frozen on the couch. Finally he shook his head. "They said you were having problems … I never realized it was so bad."

Tommy jabbed the gun forward. "Who? Who said that? Fuckin' liars. Now open the safe."

Behind Tommy's chair I was standing with one eye on Tommy and another on Tomasso. Once again Tommy had blindsided me. Where the fuck did he get that gun?

Tomasso frowned. "This is bad, Tommy. Very bad."

"It's gonna get a lot worse if you don't open that safe. Help him up, Jack."

I did it. So help me, I strode over to Tomasso and hauled him to his feet. The big man was solid, muscular. He smelled like oranges.

Tomasso wouldn't shut up. "Think about what you're doing. This is madness."

I slapped his sunglasses across the room, punched him in the belly and hauled him toward the safe.

"Open it."

"You don't know who you're dealing with."

I smashed his face into the squat grey safe. Tomasso moaned.

"Open it."

Tommy stepped forward, sneering behind his gun. "I'll take it from here. Why don't you go play a little pool?"

Yeah. I let the big man drop and slipped out the door.

Goatee was waiting for me. "Everything all right in there?"

"Yeah, sure." I cocked my head over to one of the pool tables. "How about a game?" I picked out a pool cue, checked the heft, and started to chalk the tip.

Goatee frowned. "What did you say your name was?"

I brought the pool cue down on Goatee's head. He went down hard, banging his face off the edge of the pool table. Instantly the three toughs closed in. One of them, short and squat like a bulldog, charged forward. I slammed the butt of the pool cue into his stomach and then struck upward, smashing his chin. The other two circled, holding their cues like swords. I grinned and beckoned them closer.

Wood met flesh. Blood and teeth and bits of scalp splattered the walls. Pool cues clattered to the floor. I threw my own splintered cue onto the ground next to the four unconscious men.

"The name's Jack," I told them. "Jack Palace."

Back in the back room I half expected to see Tommy shot through the head, but no, the situation was under control. Tomasso was on his knees, pulling banded stacks of dirty twenties and hundreds from the safe and piling them into a red duffel bag. Tomasso talked as he worked, his voice low and reassuring.

"People make mistakes. I understand. You're lucky it's me and not one of my brothers. Me, I'm the forgiving sort. I understand your situation. Desperate people do desperate things. But there are other ways we can deal with this. We —"

I strode over and kicked Tomasso in the face. "Shut up."

Tomasso shut up.

Tommy crouched down and zipped up the duffel bag. Tomasso crouched on the floor of his office, hands clutching his broken jaw. Tommy shouted, "You see?

You see what happens? You should've just given me the fucking money!" Tommy raised the gun. I had just enough time to shout "No!" before the gun went off.

Back in the car Tommy was zinging, hopped up on adrenalin and death. "Did you see the look in that fucker's eyes? Ha ha ha!"

I felt sick. There was a grey blob of Tomasso's brain stuck on the tip of my shoe. I pointed straight ahead into the night. "Drive."

Eddie gunned the engine and the car slid forward. He didn't say anything and neither did I. Tommy kept crowing. He was the greatest, he was the toughest, nobody better fuck with him. Just to change the subject, I said "Where to next?" All I wanted to do was go back to the office, drink four or five ice-cold beers, and have a long, hot shower.

Tommy laughed. "Yeah! Next! Next we go get some more motherfucking money and shoot some more motherfucking people. That's the way to do it, eh, Jack?"

"You didn't have to shoot him, Tommy."

"Bullshit! You think I want that guy coming after us? Fuck him and his whole operation. Come on, Jack … I thought you'd be proud of me. We got the money, didn't we?"

"How much?"

Tommy peered into the bag. "Looks like a hundred grand, more or less."

"We need more."

Tommy grinned. He looked like a gargoyle. "That's what I'm talking about! Bang bang, stick 'em up!"

Jesus fucking Christ. I couldn't do this.

"Eddie."

"Yeah?"

"Who's that guy who keeps bugging you for more jobs?"

"Who, my cousin Eric?"

"Yeah. Give him a call. Tell him it's his lucky fucking day."

Tommy chattered away in the front seat. I peeled a Kleenex from the box under the passenger seat and cleaned brains off my shoe. *Soon*, I thought, sinking into the soft leather seats. *Soon all this shit will be over.*

CHAPTER 52

I jerked awake on the couch, fully clothed, all lights blazing. Across the room on my desk the plant looked sad. Someone was knocking on the door — two knocks, then three, then one. Eddie. My bones cracked as I stood. Getting too old for this shit.

"Eddie."

Eddie's hand snaked through the doorframe. "Phone for you. It's Suzanne."

"Is she —?"

"She's fine. She's still at my aunt's house."

I took the phone and rubbed my eyes. Eddie's voice floated in from the hallway. "You want some breakfast?"

"Yeah. Scotch."

I settled into the chair behind my desk and put the phone to my ear. "Suzanne."

"Jack. Are you okay?"

"I'm fine. Don't worry about me. How are you doing?"

"Who shot me?"

"Vito's guys, most likely. They were aiming for me."

Silence on the other end. "Jack. Let's leave tonight. Let's just pack up and go."

"Soon, babe, soon. Say hi to Aunt Cecilia."

I said goodbye and hung up the phone as Eddie walked in with a tray full of food.

"Here you go, Jack. Toast and oatmeal. It's good for you."

"Where the hell is the Scotch?"

Eddie frowned. "I thought you were kidding."

A smile cracked across my lips. "I was." *Was I?* "Thanks for breakfast."

I dug in. Eddie plopped down on the couch. The springs groaned.

"Any word from Tommy?"

"That's funny," I said with my mouth full of oatmeal. "I was just about to ask you the same question."

"Eric's not answering his cellphone."

"Maybe he had to ditch it."

"Yeah, maybe." Eddie stared out the window. "I don't trust Tommy."

I swallowed orange juice. "That's because you're a smart man, Eddie." My chair scraped against the linoleum as I stood up. "Let me call him."

Tommy's phone rang and rang and then rang some more. No answer.

Eddie paced nervously across the floor. "What are you thinking?"

"Does Eric's car have a GPS?"

"Yeah."

"Then let's go find them."

———————

The GPS led us through the early morning streets, past joggers and dogs and baby carriages. We were heading north, away from the lake, up toward St. Clair and then into the twisty residential streets.

"Slow down."

Eddie did. The car crawled past the police cars, the ambulance, the crime scene tape.

"Oh no," Eddie whispered. "No, no, no."

A policeman in a yellow windbreaker had stopped traffic. Paramedics lifted Eric's body from the car and placed him on a gurney. A ponytailed paramedic with solemn dark eyes zipped up the body bag.

"No, no, no."

There was a bullet hole in the car's windshield. Blood filled the spidered cracks. The yellow-jacketed policeman waved us on.

Eddie pulled over next to a nearby park. Golden retrievers romped through the grass. A young mother in a red sweater and tan slacks pushed her toddler on the swings. Eddie hunched over the steering wheel, his body wracked by silent sobs.

I reached over and put my hand on his shoulder. "Eddie. I'm sorry."

Eddie straightened up, took off his sunglasses, and wiped his eyes. "I didn't see Tommy. Did you?"

"No, I didn't."

Eddie whipped out his phone and rattled off rapid-fire Cantonese. He closed the phone and turned to me. He looked so sad, so tired. "He wanted action. I guess he got it."

"I'm sorry, Eddie."

Eddie nodded. "Me, too."

I borrowed Eddie's phone and punched in Grover's number. "There's been a development. I need to see you."

Something in my voice put the kibosh on Grover's usual bullshit. "All right. Come on down to the marina. I'll take you on a tour of my new boat."

Wind whipped through Grover's hair as he leaned over the boat rail.

"Come on up."

I climbed up the ladder and stepped onto the new boat. It looked a lot like the last one, except shinier. I wondered if this one was also rigged to explode. "How'd you explain the new boat to your wife?"

Grover didn't look happy. He stood facing me with his arms folded. "I told her I traded in the old one. Early birthday present. What did you do, Jack?"

"What do you mean?"

"Little Vito called me early this morning. He was furious."

"What now?"

"Tommy and another guy were up all night running all over the city knocking over Little Vito's businesses."

"WHAT?"

"You didn't know? No, don't answer that. I can tell you're surprised."

"Fucking Tommy." *Fuck, fuck, fuck.*

"Vito is seriously pissed. He says he has Tommy. He's going to kill him unless you do what he says."

Just like that, the morning slid from bad to worse. I staggered over to the rail and looked back at the city.

Grover stepped up behind me, his white suit rippling like a sail. "Tommy used you, Jack."

"No shit." A gull flew by. A little motorboat putt-putted toward open water. "Those businesses … he said they were his. Said he invested in them and now he was cashing out."

"So you were there."

"I was at the first one. The pool hall. And then I got out."

"Who was the other guy?"

I pictured Eric slumped over the steering wheel, his blood covering the windshield. "The other guy's dead."

"Is that why you wanted to see me?"

"Yeah. I needed some information."

"And now?"

I flexed my arms. "I've got all the information I need."

I could see it now. Tommy and Eric, out on a spree. Knocking over gin joints and whorehouses all across town. Finally Little Vito's guys caught up. Eric didn't have a chance. It's a miracle that Tommy was still alive.

If he was still alive.

Little Vito wanted a favour. Bullshit. Little Vito wanted me dead.

Grover had a gun in his hand. I tensed, ready to charge, but the little man offered me the gun butt-first. "Here, Jack. You might need this."

"No thanks."

Grover scowled. "Go on, take it."

"I said no thanks."

"Little Vito is going to try and kill you, Jack."

"I know it." I stared at the sunlight bouncing off the water. "Grover … you think Tommy is still alive?"

"I do."

I nodded slowly. "Then I'd better go get him."

Eddie drove me over to Chinatown B to his Aunt Cecilia's house. Grover's words were ringing in my ears as we passed the shopping crowds, bumping and pushing, grabbing melons and leafy greens, grocers in long white coats with cigarettes dangling from their mouths pushing stacks of empty boxes to the curb.

"Fuck Tommy," Grover said. "Let him rot."

"It's not that simple," I replied. "I told him I'd protect him from Vito."

"Tommy used you. He lied to you."

"Yeah. Still, a deal's a deal."

I went through a similar song and dance in Aunt Cecilia's living room. Suzanne stood near the sofa with her arms folded, staring at me with disbelief. "Are you shitting me?"

"Babe. I've got to take care of this."

"No. No. Forget it. Vito's got what he wants. Don't you get it? Let him kill Tommy and then we're free."

I stared into Suzanne's eyes. "I can't let that happen."

Eddie walked into the living room with a mahogany box. Inside the box was a row of knives, glittering and sharp, resting on blue velvet. I started to strap them on. Suzanne stepped closer and put her hand over mine.

"Jack. You don't have to do this."

I yanked down my jacket, covering the knives. "Yeah. I do."

Suzanne looked sad. "This is crazy. You don't owe him anything. This is your chance. Don't you see that? You keep talking about retirement. This is it. Just walk away."

I rolled up my pants leg and strapped on another knife. "I can't do it, Suzanne."

Suzanne's shoulders slumped. "The house in the country … the kids, the tire swing … it was all bullshit. Wasn't it? You'll never quit. You can't quit. You're going to keep going until the day you die."

Eddie backed out, disappearing down the hallway. My gut turned sour. Cassandra and I had had this same conversation many years ago. We were in her apartment. Eddie was downstairs, waiting for me with the motor running. I was strapping on knives.

"This is the last job, babe," I'd told her. "I swear."

Cassandra smiled at me sadly. "Did you ever hear the story of the scorpion and the frog?"

"Let me guess. They lived happily ever after."

"No. The scorpion sat on the bank of a river, staring over at the other side. A small green frog hopped by.

"'Hey frog,' the scorpion said. 'How about you carry me across the river?'

"'Nothing doing,' said the frog. 'You're a scorpion. You're going to sting me.'

"'No I won't,' said the scorpion. 'Think about it. If we're in the water and I sting you, we both drown. Why would I do that?'

"'Hmm. All right … hop on.'

"The scorpion climbed onto the little green frog's back and together they swam out into the river. Halfway across, the scorpion lashed out with his tail and stung the little green frog.

"'What the fuck,' the frog said, his body becoming paralyzed with venom. 'You stung me! Now we're both going to drown! Why did you do it?'

"The scorpion shrugged as the water rose all around him. 'It's my nature.'"

"Great story, babe," I said, grabbing my coat. "I'll be back in a week. Stay safe."

"You, too."

When I got back a week later, Cassandra's apartment was empty. She was gone. I never saw her again.

Tears were rolling down Suzanne's cheeks. I took her by the hand but she yanked away.

"Suzanne. Look at me. It wasn't bullshit. I meant every word."

"It's a fantasy, Jack. This ..." Suzanne pointed to the now-empty box. "This is reality."

"It's all going to change."

Suzanne shook her head sadly. "No. It's not. You think you'd be happy out in the country reading the newspaper by the fire? That's not you, Jack. That's not who you are."

"I can learn."

"Did you ever have a dog?"

"What?"

"A dog."

"No."

"I had a dog once. Missy. She was a sweet old black lab. I bought her from a farmer about two hours north of the city, near Collingwood. 'I want a dog for protection,' I told the farmer. He brought out Missy, but I wasn't looking at her. I was looking past her, at her brother Boris. This huge snarling dog was penned up in a cage, barking and throwing himself against the wire mesh. 'What about that one?' I asked. The farmer just shook his head. 'You don't want that one,' he said. 'You can't tame him. You can't have him in the house. He's a yard dog.'"

Suzanne looked away. I stood in the middle of Aunt Cecilia's living room with knives strapped all over my body. I caught a glimpse of myself in the reflection of Aunt Cecilia's flat-screen television. My face was scarred, twisted and hard. Suzanne was right. I couldn't deny it any longer. *This is who I am.*

Eddie walked back into the living room, his cellphone pressed against his ear. He looked grim. "Jack. We've gotta go."

"Eddie … that twenty grand Tommy paid me."

"Yeah?"

"Give it to her."

Suzanne shook her head. "I don't want your money."

"But —"

"Forget it. You want to give your money away, give it to Sick Kids Hospital or a shelter or something. I'm a grown woman, Jack. I make my own money."

I stepped over to Suzanne. She kissed me, hard.

"I'm sorry."

Suzanne shook her head. She grinned through her tears. "It was fun while it lasted, right?"

"Yeah."

We broke apart. Suzanne reached forward and traced the scar on my cheek with her fingertip. "Take care of yourself, Jack."

As the house receded in the rear-view mirror, I jutted out my jaw and stared straight ahead. Reflections of trees bounced off the windshield.

Somewhere out there, Little Vito was waiting.

CHAPTER 53

Bits of styrofoam bobbed on the dirty water lapping against the pier. Grover, Eddie, and I stood among the rusty shipping crates. The moon hung over us, close enough to touch.

Grover's white coat flapped softly in the breeze. He looked like the maddest scientist there ever was. "Okay. Vito's holding Tommy in one of his warehouses. He wants you to come meet him, Jack. It's a set-up for sure. I'm coming with you."

I shook my head. "No."

"I'm coming with you, but you'll be walking in alone. I'll be set up on the roof across from the warehouse. Here." Grover passed me a listening device that looked like a button. "When things get hairy, I'll start shooting."

Eddie shuffled his feet and coughed. "What about me?"

"You'll be waiting for us."

Eddie shook his head. "That's bullshit."

Grover frowned. "That's the way it is. If you come galloping in with us, you'll be a marked man for the rest of your life."

My eyes met Eddie's. "I'm going to make this right."

Eddie looked away. Fog rolled across the lake. A horn sounded, deep and low.

Eddie drove us to the warehouse. In the back seat Grover hummed as he flipped open a long black case and checked his sniper rifle. My stomach churned. I felt like I'd swallowed a bucketful of ball bearings.

Willie The Driver met us on Cherry Street. He was standing beneath a streetlight, leaning against his car. Eddie and I stepped out onto the street.

"Thanks, Eddie. I'll take it from here."

"Let me come with you."

"We'll see you later, Eddie. This is all going to work out. I promise."

"And if it doesn't?"

I grinned. "Then it was nice knowing you."

Eddie and I shook hands. Then the big man wrapped me up in a bear hug. Eddie turned and walked toward Willie's car.

I climbed back inside the first car. Grover was still in the back seat. "You coming up to the front?"

"What?"

"What am I, *Driving Miss Daisy*? Come on up to the front."

Musical chairs. Grover slid into the passenger seat with his case of equipment. Across the road Willie The

Driver pulled a U-turn. Eddie's eyes met mine as their car passed us and disappeared beneath the bridge.

Grover pointed straight ahead. "Let's hit it."

Warehouses loomed all around us. Grover continued rummaging through his case. "We're outnumbered. Count on that. The one thing we've got going for us is the element of surprise. Stealth Ops. This is a delicate operation, Jack. One wrong move and Tommy is dead. Hell, one wrong move and we're all dead. You want a coffee?"

"No thanks."

Grover put his Thermos away. "Me neither." He pointed. "Pull in behind that building. We'll go the rest of the way on foot."

I steered the car past a trash-strewn loading dock and pulled in next to a green Dumpster with peeling paint. We stepped out of the car and Grover popped the trunk. Inside were racks and racks of gear. Grover shrugged off his white coat and pulled on solid black coveralls. He instantly blended into the nighttime sky. He shot me a Cheshire Cat grin. "Let's load up."

On the roof opposite Vito's warehouse, Grover and I hugged the gravel and scanned the perimeter with our night-vision goggles. Outside the warehouse two toughs were patrolling a narrow stretch of dead grass. One of them was smoking a cigarette, a shotgun slung across his shoulder. The other one was talking animatedly, miming stabbing a guy in the back. The guy with the shotgun laughed.

Through my goggles I peered through the warehouse window. Four heat signatures. No, wait ... six. Red and orange human-shaped blobs moved together and broke apart like lava lamps. Two of the blobs were sitting down. One of them was probably Tommy.

The roof gravel crunched slightly as Grover rolled toward me. "Six inside, two in the front. Maybe more in the back. You got that?"

"Yeah."

"All right. I'll cause a distraction. You go in through the side window. You see it? The one that's slightly open. Be as quiet as you can. When you see Tommy, give me the signal and I'll start shooting. We'll take 'em all out. Every last one of them. Any questions?"

"Yeah. What's the signal?"

"Code Four."

"Code Four?"

"That's right. Say 'Code Four' and I'll start shooting." Grover grinned. "Good luck."

Adrenalin pumped through my body. Each individual brick in the warehouse wall stood out sharp and clear. I slipped from shadow to shadow, heading for the window.

I was close enough to smell the guy with the shotgun's aftershave. The man smelled like saddle leather and cigarettes. His short little buddy was still blabbing. "So I said, bitch, if you don't get back into that kitchen and fix me an egg I'm going to kill your dog. You better believe that got her off her ass."

Shotgun cocked his head. "Shut up a minute. You hear something?"

I froze. Time slowed to a molasses crawl.

Shorty peered into the darkness. "You're paranoid, man. I don't hear shit."

Grover's voice boomed out, "Hey! Any of you mother-fuckers got a light?"

Shorty almost jumped out of his skin. Shotgun snarled and levelled his weapon. "What the fuck?"

Shorty pointed. "Over there! C'mon!"

I let out a breath as the two guards stomped off. With a knife in my hand, I slipped through the ware-house window.

Inside was dusty, musty, and dark. It smelled like the inside of a canvas army surplus tent. Ancient machinery sat abandoned, gathering dust. I heard rats scuttling in the shadows. My hand tightened around my knife as I stepped deeper into the darkness.

I heard voices coming from somewhere above me. A crack of yellow light filtered down through the floor. The rickety stairs creaked as I crept cautiously upward, hugging the damp warehouse wall.

Upstairs was a hallway lit by a single bulb. All doors were closed. Behind one of the doors Vito and his men were waiting.

Muffled voices. A door creaked open and I froze. A hawk-nosed man with jet-black hair was looking over his shoulder, back into the room.

"I gotta take a whiz. Be right back."

While he was still looking over his shoulder I slid past the doorway and got behind him. The floorboards cracked. Hawknose turned and his eyes went wide. His hand jerked toward the gun in his jacket.

He didn't have time to shout. He tried to step back but it was too late. My blade flicked like a cobra's tongue. Hawknose gurgled as he went down, blood pumping from his neck.

All right, Jack. This was it. With knives in both hands, I barrelled through the door.

Little Vito was sitting behind a desk against the far wall near the window. Next to him, tied to a chair, was Tommy, beaten black and blue. Two goons in blood-stained suits stood over him, pointing guns directly at Tommy's battered face. Where was the sixth man?

"Don't you fucking move." Breath like sour milk whispered inches from my ear. I waited for the press of the gun barrel to my back that would pinpoint the location of the man behind me, but it never came. The gunman kept his distance.

Little Vito and the others were staring at me. Tommy gurgled through swollen lips. Vito smiled and stood up. "We were wondering when you'd get here, Jack. Tommy over there was getting hungry. I was starting to think we might have to send out for pizza. Come on in. Don't be shy."

With each step I took I was calculating angles and trajectories. I still couldn't see the man behind me. Whoever he was, he was good.

Little Vito stepped closer, but not too close. In the sour-lemon light he looked like The Devil himself. He kept smiling. "It's been quite the ride, Jack. But it's over."

I tilted my chin at Tommy. "Let Tommy go."

The warehouse echoed with guffaws. Vito smiled. "You got balls, Jack. You got some fuckin' balls."

My mind was still calculating. Two guns on me — one from the back, one from the fat man in the bloodstained suit standing next to Tommy. One gun on Tommy. Vito's hands were free. A gun in his jacket? Count on it. Grover in position? Count on that, too.

Suddenly the smile was gone from Vito's face. He squinted at me with flint-hard eyes. "I could kill you right now. I could kill you fucking dead. Do you know that? Can you feel the truth of what I'm telling you, way down deep inside? Can you feel it in your bones? Because it's the truth, Jack. One word from me and you're bleeding all over this warehouse floor."

Bound to the chair, Tommy gurgled and spit blood. The gangster with the gun on Tommy smacked his face. "Shaddup."

Calculate, calculate. I was still alive. Why? Vito wanted to gloat. Torture? Maybe. Play along.

Little Vito leaned against the edge of his desk. "You know who I am, Jack? I'm a businessman. And as a businessman I've got a very practical mind. You know what I'm saying? Sure, I was pissed at you at first. That scene at Tommy's club … that was ugly. A lot of good men lost their lives. You should've heard Nemo's wife wail when I told her the news. But I'm not mad at you anymore, Jack. You know why?"

Once again I tilted my head at Tommy. "Because now you've got what you want."

Vito's left eyebrow shot up. He nodded slightly. "Yeah, maybe. Maybe that's part of it. What I was going to say was, I've been thinking about your phone call. I'm a businessman, and so are you. For you it's not personal. There's no grudges and blood oaths and vendettas and all that bullshit. Once you get into that shit, it never stops. Right? It never stops until everyone is lying sprawled out on the fucking pavement. That's no way to run a business."

"So what are you saying?"

Vito smiled. "Cut right to the chase, eh, Jack? What's the bottom line? See, I was right. You are a businessman. You want the bottom line? Well, I'll tell you. After tonight, you and I are through. After tonight we both walk away back to our own lives. Sound good?"

It sounded like lies. "Sure. Sounds good to me."

"I'm serious here, Jack. This bullshit with Tommy, it's caused me nothing but grief. Time and money right out the fucking window. My bosses aren't happy. And if my bosses aren't happy, then nobody's happy. It's time to put all the bullshit behind us and get on with our lives."

Could it be true?

Vito continued, his voice seductive and low. "There's just one thing I need you to do. A personal favour. You do this thing and the slate is wiped clean."

"Oh yeah? What's that?"

Little Vito pointed to Tommy. "Kill that piece of shit."

CHAPTER 54

Inside the warehouse time stood still. Tommy goggled at me, silently pleading. He looked like a whipped dog.

Little Vito reached into his jacket and pulled out a nickel-plated revolver. "Let me tell you how this deal goes down. You kill Tommy and you walk out of here a free man. If you don't ..." Little Vito raised his gun. "I'll kill you both myself." The gangster shrugged. "Up to you."

I took two steps closer to Tommy. His face was a mess. Purple bruises and red welts beneath the crusted blood. One of his eyes was swollen shut. The other eye was wide open and brimming with tears. The knife glittered in my fist. "I'm sorry," I told Tommy. With a fluid arc I brought the knife down.

The knife blade cut through the ropes tying Tommy to the chair. The ropes fell away and I kicked the chair over, sending Tommy crashing to the ground. I dove backward, throwing knives as I fell. "CODE FOUR! CODE FUCKING FOUR!"

The gunman next to Tommy slumped to his knees with my knife in his neck. The gunman behind me with the sour milk breath was screaming and shooting the ceiling, the hilt of a knife sticking out of his eye.

I didn't even hear the shots. The right half of Little Vito's head exploded in a red mist. Mr. Sour Milk went flying backward. Something slammed into my chest and knocked me back against the warehouse wall. The fat man in the bloodstained suit grinned and shot me again. He missed, and then his head exploded.

Somehow I had a fresh knife in my hand. The knife wavered as I gasped for breath. My chest felt caved in, like I had been kicked by a mule. Blood and bodies were everywhere. Someone was crawling toward me. Tommy. He was saying something but I couldn't hear him. My ears rang. Darkness was creeping around the edges. Tommy looked like he was at the end of a long, dark tunnel. *Great,* I thought. *The last thing I'm going to see before I die is Tommy's big ugly mug.*

When I came to I was outside, staring up at the stars. Cool night air gently caressed my face. Grover and Tommy leaned into my view. Grover smiled. "You're going to be fine, Jack. Aren't you glad you wore that bulletproof vest?"

I nodded. My voice croaked like a drunken bullfrog. "Let's hear it for your trunkload of gear."

"Damn straight. Can you walk? Come on, we've got to get out of here."

I crawled into the back seat of Grover's car. Tommy limped into the passenger seat and Grover punched the accelerator. I closed my eyes and heard the approaching sirens, rising and falling, rising and falling.

CHAPTER 55

Waves lapped against Grover's boat. Moonlight glittered and danced across the water. Tommy winced as Grover stuck a needle into his skin and stitched up the cut over his eye.

"Hold still. We're almost done." Grover cut the thread and looked over at me. "How are you doing, Jack?"

I looked down at the angry purple mass rising from my chest. "I'm just peachy."

"You sure you don't want to go to Doc Warner's?"

"Don't you worry about me."

I stood up and buttoned my shirt. I walked across the cabin and stared at Tommy's face.

Grover admired his handiwork. "What do you think?"

"He looks like he's been in a bar fight, but he should pass."

Tommy frowned. "Pass? Pass what? What are you guys talking about?"

"Pass through security." I pointed toward the door. "Come on. We're going to the airport."

"Right now? Come on, Jack. I'm grateful for your guys' help — don't think I'm not grateful — but we can't go to the airport now. I'm not packed, I don't have any money —"

Grover slapped a pack of banded bills on the table. "Pay me back when you get to Costa Rica."

Tommy grinned. "You guys are the best. You know that? The fucking best."

Grover nodded. "Yeah. We know."

I was standing by the open door. The night air ruffled my hair. "Come on. Let's go."

I climbed into the driver's seat of Grover's car and Tommy jumped into the passenger seat. "Man! You really saved my ass tonight, Jack. I'm not going to forget this. I mean it. I owe you one."

"You don't owe me squat." I peered straight ahead through the windshield. At this hour there were no other cars. A family of raccoons trundled across the road. After they passed I gunned the engine and we zoomed off into the night.

Tommy leaned back and grinned with his busted lip. "Little Vito … ha! Fuck that guy. We showed him who's the fucking boss."

"We sure did."

I turned the wheel. The car cut into a maze of warehouses. Tommy grinned. "You going to visit me in Costa Rica, Jack? Pina coladas and babes on the beach." Tommy's eyes flickered out the window. "Where the hell are we?"

"Short cut." Ahead of us two massive steel doors were opening. I gunned the engine and we sailed inside.

Tommy twisted nervously. "What the fuck, Jack?"

"Relax. I've got to make a stop." I cut the engine. We were parked in the middle of a brightly lit modern warehouse, all concrete and chrome. Behind us the massive steel doors rumbled closed.

Tommy slammed the passenger door open and scrambled out of the car. His face was stamped with panic. "What the fuck? What the fuck? You can't kill me, Jack! You promised! You fucking promised!"

I climbed out of the car and held out my empty hands. "I'm not going to kill you, Tommy."

Tommy relaxed. A door on the side of the warehouse swung open. Tommy's face fell.

"I just want to introduce you to some friends of mine. You already know Eddie."

Tommy turned to run. Willie The Driver stepped up behind him, hit him with the butt of a gun and dragged him toward a chair.

"And you know Willie. But I don't think you've met David." A huge man stepped forward. The dragon tattoo on his bare chest shone in the warehouse light. "He's Eric's brother. Remember Eric?"

David The Dragon pulled on a pair of surgical gloves. Tommy's head was whipping back and forth. "No. No. No." He tried to rise but Willie The Driver held him tight.

"See, Tommy … Eddie got an interesting phone call back at his Aunt Cecilia's house. Seems Eddie, being a friendly guy, has friends everywhere. Including the police department. And this friend of Eddie's at the police department called him up with some interesting news. That bullet hole in the car windshield where they found Eric's body? That bullet came from inside the car."

Tommy was rocking back and forth. A high-pitched keening escaped his battered lips.

"From inside the car, Tommy. You killed him. You. You shot Eric and then you were going to steal Vito's money and disappear. Only it didn't work out like that, did it? Vito's goons found you first."

Eddie stepped forward. He was wearing a butcher's apron tied over his charcoal grey suit. Behind his sunglasses his eyes were grim. "Thanks, Jack. We'll take it from here."

Tommy twitched. "Jack! JACK! You can't do this! JACK!"

I headed for the side door. Tommy started to scream.

I walked through the door and I didn't look back.

ACKNOWLEDGEMENTS

It takes a village! A huge thank you to my agent Kelvin Kong of K2 Literary and big thanks as well to Sam Hiyate at The Rights Factory. One million thank-yous to Kirk Howard, Beth Bruder, Scott Fraser, Allison Hirst, Michelle Melski, Kendra Martin, Laura Boyle, Jenny McWha, and all the other fine folks at Dundurn. This book would not exist without you!

Thanks to Iain Deans for invaluable feedback on early drafts. Thanks to Chris Turner for being, as he put it, a "brother-in-literary-arms."

Thanks to the crew from The Old Neighbourhood: Saira Hassan, Matt Stokes, Beau Levitt, Julia Chan, Jay Lapeyre, Ron Cunnane, Kristiina Hämäläinen, and Angela Pacini.

Thanks to my fellow writers Jacqueline Valencia, Mat Laporte, Andrew F. Sullivan, Paul Vermeersch, Lisa de Nikolits, Terri Favro, Gary Barwin, Evan Munday, Elan Mastai, Carolyn Black, and Sandra Kasturi. You awesome people inspire me daily!

Special thanks to five early supporters of my writing: Anne Yourt, Ashley Bristowe, Phil Hofton, Conrad Schickedanz, and Jennifer Holloway Flood. Having you in my corner has really meant a lot.

Thanks to my family for all the love, support, and understanding: Frances MacFarlane, Don MacFarlane, Don Pasquella, Dennis Boatright, Andrew Pasquella, Margie Niedzwiecki, Randy Niedzwiecki, Jacob Niedzwiecki, Thaba Niedzwiecki, and Phet Sayo.

Extra big special thanks to my wife, Emma Niedzwiecki, and to my kids, Leah and Matthew. I love you all so much!

BOOK CREDITS
Acquiring Editor: Scott Fraser
Editor: Allison Hirst
Project Editor: Jenny McWha
Proofreader: Catharine Chen

Cover Designer: Laura Boyle
Interior Designer: Jennifer Gallinger

Publicists: Michelle Melski and Tabassum Siddiqui

DUNDURN
Publisher: J. Kirk Howard
Vice-President: Carl A. Brand
Editorial Director: Kathryn Lane
Artistic Director: Laura Boyle
Production Manager: Rudi Garcia
Director of Sales and Marketing: Synora Van Drine
Publicity Manager: Michelle Melski
Manager, Accounting and Technical Services: Livio Copetti

Editorial: Allison Hirst, Dominic Farrell, Jenny McWha, Rachel Spence,
Elena Radic, Melissa Kawaguchi
Marketing and Publicity: Kendra Martin, Kathryn Bassett, Elham Ali,
Tabassum Siddiqui, Heather McLeod
Design and Production: Sophie Paas-Lang

dundurn.com   dundurnpress
@dundurnpress   dundurnpress
dundurnpress   info@dundurn.com

FIND US ON NETGALLEY & GOODREADS TOO!

DUNDURN